BEHIND THE HILL

B. IVY WOODS

BRETAGEY PRESS

Book Cover Design: Books-Design by Ana Grigoriu-Voicu

First Digital Edition: July 2020

❀ Created with Vellum

For my dad.

I did it and I hope you're proud.

Rest In Power

CHAPTER 1

*S*he stopped suddenly to take what looked to be a breather. She stretched her limbs and adjusted her earphones while she tried to catch her breath.

She didn't notice me because of the residents and tourists that caused a distraction as she worked out. She never noticed me. But I kept a close eye on her. I learned her routines, how she liked her coffee, what time she went to work in the morning, and other details that wouldn't necessarily come in handy.

But some of it will.

And when it does, it just might save her life.

NAOMI PORTER SLOWED DOWN to catch her breath. There wasn't much that could top jogging past the Washington Monument at dusk on a beautiful fall evening. Exercising after work allowed her to wind down a bit before heading home after a busy day at the office. She loved feeling the wind in her curls the closer she got to her goal. A new half marathon personal record was in her sights.

Since her job kept her stuck in front of a computer all day, running gave Naomi an outlet to burn off some stress. Although her work as a software developer for Edmon Cybersecurities was very rewarding, it didn't give her many opportunities to get outside and exercise. As she caught her breath, a sense of uneasiness sent goosebumps running down her arms. She looked around and noticed a few people jogging nearby, but that wasn't out of the ordinary. Still feeling a bit off, she stretched before starting her journey home.

Naomi maintained a pace that would keep her heart rate above normal and took a moment to tighten her ponytail. Although she liked to change her hair up on occasion, leaving it in its natural state was the easiest thing to do, especially while exercising and sweating.

Naomi arrived at her apartment a few minutes later. Her apartment near The Wharf gave her the best of many worlds. If she wanted to act like a tourist for a few hours, she was able to get from the National Mall to her home within minutes. It also made it easy to walk to work when she wanted to since it was only a twenty-five-minute walk.

She waved hello to the man stationed at her building's front desk and hurried up to her apartment. She took a look at herself before she walked past her hallway mirror and laughed at the sight. Although she had tried her best, stray curls had fallen out of her ponytail, and a thin sheen of sweat broke out on her golden-brown skin. Her brown eyes looked tired but relaxed. The pink t-shirt and black running shorts showed off her toned physique, but she needed to shower. She threw her phone on the couch in the living room and strolled into her bedroom, removing her exercise gear along the way. Her phone was a top-of-the-line device that not only made calls and sent text and video messages, but it also opened her apartment door, displayed holographic images, and more. The device was also encrypted due to her line of work.

She placed a shower cap on her head and headed into the bathroom. Naomi programmed her shower to 102 degrees before stepping under the spray. "Simon, turn Shower TV on, please," she said as she turned around so that the water landed on her back.

Simon was the automated system in her apartment that helped her with many everyday activities such as fixing meals and drinks, turning on electronics, and finding specific clothes in her closet. Naomi was a big techie, and the fact that Simon came preinstalled convinced her she needed to live in this apartment.

The TV turned on, and the newscasters were in the middle of a conversation about the latest political news. Naomi half listened and continued to let the water flow over her body.

"In other news, Congress is working on a bill that will keep the federal government open through March 30, 2098. Republicans, Democrats, and Independents are working together to avoid a government shutdown that will affect hundreds of thousands of federal workers. Once the bill passes both houses, it will go to the president for her signature. And on to our next story..."

Naomi let the news play until she finished showering.

After drying herself off, moisturizing, and putting on her sweatpants, tank top, and hoodie, Naomi walked into her kitchen.

"Simon, please pour me a glass of wine."

While she waited for her wine to appear, Naomi sat down on the couch, picked up her phone, and scanned her emails and messages to see if anything important happened while she was on her run. Seeing nothing pressing, Naomi messaged her best friend, Paige Harris.

Naomi: *Are we still having girls' night tonight? Or did something come up at work?*

The two had met when Paige moved down to DC from New York five years ago and Paige answered Naomi's request for a roommate through a post online. The rest was history. The women had moved three times together throughout their friendship and had been in their current apartment for over a year. Naomi was happy when they decided to decorate the apartment in a manner that would match both of their styles. Naomi's more modern approach with sprinkles of Paige's romantic style helped make the space uniquely their own.

Paige: *Didn't get held up at work. I'll be home in about 30 mins. See you soon! Happy Thursday!*

Naomi grabbed a blanket off their couch, stopped in the kitchen to get wine, and headed outside to sit on the balcony and watch the sunset. Although it was a bit chilly out, watching the sunset over the Capitol was one of Naomi's favorite things to do. It provided a sense of tranquility, giving her something to focus on when other aspects of her life were making her anxious. The realization that this was a coping mechanism continued to help her get a grasp on better managing her anxiety.

There wasn't a lot Naomi could complain about with her life. She had her health, her family and friends, a great job, and a roof over her head. But she felt like she needed to work toward something more. When she had her fill of the majestic pink, purple and orange scene in front of her, she gathered her things.

Naomi entered the apartment and was startled to find Paige there.

"I was just about to message you," Paige said. She took off her coat and placed it in the front closet and pulled her long blond hair into a ponytail. Paige made her way into the living room and Naomi shot her a grin. After the day she had at work, a girls' night with Paige would improve her mood.

"Sorry, I didn't hear you, I was sitting outside on the balcony. How is everything going with you?"

"Things are hectic. We're dealing with another potential government shutdown. Another! I'm surprised I was able to get out of work on time today. I haven't had time to breathe in years."

Paige worked on Capitol Hill as a legislative assistant for Senator George Butler of Virginia. It was no surprise that because of the budget deal that needed to be passed by Congress that many congressional members and their staffers were putting in long hours to finalize the bill.

Naomi raised a skeptical eyebrow in a you're-being-dramatic way. "Are you sure about that?"

"Okay, maybe I've had only a little less time than usual to relax and have fun. You know I'm trying to send my twenties out with a bang. In more ways than one, if you know what I mean."

"Oh, trust me, I know. Simon, please pour me another glass of wine and make a margarita," Naomi said. She walked to the kitchen and finished the rest of her wine.

"How did you know I wanted that?"

"'Cause you always do."

"True. Anyway, you should be getting out more too. You haven't been with someone in what has it been? Nine months? I know you love being behind the scenes and in front of your computer, but maybe stepping out of your comfort zone by going out more might help with your anxiety. Or at least provide a distraction for a little while."

Naomi shrugged. Paige had told her time and time again that she should do more to get out of the house and meet people. Naomi would rather place more effort into programming instead of into her relationships with other people.

One of the best parts of girls' night was that instead of having Simon fix something for them to eat, the two of them always chose a new recipe to cook together. They both found cooking relaxing, and it allowed them to catch up on each other's lives. Although they lived together, sometimes they could go days without seeing each other.

"Naomi, I met this guy while I was grabbing some coffee in Dirksen. He was cute! Tall with short, curly hair. He had pretty but intense darkish brown eyes. Maybe they were the same color as your eyes? Like I can't describe them, but they were almost...hypnotic. I think I also paid more attention to his eyes because he had a small scar near his left eye. Anyway, he asked if we can grab coffee sometime next week." Paige's office is located in Dirksen, a Senate office building.

"That sounds...a bit nerve-racking," Naomi said. She found the recipe on her phone and began to take the ingredients out of the refrigerator.

"We traded numbers, and he said he'd contact me tonight, so we'll see if that happens. If it works out, maybe he has a single friend that we can set you up with if you want."

"Yeah…maybe. Let's talk more about it when we get to that point." Naomi continued to follow the recipe and Paige hopped in and helped where she could. The two chatted about their day and their plans for the upcoming weekend. When they finished making the shrimp scampi, Naomi and Paige served themselves and walked into their living room to watch a political drama.

"That show was truly mind-blowing. I can't believe those things could happen on Capitol Hill." Naomi shook her head in disbelief.

"You'd be shocked what happens on Capitol Hill. Nothing as out there as what happened in some of those scenes, but things can get very interesting. Especially recently."

That earned Paige a look. "What do you mean?"

Paige leaned over and said in a low voice, as if there were other people in the room. "This conversation doesn't leave here. George is having a bit of trouble with some cybersecurity legislation that he's sponsoring."

George, better known as Senator George Butler, is Paige's boss of the last three years. The senator was only the third senator from Washington, DC, after it became a state in 2060. Paige worked on several policies and issues, including cybersecurity, for his office. Although Naomi and Paige didn't talk specifics when it came to their jobs because of their security clearances, they both shared a love for technology and certain aspects of computer science.

"What kind of problems?"

"George and I were in a meeting with another senator and her legislative assistant. Her office had been on the fence about the legislation and wanted to meet with us to discuss it more." Paige paused and took a sip of her margarita.

"I thought it was weird that she wanted to be more involved since we usually keep things like this on the staff level, but hey whatever the senator prefers. We did what she wanted. Everything started amicably, and then all of a sudden, she lost it. She started yelling directly at me about how wrong this was and how there would be hell to pay if this bill becomes a law. Her staffer was eventually able to calm her down. It was interesting, to say the least," Paige said and shook her head.

"Who does that? Especially someone who would want to maintain a professional relationship? Did she at least apologize? What was Senator Butler's reaction?"

Paige's sudden switch to nodding her head would have been comically if it hadn't been for the story she was telling. "It came across as being sincere, but who knows if it was. You know that feeling when you get so angry or embarrassed that you start crying?" Paige waited for Naomi to nod before she continued. "That was me. George and I talked about it afterward, and he wasn't expecting her to go off like that either. He told me he'd call her later, and hopefully, she'd be calmer by then."

"I'm so sorry. How awkward and unprofessional."

"Yeah, I'm still not completely over it." Naomi studied Paige for a second and saw tears welling up in her eyes. She decided to change the subject.

Naomi stood up and stretched. "Do you want another drink? I think you deserve it."

"Sure. Are you getting one?"

"No, but I'm happy to get you one." Naomi grabbed their dirty dishes and took them to the kitchen sink. While Naomi waited for Paige's margarita, she grabbed a cup and placed it under the refrigerator's water spout. A couple of minutes later, Naomi walked back into the living room, where she found Paige standing near their balcony door daydreaming. Naomi handed her the margarita and drank from her cup of water.

"Is everything all right?"

"Yeah, that encounter with her took a lot out of me. It made an already stressful time between all the budget shit even worse. How are things at Edmon?"

Edmon was one of the biggest cybersecurity firms in the world and one of their headquarters was in Washington, DC. Naomi worked for them as a developer and her main project was keeping data secure in cloud databases. A company or a government agency would hire Edmon to have a developer create a program that would not only help import their data into a cloud database but would also ensure there were no vulnerabilities in the code before the process began.

"Same old, same old - I heard we had gotten a bunch of new government contracts recently, so it seems that business is going well. I'm not working on any of those, however. I've mostly been focused on some database work and trying to make sure the data we receive gets handled in the most secure way possible. I assume some of the leaders at my company are very interested in this bill that Senator Butler is trying to pass."

"Have you heard anything about the promotion you were trying for?"

"Uh...no. I've been procrastinating officially applying for it."

"Why? You could go from being a developer to a senior

developer, which would boost your resume, provide more challenging work, and, I'm assuming, a pay raise."

Naomi placed her water cup down and massaged her temples. "I don't know. I guess I'm nervous. What if I fail or not prepared for this jump? Thinking about applying for this has increased my anxiety tenfold."

"But how will you know unless you try? The worst they can do is tell you no. And if you get it, I'm sure there will be a bit of an adjustment period to give you time to get your feet wet. Your boss has been great about supporting you, so I think it's worth at least applying for the opportunity."

Naomi offered Paige a warm smile. "I know you're right, and my feelings are irrational. But I just can't shake it."

"Maybe talk to your psychiatrist about it? When is the deadline to apply?"

"Two weeks. I've briefly mentioned it to Dr. Evans, and she gave me some advice about how to manage my anxiety while applying for it. I'll see if I can set up an appointment with her and then work on my application."

"That's my girl!" Paige exclaimed and gave Naomi a high five. "If you need any help with it, let me know."

"Will do. I should probably head to bed. But can we chat about it more tomorrow if you get home at a decent hour?"

Paige smirked. "Can't hang like you used to, eh? How about a happy hour if I can get out of work on time? I can confirm with you sometime tomorrow."

"Sure, that works."

"Who knows? Maybe we'll find some cute guys to talk to as well."

"Good night, Paige," Naomi said as she headed toward her bedroom.

Naomi walked into her bedroom and shut the door.

"Simon, turn on bedside table light." The lamp turned on, and she walked over to her bookshelf. Naomi picked up a book that she hadn't had a chance to read yet, grabbed her headscarf, and put it on before getting comfortable in her bed. She cracked open the book and started reading.

Naomi didn't know how long she had been reading when she felt the hairs on the back of her neck stand up, and she lowered the book. She looked around her room and noticed that her bedroom window shade was open. She huffed, got out of bed, and approached the window. Her window faced an apartment building directly across the street from her own. While looking across, she noticed a red laser flashing around one room in particular. She leaned over and turned off the light on her bedside table and her eyes darted back to the window. She saw the red light appear again on one of the walls in the building before the light suddenly appeared on Naomi's windowsill.

Naomi ducked and exclaimed, "Simon, close bedroom window shade now!" Her heart was racing. Her adrenaline pumping. Her stomach was turning into knots. The window shade closed, and Naomi slowly crawled over to her bed, thankful that the window was on the other side of her room. She climbed into her bed and threw the covers over her head.

"This is stupid," she said and removed the blanket from her head. Her heart was still beating fast. Naomi tried to figure out a way to go to sleep after that incident. But all she could do was toss and turn before she lay in bed, staring at her ceiling.

"What the heck was that?"

Not being able to shake the unsettling feeling, Naomi slid

out of bed and walked to her bedroom door. She silently opened the door, hoping that Paige was still awake, but her hopes fell by the wayside when she saw that her bedroom light was off. Naomi turned around and closed her door. She hurried back to her bed and watched the window shade to see if another red dot appeared. She didn't know how long she stared at the window before she fell into a restless sleep.

CHAPTER 2

"Doug, I was able to make that fix, so the deployment should be good to go tomorrow."

"Perfect. Thanks, Naomi."

"No problem. Happy to help with anything else."

Her boss, Doug, strolled down the hall while Naomi swung left down a row of cubicles.

Naomi walked back toward her cubicle and placed her laptop on her dock. Her desk setup was simple besides her laptop and second monitor being one of the latest models on the market. She had a few photos of her close circle of family and friends on her desk, along with a tabletop carousel for her pens, pencils, and highlighters.

Thoughts of the red laser on her windowsill the night before faded to the back of her mind once her workday picked up. Since she had been in a meeting for the better part of an hour, the first thing she did was check her email. Seeing nothing critical, she opened Eclipse, an application that would allow her to write and change the code she was currently working on.

After staring at her code for another project for longer than intended, Naomi decided she had had enough, and it was time for a lunch break.

She grabbed her phone and her coat and walked toward the elevators. As she was putting her coat on and fixing her dress, a familiar voice called Naomi's name. Naomi turned around and noticed June Liu standing next to her. June was a product manager at Edmon, and she and Naomi often worked on projects together. June's jet-black hair was usually in a high ponytail with a pencil sticking out of it. She was quieter than Naomi and mostly kept to herself, but whenever they had conversations, Naomi thought that she was sweet and sincere.

"Hey, June. Are you going to grab lunch? We can go together if you want."

"That would be great. Thanks for the invite."

Naomi and June made small talk as they walked out of their office building toward a line of food trucks. There they were able to find a list of trucks for that day and what they were serving. Both women quickly typed in their orders on the computerized menu and sat down at the first available table they saw. They chatted quietly about work while they waited for their food. Their conversation was interrupted by Naomi's phone ringing.

"I'm sorry, but it's my mom, and I need to take this since she's out of the country," Naomi said while she checked the screen and rose from her seat. June nodded and Naomi walked a short distance away to answer her device. Within a few seconds, Jada Porter appeared on the screen. "Mom, how is everything going?"

"Sweetie, everything is going great. Things are pretty quiet here. How about you?"

"Things are…going. Work has been so busy that I don't know whether I'm coming or going half of the time. How is everything with you and Logan? How is the cruise?"

"It's so beautiful. I don't know why it took us so long to go on this trip."

Her mother and stepdad had been put off going on vacation for a while due to work commitments. Jada started a nonprofit called Hazel's Temple fifteen years ago in support of raising money for cervical cancer research. She named the charity in honor of Naomi's grandmother, Hazel, who died when Naomi was a teenager. Naomi's grandfather had died several years before her grandmother, and she didn't know if her grandparents on her biological father's side were still living. Logan served on the board of directors of the nonprofit and was a partner at a law firm in the city. A few months ago, they finally took the plunge and decided to book their cruise to Grand Cayman. Seven days away was what they needed to rest and recharge.

"Mom, you don't know how happy it makes me to see you smile. You seemed to be more stressed recently, and I'm glad to see that some of the tension has lifted. I've been worried."

Jada sighed. "Life is always going to have its stressors, and there will always be plenty of things on my mind, especially when it comes to you. There's nothing you need to worry about, and we are fine, okay, sweetie? Logan wants to talk to you." Jada passed the phone to Logan.

"Naomi! How are you doing? I'm sure I can speak for your mother when I say that we wish you were here with us."

Naomi chuckled. "Everything is fine here. I wish I were there with you guys too."

Logan had entered Jada's and Naomi's lives a couple of

years after Naomi's father had abandoned them. Based on what Naomi was told, when Jada met Logan at a work event sparks flew although Jada was very cautious about dating given the circumstances of her divorce. Jada gave him a chance and their relationship blossomed. He became a father figure in Naomi's life and was there for her whenever she needed him. If anyone asked her who her dad was, she referred to Logan as such, although she didn't call him Dad.

The three spent a few more minutes talking about the cruise before Jada and Logan had to go. After hanging up, Naomi walked back over to her table. When she sat down and returned to her conversation with June, she saw something out of the corner of her eye. Naomi stopped mid-sentence and surveyed the area.

"Is everything okay?" June asked.

"I think so," Naomi answered. "Did you see anything strange?"

June tilted her head as if she were trying to figure out a math equation and said, "No. Did you?"

"I guess not."

Nothing seemed out of the ordinary, and before Naomi could think about it more, she heard their names called. The women grabbed their lunch orders and made small talk while they ate.

When Naomi and June were finishing up their lunches, Naomi's phone pinged with a message from Paige confirming a happy hour later that day at the rooftop bar at the V Hotel near the White House. Naomi thought it might be a good idea to invite June out, as she thought about what Paige said yesterday.

"Hey, June. My best friend and I are going out to happy

hour tonight. Would you like to join us?" Naomi tossed the napkin she wiped her mouth with on the tray.

"I would love to, but I already have plans. Please let me know if you guys do it again sometime." Both women gathered their trash to put in the compost bin. As the two headed back to the office, every so often, Naomi would look over her shoulder, unable to shake the feeling that someone was watching her.

* * *

NAOMI LEFT WORK a little early to meet Paige. She rode the metro to the V Hotel, where she took the elevator up to the rooftop and found a seat right at the bar. Thankful that the rooftop was enclosed given the time of year, she took off her coat and thought about what she wanted to order. Her first instinct was to order a glass of wine, but since she was trying to step outside of her comfort zone, she decided to look at the computerized menu for a drink to try. After browsing for a bit, she decided to have a signature cocktail with bourbon and ginger beer in it. As the bartender took her order, her phone pinged.

Paige: *I'm so sorry, but I'll be there a little later than planned. Have a drink on me.*

Somewhat disappointed, Naomi thought about playing a game on her phone as a way to ignore the world but thought better of it. She wanted to continue the trend of stepping out of her comfort zone, so she decided to people watch instead. The rooftop began to fill up and there was standing room only near the bar. Naomi was finishing up her first drink when her right shoulder was bumped from behind, causing her to spill a few drops of her drink on her dress.

"Oh, I'm sorry."

"Don't worry about it," Naomi said. She cleaned herself up before she turned her head toward the voice. Standing next to her was a handsome man about six-two with broad shoulders, dark brown hair, and light-colored eyes. He wore a light blue shirt and dark blue slacks. She looked down and noticed no wedding ring but a fancy Angie & Pam watch on his wrist before he placed his left hand in his pocket. The only reason Naomi recognized the emblem of the company was because Paige loved the brand. *Was this man talking to her?*

"Please let me buy you your next drink to make up for it. What would you like?"

"You don't have to."

"I want to." The stranger gave a sly smile and waited for her reply. Naomi returned the gesture and scanned the menu once more.

"I'll take a glass of the Malbec." One small step out of the comfort zone, one small step back in.

"Excellent choice. By the way, my name is Reed," the stranger said as he held out his hand.

"I'm Naomi, and it's nice to meet you." Naomi shook his hand.

"So, Naomi, you know I need to ask you the quintessential DC question. What do you do?"

"I am a developer for a company that works in the cyber-security field."

"Do you like what you do?"

"Well, …yes. The internet plays a role in a lot of what we do every day, and it is crucial to keep our data safe online. I guess I feel...important in that sense. Like I am doing something for the betterment of society even though it is just a small piece."

"I like the way you phrased it. At times, my job description includes keeping data safe too."

If Naomi hadn't been laser-focused on Reed, she was now. "Oh? What do you do?" Before Reed could answer, the bartender stepped over. Reed gave their order and asked for their drinks to go on his tab. After the bartender left, there was a brief silence before Reed spoke up.

"What brings you to the V?"

"Oh, I'm here to meet up with my roommate. She should be here at any minute."

The bartender brought them their drinks. Naomi hadn't heard what Reed ordered for himself.

"Is that whiskey?" Naomi asked and gestured to his drink. She looked up into his eyes and did everything in her power not to get lost in them. Was this drink hitting her already?

"That it is." Reed took a sip.

Naomi and Reed chatted while enjoying their drinks. She noticed when he placed his hand on the corner of her chair, grazing her shoulder. Naomi stopped herself from trembling due to the spark that she felt at his soft caress. Naomi smiled at the gentle touch before she glanced down at her phone and realized quite a bit of time had passed and apologized.

"I didn't realize how long I kept you from whatever you were doing."

"No worries. I'm where I want to be, and I've had a great time talking with you. Do you want to exchange numbers?"

Naomi was stunned. It was rare that she would get

approached by someone, let alone have someone ask for her number.

"Uh, yeah, sure." Reed fiddled with his phone, and when he held out his phone, a prompt on Naomi's screen asked if she wanted to accept Reed's number. As she clicked accept, Naomi glanced up and saw Paige trying to maneuver through the crowd to get to her. Naomi waved her over.

A moment later, Paige appeared at Naomi's side and her head swerved between Reed and Naomi, trying to piece together what was happening.

"Reed, this is my best friend and roommate, Paige. Paige, this is Reed. We met about thirty minutes ago."

"It's a pleasure to meet you, Paige," Reed said and he shook Paige's hand.

"Likewise."

"Naomi, it was great talking with you." Reed gave both women a slight wave although his eyes lingered on Naomi. He turned around and walked away into the crowd. Naomi did her best to not stare too hard before turning her attention to Paige.

"What – Was - That!" Paige exclaimed as she stared at Naomi wide-eyed.

"He bumped into me by mistake while trying to get to the bar and spilled my drink. He apologized and offered to buy me another drink."

"Please tell me you exchanged numbers!"

"We did."

"Yes! Even if nothing comes of it, I'm so happy you put yourself out there a bit and didn't try to run away." Paige hugged Naomi before scanning the menu and ordering a margarita when the bartender came by.

"It was nerve-racking, but I think I made it through the encounter without mumbling too many uhs or ums."

"Do you think you'll call him if he doesn't call you first? He clearly enjoyed your company."

"I haven't decided. I think that might be a bit too bold for me right now, but you never know," Naomi said with a smirk. The bartender placed a margarita in front of Paige.

"Awww yeah! You can run your message to him by me if you want," Paige laughed before both she and Naomi toasted each other.

"So, how was your day?" Naomi asked and set the glass of wine down.

"I can't complain too much. Things went pretty well today," Paige said after she swallowed another sip of her drink.

"Heard anything from a certain senator that yelled at you and your boss?" Naomi still couldn't believe that a senator would act like that to someone who was considered her peer.

"Not really. Well, at least I haven't heard anything. Which to be honest, I'm thankful. I don't want that type of drama in my life, but especially not at my job."

"I hear that. I can't imagine how you feel."

"I'm mortified," Paige admitted, "and I know I have done nothing wrong. I was just doing my job."

"It's so strange."

"Yeah, and that whole episode just seemed a little too personal for comfort," Paige paused and looked around the bar. "Well, anyway, that's in the past, and we should talk about something else. Something happy...like Reed."

"What about him? I just met him tonight." Naomi brought the glass of wine to her lips.

"I know. And I wish you would have gone home with Reed." Paige gave Naomi a knowing look and flipped her long blond hair over her shoulder. "I'm kidding. I know that's not your style. But I do wish it was so you could let me know how it went."

Naomi choked on her wine, and Paige had to pat her back to clear the liquid from her throat. "Could you give a girl a warning before you say that? Damn."

Paige laughed and apologized.

"Plus, you get enough action in that area for both of us. And this isn't me shaming you at all, girl. You do your thing, and I do mine, and that is completely fine."

Paige nodded and said, "I know. Speaking of, the guy who wanted to meet for coffee just asked if we could go out tomorrow. I think I'll take him up on that. I'll let you know when and where it is, just in case." Naomi nodded as Paige continued, "But back to you. I just think it might help you to let loose a little bit. The world is your oyster, and you should take it by the horns."

Naomi just shook her head at Paige. "I'm pretty sure that isn't how the saying goes."

"So?" Paige asked. "My point still stands. You only live once, or so the cliché goes."

ON MONDAY MORNING, Naomi woke up, changed into her workout gear, and got ready for a quick run around the National Mall. Before leaving her apartment, she unlocked her phone, and the conversation between her and Paige appeared from the previous night.

Paige: *Hey, are you free for breakfast tomorrow? I'm going to yoga first thing.*

Naomi: *Yeah, sounds good. Should be back from by run by then.*

As she was leaving her apartment, Naomi was happy to see her favorite security officer, Ann, stationed at the front desk this morning. There was not a wrinkle in sight on her uniform and she had pulled her light brown hair back into a low bun near her neck.

"This isn't usually your shift," Naomi remarked as she walked toward the front doors.

"Roger called out sick, so I volunteered to take his place," Ann said with a grin.

"Whew, you are a saint 'cause it's way too early to be at work, especially if it's not your normal shift. I have to do this run, but I'll see you soon!" Naomi said as she waved and walked outside. She checked her phone again and saw that it was 7:04 a.m.

Naomi jogged around the National Mall for thirty minutes before dashing back to her apartment. She saw something flash out of the corner of her eye. However, when she turned around, she didn't notice anything out of the ordinary. Uneasiness trickled through her body like a spider spinning a web. Multiple chills passed over her, causing goosebumps to race down her arms. She looked around but saw nothing suspicious. She rushed back to her apartment.

Ann was still there when she returned, and she briefly waved as she walked toward the elevators. When she got home and closed the front door, she called Paige's name, but there was no answer. Thinking maybe she got held up at her yoga class, Naomi took off her workout clothes and hopped into the shower.

After showering and completing her morning routine, Naomi put a robe on and left the bathroom. She called Paige's name again and looked in her room, but she still wasn't there.

"Strange," Naomi mumbled as she walked to her room to get dressed for work. When she finished, Naomi left her room and called Paige's name, but again, she met with silence.

Naomi: *Where are you? Are we still on for breakfast?*

Naomi asked Simon to make eggs and bacon with a side of fruit and hoped that Paige would show up while Simon was fixing breakfast. She looked around the kitchen and the hallway to see if Paige had left a note to say she wouldn't be able to make breakfast, but couldn't find anything. Simon finished making her breakfast, and she almost was done eating when Naomi realized she was running late for work. However, Paige was still not home. Maybe she had to go into the office early this morning and forgot to mention it?

She rechecked her phone but still no messages. She was confused as to why Paige wouldn't have said anything and disappointed that she hadn't heard from Reed. Deciding to call Paige on her way out the door, Naomi was surprised when it went to voice mail. She tried again and got the same result.

"Weird," Naomi glanced up just before entering the metro station. Thankfully, over many years, the metro had made tremendous improvements. It took at least thirty years of construction on the subway lines and stations for the system to become as robust and innovative as it was today. The metro trains were now nicknamed "mini-spaceships" because of their new design and how fast they transported people to and from different locations.

Naomi's train arrived at the station closest to her job, and she quickly exited. She walked up the escalator stairs and practically jogged a couple of blocks to her office. She reached her desk with five minutes to spare. She disconnected her laptop from the docking station and grabbed her phone and walked into the meeting room. Doug was already sitting at the conference table and gave Naomi a small wave as she sat down as well. She quickly sent Paige another message before getting to work.

Hours later, Naomi sighed when she opened her apartment door. She sat down on her couch without taking off her coat or shoes. She'd stayed at her office longer than she expected, and by the time she got home, it was 9:30 p.m.

"Paige?" she called and then listened for a response. Hearing none, she gathered up enough strength to walk to Paige's room and looked inside. Nothing had changed. Trying to shake the feeling that something terrible had happened, Naomi walked back toward the front door, took off her shoes, and hung up her coat.

"Simon, please cook a grilled cheese sandwich and tomato soup." Naomi walked into the kitchen and grabbed a glass from her cabinet. She placed it under the spout on her fridge. Naomi pressed the button for lemonade, removed her glass when it was full, and walked back into the living room. She turned on some mindless TV while she waited for her dinner to finish cooking. Naomi checked her phone and saw that she still had no messages.

"Maybe I should contact Diane," Naomi said out loud. Her fingers found their own beat as she tapped them on the counter. Diane Harris was Paige's mother and the two were extremely close, though Diane was still back in New York City, their hometown.

Naomi decided to send a quick message to Diane, knowing that she might not get it until morning. She also sent a short message to her parents to check in with them since she hadn't heard from them all day. Realizing that it was getting late and that she needed to get to bed, Naomi washed the few dishes that were in the sink by hand before she headed to the bathroom to shower. She got ready for bed and placed her scarf on her head. Once she was settled in bed, she grabbed her phone once more and saw that she had a short message from her parents with a picture showing how much fun they were having on the cruise. Because of the exhaustion she felt from having such a long day at the office, she fell asleep before she could set her phone back on the bedside table.

NAOMI WOKE up to her alarm and was still tired from the night before. She dragged herself out of bed and walked out into the hallway.

"Paige?" she called, but there was no response.

Vowing to call the police once she finished getting dressed, Naomi dashed back to her room to find clothes. Just as she finished buttoning her shirt, her phone pinged. It was Diane asking Naomi to call her back as soon as possible. She called her immediately.

"Hi, Diane. Thanks for returning my message. Is everything okay?"

"Good morning, Naomi. Have you seen or heard from Paige recently?"

"We saw each other a couple of days ago. We went to

happy hour after work and came home together. I saw Paige over the weekend but didn't see her at all yesterday. But with our crazy schedules, that isn't uncommon."

There was a brief silence on the other end of the line. Naomi's stomach began to cramp.

"What's wrong, Diane?" Her heart plunged to her feet. The floor seemed to shake beneath her toes. If someone had asked her, she would have sworn that D.C. was having an earthquake.

"I just received a phone call from Senator Butler's office. Paige hasn't checked in with her office in over a day. She's missing, Naomi."

CHAPTER 3

"*M*aybe this has been some sort of misunderstanding?" Naomi asked. She paced back and forth in her living room, trying to control the distressed feeling growing in her gut.

"I don't think so. Paige was supposed to check in with her office a couple of hours ago because the staff is still on call around the clock due to this budget deal. Apparently, some of Senator Butler's staffers emailed and texted her, but there was no response. You know as well as I do that that is unlike her. I already called her phone, and it went straight to voice mail." Diane sniffled.

Naomi's mind began to race as she thought about what could have happened to Paige. Before her mind started to spiral down a horrible rabbit hole, Naomi came up with an idea.

"How about I work backward and follow what she was supposed to do yesterday? Paige was going to have breakfast with me and didn't show up. Before that, she was supposed to go to yoga. I can talk to the manager of the studio and see if she went to her class. The yoga studio isn't far from our house," said Naomi. She took off her flats and replaced them with her sneakers.

"That sounds like a great idea. Thanks, Naomi."

"Okay. I'll talk to you soon."

Before she left her apartment, Naomi called Paige's phone herself again. The phone went straight to voice mail, which made Naomi think that either the device was off or that the battery had died.

Naomi raced out of her apartment to the bus stop. According to the holographic interactive bus schedule, the next bus should arrive in fifteen minutes. Naomi wished that someone would have invented flying vehicles by now, as it might make public transportation faster. Not willing to wait even longer for the bus to arrive, Naomi dashed down the street.

Naomi opened the studio doors and bent over to catch her breath. The receptionist at the front desk greeted her.

"Hi. Welcome to Yoga Salon. Would you like some water?"

"Sure. That would be great. Whew."

The receptionist handed Naomi a cup of water, which she quickly drank. Once Naomi caught her breath, she walked up to the receptionist's desk.

"Thanks for the water. I'm not sure if you can tell me this, but I figured I'd ask anyway. Can you tell me if Paige Harris made it to one of your yoga classes yesterday morning?"

"I can't tell you unless she listed you as one of her emergency contacts."

"Actually, I might be. My name is Naomi Porter. Sorry, I didn't catch your name."

"Marie. Give me one second," she said as she clicked a few

keys on the keyboard before looking at Naomi. "Can you show me your ID?"

Naomi pulled out her phone and flicked through a couple of pages and pulled up her ID.

"Ah, yes. Paige named you as one of her emergency contacts. Paige was here yesterday morning and took our 6:30 a.m. class."

"Did anything out of the ordinary happen? Would you be able to put me in touch with the teacher who taught the class?"

Marie gazed at the computer again.

"It looks like Lindsey is finishing up a class right now. If you would like to take a seat right here and wait, I'll let her know you're here to see her."

Naomi thanked the receptionist and dropped into a seat in the lobby. While she waited, Naomi messaged Diane to let her know that she had made it to the yoga studio and was waiting to talk to Paige's yoga instructor. She also sent a message to Doug to let him know that she'd need to take the day off unexpectedly. A few minutes later, a bunch of men and women started walking out of one of the yoga rooms. The last woman out of the room closed the door, and the receptionist waved her over to Naomi.

"Lindsey, this is Naomi. She wanted to know if you noticed anything strange about Paige during your class yesterday morning."

"Hi, Naomi. No, I noticed nothing out of the ordinary with Paige. She did as great as she normally did, and we exchanged pleasantries before and after class." Lindsey paused. "Wait. Now that I think about it, she seemed to a bit rushed after class. Normally she stays and hangs around a bit and talks to some other yogis, but yesterday she seemed to be in a hurry to get out of here. Is everything all right?"

"Well, to be honest, I'm not entirely sure. Did you see anyone outside waiting for her? Maybe a strange car nearby?"

Lindsey paused for a second before responding. "No. I waited until everyone filed out of the yoga studio before walking to the front. By the time I got there, Paige had left."

"Thanks so much for talking to me, Lindsey. Here is my number. Please contact me if you remember anything else."

"No worries, and I hope everything will be okay."

Naomi thanked Lindsey and Marie again and almost left the yoga studio.

"Wait," she said as she walked back to the receptionist. "Does Yoga Salon have a camera set up outside?"

Marie thought for a second. "We have a small camera that looks directly out the front door but doesn't take a wide view of the area outside. I'll check our feed, but if nothing happened directly in front of our door, we probably don't have it any footage." Marie started typing again on the computer in front of her.

"Check this out," Marie said a few moments later and motioned for Naomi to come closer. Marie turned the monitor, so it was facing both of them, and Naomi saw that she had queued up a video. Marie then clicked play.

Naomi saw Paige dash out the front and speed walk to her left, but nothing suspicious was on the film. "Do you think your neighbor next door might have a camera set up as well?"

"I'm not sure, but the business next door is a jewelry store. I ran into the owner last week, and she told me she'd be with her daughter out of state, so I think your best option would be to call her versus wait for her to open. I'm not sure when she's returning, but I can give you her contact information. Hold on a sec." Marie skimmed through her phone.

"Here it is." Marie placed the phone on the desk in front of Naomi. Naomi set her phone in scanner mode and copied the contact information for Jewelry by Jenna.

"Awesome. Thanks so much for your help." With that, Naomi left the yoga studio.

She walked for a few seconds before she fumbled with her phone and called the number for Jewelry by Jenna. It rang, and it rang. After every ring, the pain in her stomach grew and grew.

"Ugh," Naomi mumbled. She had a feeling she would hear the business's voice mail at any moment. And there it was. Naomi left a message asking for someone to return her call and that it was an emergency. She emailed the business in case Jenna or another employee checked her email while she was away.

When Naomi started walking back to her apartment, she couldn't help but feel that someone was watching her. She looked around and noticed that few people were on the street, although it was daylight. Trying to convince herself that it was because most people were at work, Naomi trudged along but couldn't shake the jittery feeling in her stomach. She jumped when a car blew its horn in the distance. Loud noises were as common in D.C. as leaves on trees and Naomi was used to this. But her nerves were shot.

Since she was feeling uneasy and worried that something might also happen to her, Naomi called Diane. She wanted to let her know what she had learned but thought talking to someone on the phone would help her feel safer.

"Hello?"

"Hi, Diane," Naomi said as she continued the walk back to her apartment.

"Did you find out anything from the yoga studio?"

"Paige took her yoga class yesterday morning, and her teacher noticed nothing out of the ordinary besides the fact that Paige seemed in a hurry after class. My first thought was that she might have been trying to get back home to get ready for work and meet me for breakfast, but who knows?"

"Thanks for checking with the yoga studio. It has now been hours since, as far as we know, anyone has seen Paige. I'll call the police and have them meet you at your apartment if that's okay. I'll be on the next train to DC."

"That sounds like a plan. And I hate that we're seeing each other again under these circumstances. I'll see you soon, and safe travels." Naomi said goodbye and took a deep breath. She didn't know how today could get any worse.

BY THE TIME Naomi arrived at her apartment, the police were already there. She unlocked her door and let them follow her inside. A woman in dark blue slacks and a dark green shirt stuck her hand out and said, "I'm Detective Alex Thompson, and I'm the detective looking into this case." Detective Thompson tucked a piece of her short red hair behind her ear and her green eyes settled on the phone she pulled from her pocket. She told Naomi that she'd look around before she started asking her questions. Then she and her team planned on sweeping the apartment for any evidence related to Paige's disappearance.

"Before we begin, I wanted to tell you how happy I am that

you're looking into this now since I know it hasn't been more than forty-eight hours."

"We do things a little differently nowadays." Detective Thompson gave her a slight smile. "When was the last time you saw Paige?"

"I last saw Paige just before going to bed a few nights ago. We went to happy hour that evening, and we both had been busy the rest of the weekend. Two days ago, she mentioned she was going to yoga the next morning and asked if we could grab breakfast after her class. I just checked with the studio, and they confirmed she was there."

Detective Thompson nodded her head and asked, "Where were you between 7:00 and 8:00 yesterday morning?"

Naomi's head jerked back, "Am I a suspect?"

"No. We just need to cover our bases."

"I woke up yesterday morning and then went for a jog."

"Can anyone corroborate that story?"

Naomi thought for a second. "Yes. Ann was working at the front desk that morning. She and I spoke briefly when I left, and I waved at her when I came back in. I'm also sure that the security cameras at the front of the building caught me both leaving and returning."

Detective Thompson nodded again and said, "We will confirm those details. Do you know of anyone that had any issues with Paige? Did she have any enemies?"

"As far as I know, no. Paige had a strange encounter with a senator while at work a few days ago, and she briefly told me about it. But that's all I know."

"How would you describe Paige's daily schedule?"

Naomi paused before responding. "Recently, she'd been leaving the apartment early to go to work and having to stay at the office late. I couldn't name exact times because they varied a lot. We would also check in with each other multiple times throughout the day to let each other know if our plans had changed. It's not like her to drop off of the face of the planet."

The questioning continued, and by the time the detective finished looking around the apartment, Naomi was exhausted. She was holding her phone close to Detective Thompson's until the detective's contact information appeared on the display when she realized that she had not told her parents what was going on.

Thankfully, technology had improved over the years, and she was able to reach her parents without an issue. Jada answered the phone immediately with a smile. That smile quickly turned into a frown once she saw the distressed look on her daughter's face.

"Naomi, what's wrong?"

"Paige is missing." Saying it out loud made everything more real.

"Wait - what?"

Naomi sighed. "No one knows where she is. Apparently, she made it to her yoga class yesterday morning, but no one knows what she did after that. I've already talked to the cops, and they just did a sweep of the apartment."

"Okay. Sit tight, and once we reach the port, we'll hop on the first plane we can get to DC."

"Mom, please don't. I know how much you have been looking forward to this vacation. Please stay and try to enjoy your cruise."

"Absolutely not. My daughter and her friend need me so I'm hopping on the first plane we can get. In the meantime, I will call Diane and contact an associate of mine who I want you to meet. Let me send him a message." And with that all Naomi heard was silence. She looked down at the phone and saw that her mother had hung up.

"Seriously?" Naomi asked as she threw her phone at her couch in frustration. She ran her hand through her dark, curly hair. Minutes seemed like hours as Naomi walked back and forth, trying to think of what she should do next to help Paige. Naomi felt her head throb as she tried to process what was happening. Her heartbeat pounded in her ears. Should she have contacted Diane or the police earlier? She swallowed hard to help soothe pain in the back of her throat. Maybe if she had gone to the yoga class with Paige, this wouldn't have happened. The urge to cry from sheer panic was intense.

About an hour and a half later, she was halfway across the room for what was probably the thousandth time when she heard a knock on her door. She opened her door, and her jaw dropped to the floor.

"What are you doing here?"

"Can I come in?" Reed asked as he gave her a polite smile.

CHAPTER 4

*N*aomi stared incredulously. The surprises just kept on coming.

"How do you know where I live? This isn't creepy to you?"

"May I come in? It might be easier to explain things if we sit down and talk," Reed said as he answered her question with a question.

"Uh...to be perfectly honest; I'm not comfortable having you in my home since I am not sure how you found out about it anyway."

"Fair," Reed said, nodding in agreement. "Your mom gave me your address. I didn't have a chance to tell you the other night, but I'm a private investigator." Naomi stared at him, blankly for a few seconds. She couldn't come up with a response to him announcing that he was a PI and that his eyes were causing a reaction in her body that she didn't want or need at this moment. It didn't help that Paige's disappearance was overwhelming her too.

"Do you mind waiting outside for a few minutes?" *There. Words.*

"Sure, not a problem."

Naomi closed the door and ran back to the couch to grab her phone. She wouldn't admit this out loud, but the knot in her stomach loosened. She called her mom and hoped that she would answer the phone.

"Naomi?"

Naomi breathed a sigh of relief when her mother answered immediately.

"Did you hang up on me earlier? Mom, what is the name of the person you wanted me to talk to about Paige's disappearance?"

"Sorry, sweetie. My mind was racing and I was trying to figure out how to get back to you, reach Diane, and contact Reed. His full name is Reed Wright. He's definitely over six feet tall with brown hair and blue eyes. Has he made it to your apartment yet? I sent you the photo I have of him. I also let Diane know that I asked Reed to look into this case, and she gave her full support."

Naomi looked at the photo and mumbled a few choice words. Well, this could not possibly get more awkward.

"Thanks, Mom. I'll try to talk to you later and fill you in on any other news that I find out. And I can't wait for you to tell me why you know a private investigator."

"Great, sweetie. And if I find out anything else on my end, I will let you know. Talk soon."

Naomi hung up her phone and went back to her front door. When she opened the door, Reed was leaning on the wall opposite the door with his feet crossed, eyes focused on his phone. This time she looked at what he was wearing. The dark washed jeans and dark blue sweater fit perfectly and brought out gunmetal blue eyes. He had a black coat on over his clothes.

"Have I been verified?" he asked as he looked up from his device.

Naomi glared at him. Was it just a coincidence that she met him at happy hour, and now he was standing at her front door? "Yes, I guess it's all right for you to come on in."

"On second thought, how about we head downstairs to the coffee shop I saw on the corner?"

Naomi was relieved that he suggested that as she still was not too sure she wanted him in her apartment. She grabbed her phone, her coat, and locked her apartment door.

Naomi and Reed quietly walked to the coffee shop down the street from Naomi and Paige's apartment. Once there, Reed opened the door for Naomi, and they found a corner table near the rear. When they sat down, Reed handed Naomi the menu monitor, and she selected what she wanted. She then gave it back to him for him to make his choice. Their drinks popped up from two planks on the table a minute later.

Naomi savored the taste of her coffee for a few seconds before she said, "I'm not even sure where to begin."

"Well...first, I can start by reintroducing myself. My name is Reed Wright, and I'm a private investigator. I apologize for not telling you when we met two nights ago." Reed held out his hand for Naomi to shake. She stared at his hand for a beat before putting out her hand to meet his. As they shook, Naomi zeroed in on how warm and callused his hand was. It was smooth yet rough. She broke contact before it became awkward. Reed gave her a curious glance and then bent over to pull something out of a book bag that Naomi had not even noticed he had. He set the pen and paper down in front of him.

"After all that has happened since last night, no worries. I'm just trying to find Paige as quickly as possible." Naomi rubbed her hands across her face.

"Understandable. And if you wanted more proof, here's my badge," Reed said as he showed Naomi his ID on the phone screen. She studied it and passed the device back to him.

"Do private investigators usually carry badges with them?"

"No. I do because of my association with MPD." Naomi was intrigued to learn that he was associated with the Metropolitan Police Department.

"When was the last time you saw Paige?"

Naomi took her time as she told him what she mentioned to Detective Thompson.

"Does she usually make plans and flake on them? Could she have possibly taken a last-minute trip and not informed you about it?"

"No. That isn't like Paige at all even with her being very busy. She is usually fantastic at communication. Even her mother has no idea where she is, and every time I call, her phone goes straight to her voice mail."

Reed went through a series of questions, similar to the ones that Detective Thompson asked Naomi earlier.

"Was she dating anyone?" Reed asked as he took notes with his pen and notebook.

"Not that I can think of - Well…Paige's yoga instructor mentioned that she seemed in a rush to leave right after the class yesterday morning when usually she sticks around to chat with people. She doesn't have any enemies that I know of." Naomi took a quick breath and continued. "We're both single, but she's dated a few guys here and there but nothing serious. And now that I'm thinking about it, she mentioned a strange encounter that she and her boss had with another colleague at work the other day."

Reed looked up from his notebook and gave Naomi a small smirk. "I didn't ask if you were single."

Naomi felt her cheeks heated after Reed called her out. "I…uh…I didn't mean it like that." *We have to focus on Paige.*

"I know, I know. I'm just messing with you. Anyway, you mentioned that Paige worked on Capitol Hill. She works for the Senate or the House?"

"Senate. She works for Senator Butler." Naomi noticed his not-so-smooth transition back to the issue at hand.

"And what encounter did she and Senator George Butler of Washington, DC, have with another senator a few days ago?"

"How do you know this? Why are you asking since you seem to know everything?"

"I'm just double-checking my answers. What happened?" Reed asked as he smoothly tried to stay on topic.

Naomi noticed he had not answered her question, but she continued. "I'm not sure who the other senator was beside her being a woman. Years ago this would have been hard to narrow down, but since half the Senate is female, who knows who it could be? Apparently, there was a blowup over legislation that Senator Butler was a sponsor of related to cybersecurity. The senator lost her shit and hinted that Senator Butler would regret supporting this legislation. Paige said it was one of the strangest things that she had ever seen at her job."

"Do you think political motivation could be a factor?"

"I mean it could be. Some people have some powerful feelings about cybersecurity and how much of it the world needs. It's the only reason I could think of that she would be missing."

"How did the police act when they interviewed you? Were they suspicious of you at all?"

"A little at first. I had an alibi for the time that Paige disappeared based on when I went out for a jog. I thought Detective Thompson would try to trip me up while she was questioning me, though."

"And they didn't mention any leads, right?"

"Nope. Not to me. I started doing my own investigating, though."

"What did you find?"

"So, I mentioned that when I went to the yoga studio, I asked if Paige attended one of the classes Monday morning, and if so, when did she leave, etcetera. I almost left before asking if they had a video feed set up to monitor their front door. The receptionist told me they did, but the camera's angle wasn't great. Even though there was nothing suspicious on the video, I could see at the very least which direction Paige walked off. I got the contact information for the business owner of the property next door that might have a video feed that would show Paige. I reached out, but the owner is visiting her family out of state. So, now I'm waiting for her to get back to me."

Reed stared at Naomi for a moment before he said, "Fantastic detective work, Naomi. That is super helpful, and hopefully, the owner gets back to you soon. I'll follow up with the police to find out where they are and if this will officially be a case."

"Great, and please let me know as soon as you find out anything."

Reed stopped writing and looked at Naomi. "You'll be the first person I talk to if I hear something from them." He then went back to writing things down in his notebook.

Naomi sat there and awkwardly watched Reed continue jotting down notes. Then he placed the pen down and looked directly into Naomi's eyes.

"Did Paige have a computer or laptop, and is it at your apartment?"

"Yes, of course. Most people do."

"And the police didn't take it with them? Hmm. Weird. Then again, they might have been able to download all of the information they needed without taking it in. Do you mind grabbing it and bringing it back here? There might be clues to her whereabouts on it."

"You know what? It might be easier if you just came back to our apartment and looked around. The police have already been there and said nothing about coming back."

Reed leaned a little closer to Naomi and said, "Are you okay with me being in your apartment?"

She did everything she could to control the shiver that attempted to make its way down her spine. She shook the feeling off before shrugging. "To be honest? Not really, but I don't have much choice right now. I'll do anything to get Paige back safely."

Reed leaned back and said, "Fair enough. Let's go."

Before Naomi had a chance, Reed grabbed the menu

monitor and flicked the screen to their bill. He quickly paid and then smiled at Naomi.

"Drinks are on me. Again," Reed said as he stood up and grabbed his book bag.

"Thanks," Naomi said as she stood up as well. They both walked out of the coffee shop and back to the apartment.

On the way back, Naomi debated telling Reed about her uneasy feeling that someone was watching her. She debated the thought for a few seconds before giving in.

"Do you feel that?"

"Feel what?"

Naomi looked to her right before she replied, "That someone was watching us?"

She watched while Reed surveyed their surroundings before he gestured in the direction of her apartment. "I don't see anything, but it doesn't mean that someone isn't watching. Let's walk faster."

She nodded her head and picked up her pace. A few seconds later, she let out a frustrated sigh. "Paige would never disappear willingly. Someone must have taken her."

Reed nodded but said nothing as they arrived at Naomi's apartment. He held the door for her as they walked through the lobby of the apartment complex. Ann was chatting with another woman at the front desk. She looked up and saw Naomi and waved.

"Sorry to interrupt, but do you have a second, Ann?"

Ann apologized to the woman she was talking to and then turned back to Naomi and said, "Sure. I was just getting ready to clock out. Hello," she said and held out her hand to shake Reed's. Reed nodded in return and shook her hand.

"Ann, this is Reed. Reed, Ann," Naomi said, quickly introducing the two. "Did you see Paige after she returned from yoga?"

"The police asked me a similar question. No. I didn't see Paige return. I only saw her leave. Later on, I saw you leave for your jog and then come back. I told them all of this."

"Thanks, Ann." Naomi turned to Reed. "We can head up to my apartment and see if there is anything we can find that might help the police."

"Good luck."

When they got back to her apartment, Naomi opened the door and hung up their coats in the front hall closet. She gave Reed a brief tour of the apartment and showed him Paige's room. It was a bit messier than usual, Naomi thought, but that could have been because of her rushing to get out the door in time for her yoga class. It didn't help that the police also searched her bedroom.

"Do you know Paige's password?"

"Maybe. I had to use her laptop a while back, and she told me what it was. Hopefully, she hasn't changed it." Naomi sat down at Paige's desk and turned on the computer. When the password prompt appeared, Naomi typed in the password that Paige had given her months ago, but it didn't work.

"Oh, no."

"Do you have any other ideas?"

"No...wait. Let me try this." Naomi started typing again and then pressed enter. It worked, and the computer loaded Paige's home screen.

"How did you figure it out?"

Naomi looked over her shoulder at Reed. "Looks like she just made a slight change to the password she gave me. Not the best thing to do in terms of cybersecurity, but hey, it worked, and we got in."

The first thing Naomi clicked was an application that allowed someone to locate their phone, which might give Reed and her an idea about where Paige was, especially if she had her phone on her, and it was on.

"Let's see if we can track down her phone this way."

But when she accessed the app, it said the last time Paige's phone was on was around the time she was at her yoga class. Determined not to get discouraged, Naomi loaded the application that synced Paige's messages between her computer and her phone.

Naomi saw a bunch of messages between Paige and various people in her life. Although she felt awkward about reading Paige's private messages, Naomi saw nothing out of the ordinary, except she noticed one from a number that no contact information listed.

"Looks like the guy she recently met while at work texted her, and they talked about getting coffee again, but nothing set in stone," Naomi whispered as she copied his number.

She opened up a new window in Paige's web browser and searched for the number, but nothing came up. She took out her phone and saved the number just in case.

Naomi took a break from looking through Paige's computer files to glance at Reed and noticed he was inspecting Paige's room. A few minutes passed, and Reed was now standing over her shoulder, looking down at the monitor. She felt his hand lightly brush against hers before he asked, "Did you find anything else that was interesting?"

Although the touch was light, it still gave her small chills. Naomi looked at how close their hands were before she replied. "Nothing really besides this guy who asked her out for coffee. But even that isn't really out of the ordinary. She talked to her coworkers, her mom, me, and her other friends. Nothing strange about that."

"And you're sure it isn't possible she had to take a last-minute trip and will be back in a few days?"

"No. It's not like Paige to go somewhere unannounced and not tell me or her mother or anyone else," she snapped. "Why don't you believe me?" Those sweet feelings she felt after he touched her fled her mind. Plus, the feeling was mutual. She didn't completely trust him either.

Reed was silent for a moment. "I believe you. I'm just verifying." Before Naomi could respond, the doorbell chimed.

"Saved by the bell," Naomi muttered as she left Reed in Paige's room and went to answer the door. Diane Harris stood on her doorstep, looking understandably distraught. Paige had gotten most of her features from her mother. From their statuesque physiques to their blonde hair and blue eyes, the only difference was that Diane wore her hair in a bob. Whereas her daughter preferred her hair to be longer.

"Have you heard anything?" Diane asked as she walked into the apartment.

"Nope. Have you?" Naomi asked. She grabbed Diane's coat and hung it in the front hall closet.

"Not much. I've been on the phone with Detective Thompson and another officer assigned to this case, but so far, I think I'm getting the runaround. I don't think the police believe anyone kidnapped Paige. I...just don't know which way to turn," Diane sighed as she sat down on the couch in the living room.

Naomi watched as Reed left Paige's bedroom and shut the door as if it were made of glass. He walked over to the couch and sat down in an armchair across from Diane.

"We will do everything we can to get your daughter back safely. You have my word." Reed briefly looked at Diane before looking at Naomi.

"Sorry, I don't think we've met. I'm Diane, Paige's mom."

"I'm Reed Wright. Jada called me and asked me to help where I could."

"That's right. Thank you so much for helping us find my daughter, and it's so nice to meet you. Your reputation precedes you."

Naomi turned to Reed and raised an eyebrow.

"Ah...well, thank you." Reed blushed. *Interesting.* She wanted to find out more about his stellar reputation.

"Do you mind if I ask you a few questions, Diane?" Reed asked as he stood up. He walked over to where he left his book bag near the front door.

"Sure, I have no problem with that," Diane said as she adjusted herself in her seat. Reed asked her about the last time Diane heard from Paige and if she knew of anyone who might want to harm her. Diane repeated the same answers that Naomi gave, not giving the group any more insight into why Paige might have disappeared.

"Thanks, Diane," Reed said as he placed his pen and notebook back into his book bag. "My first thought is that we should try to talk to Senator Butler and some of his staffers. Especially the staffers that were closest to Paige. I thought we might get an interview with the senator through Naomi, but without a doubt, the staff would make time to see you, Diane."

"I think that is a great idea, if that is okay with you, Diane.

Let's reach out to them right now." Diane nodded, and Naomi found the number to Senator Butler's office on her phone. She clicked the call button and placed the device on the coffee table.

"Good afternoon, you've reached Senator Butler's office. This is Melody speaking. How may I help you?"

"Hello. This is Naomi Porter, and I am sitting here with Diane Harris, Paige Harris's mother. We were hoping we could come in to talk with the senator and his staff to see if they might know anything about her disappearance."

There was a pause on the other end of the line before Naomi heard, "Is it all right if I put you on hold for a few minutes?"

"Sure, that's perfectly fine," Naomi said before she put her phone on mute. "I hope they talk to us, but I understand if they don't since I am sure it's crazy busy."

"I'm sure they will make time to talk to us," Reed said as he leaned forward a bit toward Naomi's phone. "If the press ends up getting wind of this and finds out that the senator didn't meet with his missing staffer's family...well, I assume the fallout will not be good."

"Well, maybe that's an option we need to explore," said Diane. "I can't just sit back and do nothing while my daughter is missing."

Naomi nodded her head in agreement and placed a hand gently on Diane's shoulder. She could not imagine what she was going through right now.

"Ms. Porter? Ms. Harris?"

Naomi unmuted her phone and responded, "Yes, we are still here."

"The senator would love it if you came by sometime

tomorrow. We will make any time work as long as it doesn't conflict with his morning committee meetings. What time would work best for you?"

"Will he be available at 2:00 p.m.?"

"Sure, that will work. Do you know where our office is?"

"I just know it's in Dirksen."

"Our office is 381 Dirksen Senate Office Building. If you have any trouble getting in or finding our office, please call this number back."

"Great, see you tomorrow," Naomi said as she disconnected the call. She looked at the two people before her and said, "Hopefully, the senator can answer some of the questions we have."

CHAPTER 5

The next day, Naomi and Diane met up with Reed in front of the Dirksen Senate Office Building. Once the trio was through security, Naomi pulled out her phone to double-check the office number. Once she knew where they were going, everyone stepped on the elevator and got out on the third floor. Senator Butler's office was a short distance from the elevator, and Reed swiped his hand on a sensor that opened the office door. A woman sat at the front desk and wiped her eyes with a tissue. She tossed her blonde curls over her shoulder before greeting the group.

"Hi, my name is Melody, Senator Butler's staff assistant. How may I help you?"

"Hello, Melody, my name is Naomi, and I am here with Diane Harris and Reed Wright. We're here to talk to the senator and his chief of staff about Paige's disappearance." Naomi glanced around the room and noted all of the memorabilia and photos of Washington, D.C.

Melody stared at Naomi for a split-second before she rushed behind her desk. She started typing on her phone, and after a few seconds, she headed toward another door in the office.

"Please follow me. I'll take you to the senator's conference room. He and Heather, his chief of staff, should be available to talk to you shortly. I'm so sorry all of this has happened." The trio followed Melody through the senator's office until they came to a door labeled Conference Room. Melody opened the door and let everyone inside. The three got as comfortable as they could in the seats surrounding the table.

Melody looked around and asked, "May I get you all anything? Maybe water?" Everyone shook their heads no. "Well, the bathroom is just out this door and to the left. If you all need anything, I'll be out front at my desk. The senator and Heather should be here shortly." And with that, Melody closed the door behind her.

"I think you should talk with her after we meet with the senator," Reed said as he dug around in his bag after a few seconds of silence. He pulled out the same pen and notebook that he had the day before and opened the notebook up to a new page. Naomi chuckled at his quirk since most people used computers to take notes on.

Naomi nodded and glanced at Reed and asked, "Random question that means nothing, but why do you use a notebook and pen to take notes during interviews?"

"Because my brain works better when I write things down versus typing them. And I just prefer it to be honest," Reed said and gave Naomi a slight smile. Naomi nodded, and the room was silent once again.

A few moments later, there was a knock on the door, and Senator Butler and a woman walked into the conference room. Both were dressed to impress in their suits and the senator's salt and pepper hair added another hint of sophistication to his look. The group stood up and Naomi rubbed her hands on her pants. The senator scanned the people in his room and went over to shake Diane's hand.

"Ms. Harris, I am sorry we are meeting under such unfortunate circumstances. Paige has been a wonderful addition to my team, and I am sorry this has happened."

"Thank you, Senator." The senator moved on and stood in front of Naomi. They shook hands.

"And you must be Naomi. Paige has talked about you, including your experience in cybersecurity. You work in the field, correct?"

"Yes, that is right. It is nice to meet you, Senator." Senator Butler then reached over to shake Reed's hand.

"And I'm sorry, but I don't believe we have met before."

"I'm Reed, and I am here with Naomi." Naomi side-eyed Reed and made a note to ask him about that later.

"This is my chief of staff, Heather. She and Paige work together often." Heather shook everyone in the group's hands, and Senator Butler led everyone back to the table to take a seat.

"I want to mention that the police came by yesterday and my office is cooperating with them. Whatever they want to know, we will tell them. How can we help you all?"

Naomi was a little intimidated by the senator. Although he was friendly, she felt awkward. Here she was sitting in front of a United States senator, getting ready to question whether or not he was involved in the disappearance of her best friend. Naomi looked at Reed before answering. He slightly nodded his head, which she took to mean that she should go first. She took a deep breath and asked the senator and his chief of staff her first question.

"Did either of you notice any changes in Paige's behavior over the last few days or weeks?"

Both the senator and his staffer shook their heads no. "She has been her normal, hardworking self. I know that she had a lot on her plate between the budget fight and this cybersecurity legislation, but she seemed to handle it in stride. Well... she didn't complain to me," Heather said as she folded her hands onto the table.

"Could you tell us about your cybersecurity bill?"

"Sure. One campaign goal was to decrease the likelihood of cyberattacks and to protect my constituents and the citizens of this country. This bill ensures more funding goes to implementing current and new ideas to improve our security. Paige, Heather, and other members of my staff have been working extensively on getting cosponsors for this bill on the staff level."

"But it sounds like Paige was the key person on this bill."

This time Heather answered. "Yes, that's right. She was the lead on it, but we worked together and checked in with each other a lot. The budget deal negotiations have taken up most of my time."

Reed sat up taller before asking his question. "Would you say this bill is controversial?"

Senator Butler paused for a beat before answering. "Depends on who you ask."

"Paige told me about a confrontation that happened a few days ago when you and she met with another senator and her staff about the cybersecurity legislation. Would you be willing to talk to us more about that?" Naomi tightened her grip on her chair arm as she waited for a response. Senator Butler and Heather glanced at each other before the senator responded.

"Yes. We met with a senator and one of her staffers recently, and...there was a moment of contention. But everything is okay now. I'd like to keep this between us, of course."

"That's fine, Senator. If you don't mind me asking, who was the senator you were meeting with?"

"I'd rather not say."

Naomi glanced at Reed before turning her attention back to the senator.

"Well, is this senator still upset about the bill? Has she spoken out against it?"

The senator and Heather looked at each other again before Heather answered.

"No. The senator still hasn't told us which way she will vote on the bill, but she has decided not to cosponsor the bill at this point."

Reed nodded again before asking, "Had you noticed anyone strange around the vicinity of the office? Has the Capitol Police warned your office that something might occur?"

Senator Butler looked at Reed for a second before responding. "I get all kinds of threats all the time. Some of those threats are more serious than others. And some of those threats include my staff. The Capitol Police and any other proper authorities are well informed. There has been nothing out of the ordinary occurring as far as I am aware."

Naomi digested this new information and thought somehow, someway, they needed to find out that other senator's name. The senator and Heather spent a few more minutes talking with the trio before walking them back out to

Melody's desk. Naomi told Reed and Diane that she would meet up with them in a few minutes. They left the office while Naomi walked over to Melody's desk, just as she was hanging up her phone.

"Melody, do you know who else was close to Paige?"

"I would say that I probably was the closest outside of Heather. She offered to become my mentor a few months ago when she found out that I eventually wanted to work in a position that was more legislative focused." Melody wiped her eyes again with the napkin in her hand.

"Are you interested in cybersecurity as well? Both Paige and I took some classes in it during college and after - well, me more so than her."

"Yes! She mentioned introducing me to you at some point because you had some experience in the field directly. It's probably the policy area that I am most focused on and one reason I wanted to get a job in Senator Butler's office. The politics at play surrounding the issue are even more interesting. You would think everyone would agree that we need more cybersecurity, but certain factions of Congress don't. I shouldn't probably say this out loud, but I was shocked by one particular senator's reaction to the bill."

"Really?"

"Yep. Senator Evie Graham. She is on record with having been supportive of increasing cybersecurity, so it shocked me when she and her staff wanted to meet with George and Paige urgently a few days ago. Not that George doesn't meet with other senators, but it just seemed strange, given how much their office was forcing the meeting."

"That's very interesting."

Melody continued, "The staff assistants sometimes talk,

and apparently things have been stressful over in that office. I don't know this for sure as I didn't hear it directly from her staff assistant, however."

"This is helpful. Here is my contact information." Naomi sent her phone number to Melody's phone before she continued. "Please let me know if you think of anything else that might be helpful. And once we get Paige back safely, I'd love to take you out for coffee so we can chat about cybersecurity."

"Really? That would be awesome. Thank you so much!"

Naomi walked out of the senator's office and saw Reed standing down the hall.

"Where is Diane?" Naomi asked.

"She went to the bathroom to fix her makeup. Said she'll be right back."

"Oh, okay. How did you know talking to Melody one-on-one would lead to some helpful information?"

"I didn't. I figured Melody probably saw who was coming in and out of the office, and she probably had a decent idea of what the senator's schedule might entail even though she is not his scheduler. Did you find out anything useful?"

"Yes. Senator Evie Graham is the senator who Senator Butler and Paige met with about his cybersecurity legislation that ended in a screaming match." Naomi pulled out her phone and started scanning news websites after performing a quick search.

Reed nodded his head as he processed that information. "That's great to know. I found it interesting that Senator Butler withheld her name."

"Well, maybe he didn't want to spread gossip. Like he was worried, we'd tell someone or leak it to the press. Speaking of which, it's amazing that Paige's disappearance hasn't leaked either. Well, at least I haven't seen anything." She showed Reed her phone screen.

"True. There is usually a bigger reason for keeping certain things quiet…at least in my line of work."

"Well, then I guess we need to figure out why he withheld her name. I will go check on Diane."

As Naomi turned away, Reed gently grabbed her hand.

"You did a great job in there."

"Thanks," Naomi said as she gave Reed a small smile and walked into the women's bathroom. Naomi heard some sniffling and called out Diane's name. Diane gave a soft reply and walked out of a bathroom stall to the sink where she washed and dried her hands. When she looked up, Naomi could see that her eyes had turned a bleary red.

"Do you mind if I give you a hug?" Diane shook her head no, and Naomi and Diane embraced as Diane quietly sobbed.

"I just don't understand why this is happening to my baby."

"I don't understand why this is happening either. I wish there were more I could do," Naomi stated as she gently rubbed small circles on Diane's back. "But we will get her back safely. I promise you." As the words fell from her lips, dread crept into her heart. Would she be able to deliver on this promise?

Those words seemed to reassure Diane somewhat as she stopped sobbing. Diane looked back in the mirror and started pulling herself together.

"I want you to be careful as well. I don't want to lose my second daughter." Naomi smiled at the compliment before Diane sniffled. "I'll only be a few more minutes. Go out and join Reed, or he might think we fell in the toilet or something."

Naomi laughed and left the bathroom. Once again, Reed was on his phone, and Naomi cleared her throat to get his attention. Reed looked up at Naomi, smiled, and placed his device in his pocket.

"So, what was all of that about?"

"All of what about?"

"I'm here with Naomi?"

"I didn't want to stroll in there and say I was a private investigator. It might put them on the defensive. And technically, I was there with you." Reed kept his tone light and matter of fact.

"I guess you were, technically," Naomi said before she dropped that topic of conversation. "What did you think of the encounter with the senator and Heather?"

"I think you learned more from Melody during your two-minute conversation than we learned during that entire session with the senator. I also don't think Paige's disappearance involved anyone that we talked to today."

Diane walked out of the bathroom and appeared to be on her phone. She wrapped up the conversation quickly and joined Naomi and Reed.

"So that was the police. They haven't found much to go on but will keep me in the loop if they do. They are trying to keep Paige's disappearance under wraps for now as it might be a political matter because she works on the Hill."

"Okay. Would you like to stay at our apartment while we continue to wait for more information? I think it would be nice to have someone staying with me during this ordeal. My parents are trying their best to get back, but who knows how long it will take as they are on a cruise."

"That's right, Jada mentioned the cruise. I'd love to stay in the apartment. I agree it would be nice not to be alone." Diane gently grabbed Naomi's hand and gave it a quick squeeze.

Naomi turned to Reed, looked into his eyes, and said, "I'll take Diane to my apartment to get settled. So, we'll see you later? And I can call you if anything happens."

"Sure, that works. I'll see you later."

* * *

COLD. That was all Paige could think of as she woke up. She lifted her head slowly because she still felt groggy. She tried to place her hands down to help herself up, but realized they were tied together somehow. *Is this a zip tie?* She frantically pulled against the plastic before coming to a stop. Some of her memories flowed back to her consciousness, but she could not tell how long it had been since they had occurred.

Paige remembered going to yoga class. Since she was planning on grabbing breakfast with Naomi that day, she practically ran out of her yoga studio to get home in time. She walked out the door and started heading to the bus stop when she was stopped by a deep voice calling her name. She looked up and saw that it was the guy who invited her for coffee a couple of days ago.

"Hey...Jett, right? What are you doing out here this early?"

Jett gave her a slight smile and said, "Hey, Paige. I was just walking to work, and I saw you. Did you just come out of that studio?"

Paige nodded and said, "Yes. I try to take yoga classes as often as I can."

Jett adjusted his baseball cap and nodded. "Understandable. I'm sure it's a stress reliever and an excellent way to stay active. Are you headed to the bus stop? I can walk you there."

Paige was not comfortable walking with Jett to the bus stop because she didn't know him well, but at least it was just two blocks away as opposed to him walking her all the way home. Paige looked to see if anyone was around, but the people from her class had walked in the opposite direction. "I guess that's okay," she said as she felt like she did not have much of a choice nor could she think of an excuse quickly enough to get out of it.

The two began walking and chatting on their way to the bus stop. When they got to the corner of the street just before the stop, Paige felt something cover her face. The rest of her memories of what happened after that was blurry.

Now she was here.

As Paige tried to gather her thoughts, she heard a bang. A door opened from what appeared to be a flight of stairs, and light flooded the room. Paige looked to where the sound and light came from and saw someone walking down the stairs.

"What is going on? Where am I?" Paige asked. She gasped when she recognized Jett.

Jett just stared at her, which made her feel even more uneasy.

"Jett?"

Jett raked his fingers through his hair and sighed. "I'm sorry," he said just above a whisper.

"Sorry? Sorry for what? Why am I tied up? Where am I?" Paige asked. There wasn't anything she could do to stop her heart from beating out of her chest. She tested the tightness of the zip ties to see if she could get free.

"Paige, there is no way you are going to able to break free.

And I'm sorry that I am the reason you're here." Jett walked away from the staircase and bent down to get on the same level as Paige. "There isn't much I can tell you that will make this any better, but I didn't have a choice."

"What do you mean you didn't have a choice? We all have choices. We make them every day. Let me out!" Paige said in full panic mode. She started wiggling her body to see if there was any way to release herself from her bonds. When she realized that so far, Jett had been right, she started screaming.

"Someone help me! Help! Help!" Tears fell from Paige's eyes.

Jett let her scream for a bit before turning to her and saying, "No one can hear you, and you should probably stop screaming. You are just wasting your energy."

Paige stopped screaming and looked at Jett. "Why are you doing this? What is going on?"

"I wish I could explain, but I can't," Jett said as he looked Paige in the eyes. "Just know that none of this is your fault, but I didn't have a choice. I will start lunch and bring it down when it's ready. Okay?"

Paige nodded because that was all she could do. She hoped that someone had heard her screams, and she knew she needed to find a way out.

CHAPTER 6

*N*aomi and Diane arrived back at Naomi's apartment in record time. Naomi grabbed some water for Diane and did her best to help her settle in. Once Diane was situated, Naomi headed back to her room to check in with work even though it was late afternoon.

While talking to Doug and June online, Naomi heard her phone make a pinging noise, which notified her that she had a new message. It was from Reed.

Reed: *Although it was under terrible circumstances, I really enjoyed hanging out with you today.*

While Naomi thought of a reply, she realized there was part of her that was beginning to give Reed the benefit of the doubt. After all, she currently only had Diane and him to help her find Paige. Plus, her mom put her trust in him, and she trusted her mother's judgment.

Naomi: *I enjoyed hanging out with you too. Have you heard anything from the police?*

Reed: *Nothing yet.*

Naomi: *Ugh, I get it, but it's still frustrating.*

Reed: *Without a doubt.*

Naomi placed her phone facedown so she wouldn't get distracted and started doing some work. She called Doug to update him on the search for Paige after she got caught up on her email and projects she was working on. After working for seven hours, Naomi closed her laptop. She stood up and walked into the kitchen to find Diane sitting in the kitchen, looking at her phone.

"How are you doing?" Naomi asked. She turned away from Diane to grab a mug from a cabinet.

"I'm...surviving. Trying to call some of my contacts who might be able to help. How are you?" Diane asked as she looked up from the device.

"I'm surviving too, I guess," Naomi said as she used her refrigerator's water filter to pour some water in her cup. "Have you heard anything from the police?"

"Detective Thompson called a few minutes ago and said they are following a couple of leads, but they don't have anything concrete yet. I know usually no news is good news, but I can't help but feel disappointed that we haven't heard anything."

"I understand that. Reed hasn't heard anything either. It's frustrating, but what can we do?" Naomi asked as she was about to change the subject. "Is there anything I can get you to help make you more comfortable?"

"I think I have everything I need. You should go to sleep because we've all had a long day. If I hear anything, I'll wake you up, okay?"

"Sounds great, have a good night," Naomi said before she walked back into her room. She sat down on the edge of her bed. The knot that had been in her stomach was a permanent fixture that she seemingly couldn't undo because Paige was still missing. She put her glass on her bedside table, placed her scarf on her head, and went to sleep.

* * *

THE NEXT MORNING, Naomi woke up feeling slightly disoriented. The first thing she did was check her work email account. Seeing nothing, she checked her personal email. She skimmed through her emails that included spam messages from different clothing stores, food delivery services, and more. Just as she was about to click off her personal email, Naomi noticed a new message had just arrived. Her heart started beating hard inside her chest. The email had come from Paige Harris. The grogginess went away immediately as she threw her headscarf on her bedside table.

The title of the email just said, "Important Please Read," but Naomi was scared to click. She pulled out her phone and called Reed. The line rang a few times before he answered.

"Hey, Naomi," he answered, his voice full of sleep.

"Oh, jeez, I forgot how early it was. I'm sorry, but you need to get over here as soon as possible."

"What's wrong? Is everything all right?"

"I got a message from Paige's personal email account. I haven't opened it yet, but I assume this email is new and scheduled to be sent to me today."

Reed waited for a beat before responding. "Let me grab a couple of things, and I'll be right there."

While Naomi waited for Reed to get to her apartment, she woke Diane up and filled her in on what she had found. The next thing she knew, she was pacing in her living room. The all too familiar anxiety pangs in her stomach had returned.

When Reed knocked on the door about twenty minutes later, Naomi quickly fluffed up her curls before answering.

"Cute pajamas," Reed said, referring to her unicorn pajamas and socks.

"Thanks for trying to lighten the mood but now is not the time," Naomi said. She did, however, look at what he was wearing. Reed had on a pair of black sweatpants, a blue sweatshirt, and sneakers.

"So, what happened? What's up with this email?" Reed asked.

"Come on in," Naomi said as she and Reed started walking to her room. Diane still had not left Paige's room.

"So, I had just woken up and decided to check my email," Naomi said as she moved out of the way to let Reed into her room. "I skimmed through a bunch of spam emails, and just as I was about to close the window, I get an email from Paige's personal account. I didn't want to open it without talking to you first."

"Okay, well, let's open it up."

"By the way, I ran this email through multiple virus scanners and found none."

"Are you sure?"

A knock on the door interrupted Naomi before she could respond. Reed got up and opened the door. Diane walked in with two mugs of coffee, and Reed hurried to the kitchen to grab the last mug. Reed and Naomi thanked Diane for the coffee when he returned.

"Anyway, I work in cybersecurity. I have helped develop some of the most secure security programs there are, so my computer is secure. Probably even more secure than Paige's government laptop."

"Touché," Reed said as he pulled out his phone and waited for Naomi to open the email. Naomi sat back down at her desk and opened the email.

Dear Naomi,

You don't know us, but we know you. My name is PAN. Paige will stay with us for a while until we get what we need from you. We have several tasks you need to perform before we let Paige go. You will have 48 hours to finish each task. And here is your first one: What does PAN stand for? Submit your response in the field box below.

PAN

"I don't even know what to say to that," Diane said.

Naomi stood up and paced. "Me neither." She walked back and forth twice before coming to a stop. "Reed, do you think it makes sense to call the police?"

"It wouldn't hurt."

"I will call Detective Thompson and tell her about the email," said Naomi as she nodded and dialed the detective's office number, but there was no answer, which Naomi guessed made sense since it was so early. Naomi left a message asking her to return the call. When Naomi hung up, she turned to Reed.

"She didn't answer. Hopefully, she calls me back quickly," Naomi said.

"I agree, and if I don't hear anything soon on my end, I will have to call an old family friend."

Naomi nodded but said nothing. Her thoughts engrossed her too much to respond to him.

"Diane, why don't you and I head to the kitchen?"

Diane agreed and said, "I'll ask Simon to make us a small breakfast? I'm sure none of us are going back to sleep anytime soon."

"Naomi, do you need anything?" Reed asked as he and Diane walked toward the bedroom door.

Reed and Diane left the room when Naomi shook her head. She was alone with her thoughts, and to her, that was dangerous. Why had Paige been kidnapped? What did this "PAN" want with her? Why was all of this happening?

She tried to do a little research. She pulled out her phone and searched for PAN, but could find nothing that might have been relevant. She placed her phone down when she felt weird pains in her chest.

Naomi's heart leapt into her throat. The shortness of breath and the feeling of losing control followed shortly afterward. Naomi knew she was having an anxiety attack and that she had to act quickly to prevent it from getting worse. She focused on deep breathing and turned to the photo of her and her parents on the dresser. She tried to transport herself back to her happy place. Back to their vacation in Puerto Rico. Back to when everything was normal.

The anxiety attack subsided within a few minutes, and she was happy that she was able to control that one. Naomi decided the best course of action for her was to put some water on her face and schedule an appointment with Dr. Evans because she was worried about it occurring again. After splashing some cool water on her face and drying it off, she walked out of her bathroom, grabbed her mug, and went to the kitchen.

Diane had set out some fruit and toast on the kitchen counter. Naomi looked around for Reed, but she didn't see him. Diane grabbed her mug and walked to the living room to sit on the couch. She turned the television to one of the morning news shows. Although the TV was on, Diane stared off into space, the show serving as background noise.

"Diane, can I get you anything?" Naomi asked as she walked to the counter to grab a piece of toast.

Diane looked around quickly before settling her eyes on Naomi and said, "No, I'm fine. Well, as fine as I can be anyway. Reed stepped outside to make some calls, but he said he would be back soon."

"Ah. Okay. I'm surprised anyone would talk to him this early. It's about 7? 7:30?" Naomi sat down next to Diane and tried to watch whatever show Diane had turned on. Naomi grabbed her phone from her pocket and quickly checked her email to see if she got another message from "Paige/PAN." There was nothing.

Naomi sighed and turned to Diane. "We're at the mercy of whoever kidnapped Paige."

Diane looked down at her mug and replied, "I know."

Naomi stood up and paced again. Diane turned back to the television. After a few moments, it clicked. Naomi headed back into her room.

Naomi sat down at her desk and opened PAN's email again. She forwarded the email to her work account and then grabbed her work laptop from her bag. A short time later, she set up a program that Edmon had been testing to find the IP address of a computer, based on emails sent from it. The program analyzed the email, and Naomi sat back in her chair and waited.

"Naomi? Are you okay?" Reed asked, his words bringing Naomi out of her daydream.

"Uh, yeah. What's up?"

"Detective Thompson just arrived. Said she wanted to talk to you and Diane."

Naomi stood up and followed Reed into her living room.

"Oh, there you guys are. I was just getting ready to tell Diane that we have some good news! We've heard from Paige."

"You what?" both Naomi and Diane screamed in unison. Reed just stared at Detective Thompson silently.

"Yes. Paige called my phone at the police station. Here is the video." The detective took out her phone, pulled up the video, and pressed play.

Paige appeared on the screen and was sitting in front of a black background. She glanced to her right side first before she began talking.

"Detective Thompson, my name is Paige Harris, and I heard that a missing person's case is in the beginning stages of being formed on me. I wanted to let you know that I am fine and just took an extended leave of absence." She held up a phone whose screen looked to be displaying a plane ticket before putting it down and continuing. "Please don't waste police resources looking for me. I will return as soon as I can. I will contact my family and friends shortly. Thank you so much." Then the screen went black.

Reed spoke first. "Have you verified this video? Have the police been able to confirm that this is Paige and that she isn't under duress?"

Detective Thompson stood up and placed her phone in her pocket before settling both hands on her waist and answered, "Yes. Our team verified that this is Paige in the video, and there is no sign of coercion. We find the circumstances of her leaving kind of strange, but with this video, there isn't much we can do at this point until she returns."

"There is no way my daughter would have left without telling anyone where she is going. I don't care what her kidnappers forced her to say on that video." Diane stood up and glared at Detective Thompson.

Detective Thompson placed a hand on Diane's shoulder. "I understand that, but this video has our hands tied. Unless we hear something else that contradicts what she said on the video, we have to stop investigating at this point. I'm sorry." Detective Thompson started moving toward the door before turning around. "If there is anything I can help you with please, let me know."

Naomi thought about telling Detective Thompson about the email she received but refrained because if Detective Thompson was willing to close this case with just that video....

Reed jumped up. "Is it possible that we could get a copy of the video?"

"Sure, I'll send it to you right now." Detective Thompson and Reed worked together to make sure he had access to the video file, and then she left the apartment.

Naomi, who had been silent since Detective Thompson arrived, said, "There is no way that video is real. It would be completely out of character for Paige to just leave."

"I don't know Paige well, but I don't think she left on her own accord either." Both Naomi and Diane looked at Reed after his admission. Reed stared out of the balcony doors.

"Why is that?" Diane tried to shake off her anger but had a hard time doing so.

"Because I can tell someone doctored the video. Naomi, let's go check out that email you received, and I'll explain."

Naomi, Reed, and Diane went into Naomi's bedroom to read the email. Naomi watched Reed glance around her room. She thought she did a good job of making it homey. Naomi had a bed, a dresser, a bedside table, a bookshelf, and a desk in it. On her dresser were photos of her family, Paige and other friends, and places she had visited around the world. Two pieces of art hung on the walls along with her diploma from college. Near the entrance of the bedroom, there were some race medals that she won over the years. Reed walked over to the dresser and grabbed the photo frame that contained a picture of her parents.

"You and your parents look so happy here." Reed showed the photo to Naomi.

She smiled at the photo before she said, "Yeah, Mom, Logan, and I went to Puerto Rico to celebrate my graduation from college. We had a blast, and I'll never forget that trip."

"Logan has been in your life for a long time now, right?"

"Yeah. Logan and my mom met when I was about five, and they got married when I was eight. He adopted me soon afterward because, apparently, my biological dad gave up his rights a long time ago. He's my dad in every sense of the word, and I remember the day fondly that Logan officially adopted me. Logan said that I should continue to call him Logan in case my biological dad came back into our lives. He never did."

Reed nodded and put the photograph back on the dresser. She walked over to her desk and sat down. Once she had the email up, she clicked a button and waited a few seconds for the results.

"What the hell?" Naomi asked as she stared at her screen. "I think whoever is sending these emails has some experience in the tech field."

"What makes you say that?" Reed asked as he walked over to her desk to look at the computer screen. On her monitor, there was not just one IP address; there were many.

"Someone tried to mask their IP address, but I don't think they were smart enough," Naomi said as she began typing on her computer.

"What are you doing?"

"Narrowing down the IP addresses until we find the accurate one. Edmon is still beta testing this software, but hopefully, the functions we need will work. The other downside is that I am not well versed in this application as I didn't work on this project directly, but there is no time like the present to figure it out."

Naomi kept typing, and Reed stood back as he watched her work. After a few moments, Naomi let out a whoop.

"Yes, I found the IP address! Now let's see if I can find the internet service provider it belongs to."

Naomi typed a few more functions, and Reed continued to look over her shoulder. She could feel his breath on her neck, and she wondered if he was this close to her on purpose. She glanced up at him on her left and saw that he was watching her and not the screen. So, he was doing it on purpose. With that, Naomi gave Reed a small smile and shook her head as she focused on the task at hand.

It took some time for Naomi to figure out the internet service provider that the IP address was attached to, but when she did, she let out a sigh of relief. It belonged to an internet cafe called Cyber Sonic in Washington, DC. Naomi turned in her seat to Reed, who had, at some point, sat down on

Naomi's bed and was on his phone. He looked up when she turned her chair around.

"Want to go to an internet cafe?" Naomi asked as she started grabbing her things.

"The IP address belongs to the cafe? Interesting," Reed said as he put his phone in his pocket.

"Why is that interesting?"

"First, I didn't think they still existed. Second, it might be hard to find out who sent this email, but let's see what we can dig up."

And with that, the two left Naomi's apartment and took the metro to Cyber Sonic.

CHAPTER 7

*C*yber Sonic's location is on a small side street just
past the Capitol. Reed held the door while Naomi
walked into the cafe. She examined her surroundings and
what she saw impressed her. The owners divided the cafe into
stations, and each desk had one of the best computers on the
market today. Each station had automated menus and there
were slots on the desk where Naomi assumed the food
appeared once they ordered it. The cafe was dazzling with
neon-colored art decorating the walls. Naomi glanced around
and saw a woman about her age standing at the front desk.
She tapped Reed's shoulder, and she walked over to the desk.

"Hi, Isabelle," Naomi said, reading the woman's name tag.
"I was wondering if you could help us."

Isabelle briefly acknowledged Naomi before turning her
attention to Reed. "I'm happy to help you in any way, shape,
or form."

Naomi sighed and shook her head just before she looked
at Reed. She thought it might have amused him, but his eyes

showed a hint of annoyance. "Were you working here earlier today?"

Isabelle turned toward Naomi before focusing her attention on Reed again and said, "Yep."

"Did you see anyone or anything that was suspicious? Acting strange, maybe?"

"Nope." Isabelle kept focused on Reed.

Naomi knew this score. Isabelle was interested in Reed and wanted her to disappear as quickly as possible. So, they should use it to their advantage.

"Reed, did you have anything to add here?" Naomi hoped Reed would pick up on Isabelle's actions and "flip the switch."

Reed smiled at Isabelle and showed his license on his phone. "Well, Isabelle, my friend and I need some information about a person who was here a few hours ago. We noticed that the cafe is open twenty-four hours. What time did you start work?" Reed asked.

"My shift is from midnight to 8:00 a.m. on Tuesdays and Thursdays. This job is a part-time gig for me." Isabelle's gaze never wavered from Reed.

"So, was this morning slow? Do you have any cameras in here or at the door?"

"In terms of customers? Yes. That's just one reason I like this shift. There's usually no one around. And our security camera has been busted since yesterday. We are waiting for a piece that should be delivered today."

Naomi shook her head at that news and listened to Reed as he continued to question Isabelle.

"Could you tell me anything about any of the customers that came in?"

"There were only three people in here until about 6:30

a.m. I mean, there was nothing completely out of the ordinary with any of them," Isabelle said before pausing for a few seconds. "One customer paid with cash, which was strange since most people pay with either their phone or a credit card. He didn't say much, which was fine by me. The other two customers were together and were really excited about a gaming event that was going on around the time they arrived."

Reed peeked at Naomi, who briefly widened her eyes. "Could you tell me more about the person who paid with cash?"

"Uh. He was a black man and looked to be in his fifties or sixties. I didn't get a good look at his features, but I can probably find out when he checked out. Gimme a sec," said Isabelle with a smile, and then she walked over to a computer to find the information.

Naomi turned to Reed and whispered, "Do you think this might be the person who kidnapped Paige?"

"It could be. I wouldn't want to leave any tracks if I had kidnapped someone. I would pay in cash too."

"Touché," Naomi whispered. "She likes you."

Reed smirked at Naomi and said, "Jealous?"

"Of course not. What is there to be jealous of?"

"Ouch. That hurt. A tiny bit. But it hurt."

Naomi rolled her eyes. Isabelle walked back to the front desk, and the duo turned their attention to her. "So, this guy logged into the computer at 5:10 this morning and logged out around 6:45 a.m. Since he didn't need to sign up for a computer because we had plenty available, we have little information on him. We can't pull any data from the computer about what websites he visited or what he did because the search history deletes as soon as you log out. Even if we did, I probably wouldn't be able to tell you without a warrant."

The fact that the cafe's computers deleted the search and website history once the person signed out didn't surprise Naomi. But it disappointed her.

"Would you be able to show us the computer station he used?" Reed asked.

"Sure, it's right over here," Isabelle said as she walked from behind her desk and directed Reed and Naomi over to a desk in the corner of the cafe. "Let me know if I can help you with anything else." Isabelle smiled at Reed and returned to the front desk.

Naomi studied the desk. "Is there anything, in particular, we're looking for?"

"If I had to guess, looking for fingerprints would be fruitless since who knows how many people have used this computer station. But maybe he left something else." But try as they might, the station was clean.

"Crap," Naomi mumbled. She placed her hands on her hips and groaned. Although she wouldn't admit this out loud, their lack of evidence disappointed her. They still weren't any closer to finding Paige.

"At least we have a description of the guy who was here. It's a broad description, but we have something to go on," Reed said as he sat back on his heels. He had been looking underneath the desk to see if maybe the suspect had dropped anything.

Naomi held out her hand and helped Reed up off the floor. He held her hand longer than was necessary and gently rubbed his thumb along her knuckles. Naomi looked down at their hands and then back up at him. He smiled at her, gave her hand a gentle squeeze, and let go. And with that, he headed back up to the front desk. Naomi just stared at him before following along.

Isabelle smiled at Reed as he approached. "Did you find everything you needed?"

"Yes, thanks, Isabelle. For all of your help. Here is my contact information in case you remember any more details." Reed pulled out his phone and placed it over a scanner on the desk. The scanner made a slight ringing noise, and Reed removed his phone.

"Thank you, Reed. Wait! Here is the cafe's contact information. If you ever need anything else, don't hesitate to reach out." Isabelle handed him a piece of paper.

"Thanks again." Reed opened the door for Naomi and gave Isabelle one final wave.

"Yes, thanks for helping us." Naomi nodded at Isabelle and walked through the door.

Naomi glanced at Reed and noticed he was looking at the piece of paper Isabelle handed him. "Well, that's certainly an old school way of getting contact information. And why wouldn't we already have their information? We made it here, didn't we?"

"She wrote her phone number on the piece of paper."

"Of course she did. Brilliant." Naomi marched down the street.

Reed caught up with her quickly and said, "You're so jealous."

"I have no reason to be jealous. We're not dating."

Reed smirked and said, "True, but I think I've made it obvious that I want to get to know you better."

"You've hinted at it. Well, you did the night we met. You haven't hinted at it since." The last sentence flew out of Naomi's mouth before she stopped it. She mentally shook her head at herself.

"Oh, so you've been thinking about it too?" Reed gently grabbed her hand to stop her from walking away. Naomi gazed down at their hands before looking at Reed. She studied his eyes. She hadn't noticed before that they had specks of gray, which added another dimension of color in them, like waves in an ocean.

Naomi didn't answer right away. She smirked when she replayed what he said in her head. "Too? So, I guess that means you've been thinking about it."

"I guess you caught me there." Reed smiled at her.

Naomi smiled back before replying, "Anyway, what should we do now? We kind of hit a dead end here."

"How about we go for a run? I assume you didn't go for a run this morning since when I came over, you were in your pajamas. I do some of my best thinking while exercising."

Naomi felt somewhat self-conscious. Reed looked more fit than she, and she didn't know if she could keep up with him. Plus, she was already feeling anxious, given their flirty but non-flirty relationship. Plus, her primary focus was finding Paige.

"Come on. It will be fun and give us an opportunity to think of our next steps in the hunt to find Paige. And maybe we can get an early dinner afterward? I love running around the National Mall, and you live close to it."

"That sounds like a great idea."

Reed beamed before saying, "Okay. How about I meet you at your apartment at 3:00 p.m.?"

"Sounds perfect. See you then."

Reed and Naomi went their separate ways. On the way back to her apartment, Naomi tried to think of what she could do to help Paige. What would emailing Paige's personal account do? She didn't want to make the situation worse, but on the other hand, what else could they do? She should probably run this by Reed.

But could she trust him? He hadn't led her wrong yet, but in the back of her mind, she was concerned about how he seemed to know an awful lot about her. But who else was there to trust?

Naomi continued to ponder these questions as she approached her apartment building, waved hello to the security officer at the front desk, and took the elevator up to her apartment. When she opened her front door, she saw Diane sitting on a barstool at the kitchen counter.

"Hey. How's it going?" Naomi asked. She walked to her dish rack and found her water bottle and set it out on the counter.

"Okay. Do you want anything to eat? I can ask Simon to put something together for you," Diane said before she took a sip of her orange juice.

"Thanks, but don't worry about it. I can grab a snack for myself. I'll work for a bit and then go for a jog with Reed in a couple of hours."

Diane gave Naomi a soft smile. "I'm glad you're trying to maintain some sense of normalcy through all of this."

"Yeah. I know we're doing all we can to find Paige, but I'm using jogging as an opportunity for some self-care. Even though I'd rather be on the couch, underneath a blanket, crying my eyes out." Naomi's eyes teared up.

Diane nodded her head and stood up. She walked over to Naomi and gave her a big hug. "We'll find Paige, and she will be okay. We have to be optimistic. We need to believe that she's all right. She is all right." Diane broke the hug and wiped tears from her eyes.

"I'm working on a few things that I'm hoping will help with the case. When I know more, I'll let you know, okay?" Diane paused as she wiped the tears that had fallen down Naomi's cheeks and then gave her another hug. "We'll all be okay."

Diane walked back over to the kitchen counter and grabbed her phone. "I'm going to work on a few things myself, including lining up some opportunities to talk to the press. I think tomorrow I'll take your self-care recommendation for at least part of the day. I'm going to go for a walk around the Mall. Oh! Did you hear that your parents will be back in a couple of days? I'll probably head over to the airport to meet them there."

Naomi smiled at Diane and said, "That sounds like an excellent plan. Wait a minute, my parents got a flight out?"

"Yes? Haven't you heard from Jada? I swore she mentioned that she sent you a message."

"Oh, okay. Thanks," Naomi said and she walked toward her bedroom. She stopped in the hallway and pulled out her phone to check her personal email. There was a message from Jada that she received around the time Naomi was at the internet cafe.

"Strange that I didn't get a notification about this email," she said to herself. Her parents were arriving at DCA in two days. "I'm glad that, at least, worked out."

Naomi entered her room and headed straight for her

dresser to grab her workout gear. She put her dark brown curls into a ponytail and slipped a baseball cap onto her head. Naomi grabbed her headphones to use with her phone and sat at her computer to do some work before Reed came to her apartment. She chatted with her boss, Doug, and filled him in on the latest news regarding Paige. Naomi was thankful that he allowed her to take as much time off as needed due to the company's lax leave policy, but she still wanted to be available to the team due to the number of projects she was involved in currently. Plus, Paige would have wanted her to keep moving toward the promotion she had set her eyes on at work. She also checked in with June to make sure the projects they were working on were still going smoothly.

* * *

A FEW HOURS FLEW BY, and next thing Naomi knew, Reed sent her a message to tell her he was heading to her apartment. When he knocked on the door, Naomi answered with a smile that quickly turned into a look of confusion as she saw a small duffel bag near Reed's feet.

"What is that for?"

"Figured it wouldn't hurt to bring a change of clothes and a water bottle."

"That makes sense."

"Awesome. Thanks. How about I fill your water bottle while you leave my bag in your room? I should probably fill mine too." He grabbed the water bottle and handed his bag to her.

Naomi nodded, took the bag, and headed to her room. She stopped by Paige's room to ask Diane if she wanted to join the couple, but she declined. A few minutes later, the duo was walking along the National Mall to warm up for their jog. She turned around and surveyed her location but noticed nothing out of the ordinary. Joggers were running, and tourists were sightseeing, kids were laughing. It was a beautiful day in the nation's capital.

"So, what else can we do now to help Paige?" Naomi asked to break the silence.

"I'm not exactly sure where to turn. I reached out to my contact at the police department, but they've been radio silent, which is worrisome, to be honest. And without someone like Isabelle remembering more substantial details, we're kind of at a dead end. I'm hoping some exercise will get the juices flowing."

"Why is it worrisome that the police haven't reached back out to you yet? No news is good news? How did you get 'in the know' with the police?"

"To answer your first question, yes, I agree it usually is. But I also hear tidbits here and there from the police about where they are on certain investigations, especially if they know I'm involved. Having no update is very strange. And I sometimes work with the police on some of their cases. That's also why I show my badge when it isn't required."

Naomi nodded and asked, "Should we jog?" Reed nodded, and the two began their workout. She was happy with the pace they were jogging and felt less self-conscious about her athletic ability.

The two jogged for a little while and didn't say much beyond giving each other a little encouragement. When the two stopped at a stoplight, Naomi turned around and saw a woman with brown hair wearing a black baseball cap, a black jacket, and black capri leggings behind her. Once the light turned green, Naomi and Reed continued their jog.

A few minutes later, they turned down a street to continue running on the Mall, and Naomi felt a strange sensation. She glanced behind her and saw the same woman was still behind them. A few moments after that, Reed slowed down to a walk, and Naomi followed his lead.

"You doing all right over there?" Naomi asked. She briefly looked behind her again. This time she noticed the woman looking back at her. When Naomi turned to get a good look at her, the woman quickly averted her eyes.

"Reed," Naomi whispered to not bring attention to herself. Reed looked over at her, and she said, "I think someone is following us."

"You noticed that woman behind us in the black baseball cap too?" Reed asked. Naomi nodded her head, and Reed said, "On the count of three, we run toward her, okay?" Naomi nodded again even though she thought this was a crazy idea. Reed counted to three with his fingers, and both he and Naomi turned around and started sprinting toward the unsuspecting woman.

But the woman recovered from her surprise in record time and took off running. Naomi and Reed sped up, but there was a street up ahead. The duo was gaining ground on the mysterious woman, but as they got closer, a car flew down the street and screeched to a stop. The woman hopped into the car, and it sped away.

Naomi and Reed came to a stop at the corner and tried to catch their breaths.

"What the hell was that? Also, was that car literally flying?" Naomi exclaimed in between, trying to take deep breaths.

"That was us getting chased, and I'm not sure. It confirmed at least one thing."

"What's that?"

"That our little trek to that internet cafe means that we're on the right track, and someone is following you." And with that, Naomi and Reed headed back to her apartment. Once they had reached their destination, Naomi waved at the front desk security guard and walked with Reed to the elevators. When they were inside her apartment, Naomi headed to her room to grab her laptop after leaving Reed with Diane in the living room. Thinking nothing of it, she pulled up her email and sat back in shock. Another email from "Paige" was in her inbox.

"Um. You guys won't believe this. But I just got another email from 'Paige.' Like within the last five minutes." Diane and Reed gathered around Naomi's computer to read the new message.

CHAPTER 8

Naomi,
*   That video from Paige is just a small taste of what*
we can do. If you alert the police about the email, Paige dies.
Complete your first task.
PAN

Diane stepped back. "That's it? That's all we get?"

Naomi just stared at the monitor. She saw movement out of the corner of her eye and turned to find that Reed had grabbed his phone. He pointed to the door and left the room. Naomi turned to Diane and said, "I have no idea what is going on or what they want from me, but I am so sorry."

Diane stood tall and laid a hand on Naomi's hand. "It will be okay, sweetheart. I'm going to step out on the balcony and get some air. Let me know if you need anything or hear anything else." With that, she exited the room.

Naomi didn't know what she should do. Her gut instinct was to tell the police about the email. But she didn't want to cause any harm to Paige by doing so. Plus, they had closed the door on their investigation.

The pangs in Naomi's stomach began. She knew that another anxiety attack was on the horizon but and started doing her breathing exercises to try to calm herself down. They didn't work, and the pain only grew more intense. Her body grew feverish in the time it took her to center her mind and figure out what she needed to do next. The stabbing feeling in her stomach made it difficult to get to the bathroom, but once she did, she grabbed the lone medicine bottle on her counter. She popped a pill in her mouth before she slid down to the floor. After a few minutes, she could breathe a little easier. Her stomach pains lessened, and her heart rate slowed down. Naomi couldn't determine what was sweat or tears as she tried to pull herself together. She slowly got up and leaned against the counter. She hadn't experienced an anxiety attack that bad in a long time, and thankfully her prescribed medicine usually worked quickly.

Waving her hand over the faucet, she took a second to watch the water flow from the spout before and throwing some water on her face. She took some more deep breaths as the soothing sensation cooled her hot skin. She grabbed a hand towel and gently dried her skin before deciding that she looked presentable enough and walked into the living room.

Reed looked up when Naomi entered the room. "Are you okay? You look like you might faint." He walked over to her and put a hand on the small of her back. His touch briefly made her mind short-circuit, something she couldn't afford to have happen given the stakes. She watched as Reed looked at his hand placement and then back into her eyes. His look of concern drifted from her eyes to examine her face, looking to see if anything else was out of place, she assumed.

Naomi saw Diane step back into the apartment with a look of concern on her face as well.

"No, no. I'm not going to faint. I just need to go outside for some fresh air."

"Do you mind if I join you?"

"Sure."

"While you guys are outside, I'll make some tea. And it won't be that autogenerated stuff that Simon makes," Diane stated as she headed to the kitchen.

With a nod, they walked out onto the apartment balcony. After all the craziness today, Naomi didn't realize how late it was and was shocked to see that the sun was setting. The breeze from the evening air felt cool, giving her a bigger reprieve from the anxiety attack she had a few moments ago.

"At around this time several days ago, I was sitting outside enjoying the sunset, thinking about everything I was grateful for as a way of relaxing. Now we're dealing with my best friend's kidnapping, and the police think she took an extended vacation. Besides, the kidnappers want me to help them do something that I don't completely understand. All of this is happening while I am trying so hard to control my anxiety."

Reed stayed silent for a moment. "There is nothing I can do or say to fix this situation, even though I want to make this all go away. I wish we could go back to happy hour at the V Hotel, where things seemed less complicated. And all I was trying to do was make you smile."

"Uh...you were?" Naomi questioned as she glanced over at Reed.

"Yep. You were the most stunning woman in that room."

"You are laying it on thick, sir," said Naomi. She laughed at Reed, and one of her curls fell out of her ponytail.

He winked. "Doesn't mean it isn't true. I would have tried to get to know you the old-fashioned way, but it seems like fate had other plans."

Naomi glanced at Reed again and whispered, "Yeah, I guess fate did."

Reed took a step toward Naomi and cupped her cheek. With his other hand, he pushed the curl behind her ear. Naomi gave a timid smile, and they both leaned in. Just as they were about to kiss, the sound of a teakettle going off startled both Naomi and Reed, breaking the moment.

Naomi and Reed stood quietly before Reed cleared his throat. "Saved by the tea. Anyway, so let me explain to you how I knew Paige's video was fake." He pulled out his phone and scrolled through until he found the video that Detective Thompson sent to him. He pressed play.

Reed let the video play for a few seconds before pressing pause. He then rewound the video and let it play again and stopped it at the same spot. "Do you see anything weird?"

Naomi analyzed the screenshot for a few seconds before declaring, "There is a weird green line in the lower left-hand corner."

"Right, which makes me believe that the background behind her is fake. Whoever made this did it to hide where she is. Now watch the rest of it until the end."

Reed pressed play again, and the video continued until the screen went black. "Did you notice anything odd there?"

Naomi rewound the last two seconds of the video and played it again before replying, "Yes. She nodded her head at the end."

"Exactly. It was almost like Paige was telling the person on the other end of the camera she was done. I picked up on this after watching the video once versus the police department, who I am sure combed over this video multiple times, which is troubling. I need to make a few phone calls. Are you okay?"

"Yes. I guess I have to be. There's something I forgot to tell you with all of this craziness."

"You don't have to be anything other than what you want to be. If you aren't okay, then you aren't okay. And that's perfectly fine. What did you forget to tell me?"

"I've suspected that someone has been following me for a while now. Now, I don't have any solid proof, just a feeling. Goosebumps were popping up on my arm. Chills down my spine. The feeling that someone was watching me, that type of thing. Then the night before Paige disappeared, I got the feeling that someone was looking at me, and I noticed that my window shade was open. So, I go over to close it, and I see a red laser shining in the apartment across from mine." Naomi took a deep breath.

"So, I'm looking out the window, and suddenly, someone or something points a red laser at my windowsill. I didn't know if this person would shoot or what. The thought crossed my mind. I still don't understand what that was all about." Naomi didn't realize she was crying until she felt a tear fall on her hand.

"Is it all right if I give you a hug?" Naomi nodded, and Reed hugged her. "You're going through a lot right now, but I promise things will get better." Reed held her for a few moments until Naomi took a small step back. He placed a stray piece of Naomi's curly-coily hair behind her ear.

"Are you okay?"

Naomi nodded her head and sniffled but said nothing. She tried her best to wipe the tears from her eyes, but she realized she missed one when Reed wiped a stray one away.

"I have a couple of calls to make related to the case that I want to get a jump on making. We can talk more about all of this when I finish if that's okay with you. I'll try to make these calls quick. If you're not okay, I'll stay here."

"No, please go. If it means this nightmare will end faster, please do it."

Reed grasped her hand and squeezed it before walking back inside the apartment. Naomi turned back to look at the sunset. A few more tears fell from her eyes. Not only was she upset that someone had kidnapped her best friend, but now if she didn't perform the tasks at hand, there might be repercussions against Paige. There was a reason "PAN" contacted her. Naomi felt like she was in way over her head. Part of her wanted to go back to the police and beg them to take a second look at the video and tell them about the emails she received. The kidnappers told her not to inform the police, and these people knew what they were doing since they sent that video to Detective Thompson.

She was also overwhelmed with whatever was going on between her and Reed. They had almost kissed, which complicated this situation even more. And there were still several questions she had for him. For example, how had he and her mom met? She truly didn't know much about him, yet he had picked up on quite a few things about her. Was it just a part of his job?

Shaking the thoughts of her relationship with Reed out of her head, she focused more on the choices she needed to make to get Paige back.

Naomi knew she had to do whatever it took, even if she didn't have the backing of the police. But what was the kidnappers' end game? What would the final project be to ensure Paige's freedom? And why were she and Paige chosen to be a part of this little game?

Naomi needed to complete this first task. Who even calls themselves "PAN"? What did PAN stand for? Naomi started pacing outside on the balcony.

Everything about this situation stumped Naomi. She felt as if the answer was right in front of her face, but she couldn't see it. But she knew that finding out the answer would be the key to finding Paige. And she had every intention to do just that.

CHAPTER 9

*E*xhaustion flowed out of every pore on Paige's body. She had barely gotten any sleep last night and was feeling it now. Jett and another man, Morris, set up a green screen in the room she was in and sat her down on a chair in front of it. Morris removed the zip tie on her wrists, and she was thankful for a chance to massage them. A woman with dark brown hair walked in a few minutes later and set up a camera in front of her. Paige tried to make eye contact with the woman, but she refused to look at her.

The brunette set up a laptop on the floor to Paige's left while Jett put the finishing touches on the camera lights set up in front of her. Just as she tried to wrap her head around what was going on, Morris's phone rang.

"It's the boss. I'll take this upstairs," Morris announced to the room, and he headed up the stairs. Jett came over and started fiddling with some equipment near Paige. A few seconds later, she heard him whisper, "Are you okay?"

"I'm okay as I can be, given the situation. Why can't you just let me go?"

"You know I can't."

"But you won't tell me why."

"That's because it's complicated," Jett said as he clipped a small, cordless microphone to Paige's shirt.

"Jett! Come here!" Morris yelled from upstairs.

"Be back in a minute," Jett whispered to her as he stopped what he was doing and headed toward the stairs.

"Tiffany, can you finish setting up?" The brunette gave Jett a curt nod, and Jett gave Paige a slight wave as he ascended the staircase.

Tiffany walked over to Paige and started fiddling with her microphone.

"Can you explain what is going on? What is up with all of this equipment?" Paige got a closer look at Tiffany and realized that she couldn't have been much younger than her. Tiffany glanced at Paige and sighed.

"We're doing it to create a video of you to send to the police."

"And why is that?"

"To send to my coworkers to ensure they close the investigation of your disappearance."

It took Paige a few seconds to process what she said. "Wait. You're a cop?" Paige asked as she sat up a little straighter in amazement. "Why are you doing this?" Her stomach dropped to her knees. Someone involved in her kidnapping worked for the police department?

Tiffany nodded and attached the microphone to Paige's yoga T-shirt. "The boss has some stuff on me that I would like to keep buried," she said as she backed up from Paige to look at her handiwork. "Although you were kidnapped, your kidnapping is only a piece of the puzzle. There is a bigger plan going on that I'm not even in the loop on."

"So, this boss is blackmailing everyone?" Paige asked as she tried to understand the situation. "Who is this person?"

"I'm not sure what he or she is doing with those two"— Tiffany gestured to the two men who were upstairs— "but that is how I got involved in this mayhem. I am trying to keep my head down and mind my business and just get this over with."

Paige knew there was nothing she could do to convince Tiffany to let her go. Whatever this "boss" had on her was strong enough for her to risk her job and livelihood to continue with this manic plan. Tiffany walked over to the laptop and grabbed some whiteboards that Paige hadn't noticed before.

"Do you know how many other people this person is blackmailing? Aren't you worried about the police department finding out what you're doing?"

Tiffany paused briefly before responding, "I have no clue, but I wouldn't be surprised if there are more people. And honestly, this was a tough choice to make. But losing my job is the least of my worries at this point." Tiffany continued what she was doing to prepare for the video shoot.

"Jett will be behind the camera, Morris will hold these cards for you to read, and I will watch on my laptop. What you will do is say these words in your regular voice so you won't raise suspicion. Don't try anything funny."

Paige nodded slightly. A few minutes later, Jett and Morris came back downstairs in a hurry. "We need to do this quickly and then clean up," Morris said as he grabbed the white poster board from Tiffany.

"Why? What's wrong?" Tiffany asked as she put her laptop in her lap.

"We need to clean up quickly because we'll have another guest soon," Morris said as he got into his position near the camera. "Oh, show this to the camera at the end of your speech," Morris said as he handed Paige a piece of paper.

Paige looked down to read the device and noticed it was a plane ticket. She couldn't stop the tear that rolled down her face. When she looked up, Jett was staring at her. She raised an eyebrow at him, and he went back to whatever he was doing behind the camera.

A few minutes later, Paige was telling the camera in front of her she had gone on a trip and would be back soon. She also told the camera that she would reach out to her family and friends shortly and that there was no need to open a missing person's case on her behalf as it would be a waste of police resources. At the end of her spiel, she showed the phone with the plane ticket, and Morris yelled cut.

"Good job, Paige. How did that look, Tiffany?" Morris asked as he moved from his position near the camera.

"It was perfect. And it only took one take," Tiffany confirmed as she glanced at Paige before looking back at her laptop.

"That it did," Morris said. He set the cards down and walked over to Paige. He put a new zip tie on her wrists and looked at Tiffany. "Would you be able to have this video ready to go in an hour?"

"That shouldn't be a problem," Tiffany said as she closed her laptop. "I'll work on it as soon as we put all of this equipment away."

"Perfect," Morris said as he led Paige to another corner of the room and sat her down on the floor. "Let's get to work."

Paige watched as they took down the equipment that they had put together thirty minutes before and wondered who this new guest was.

* * *

ONCE AGAIN, Naomi was having a hard time falling asleep. She looked at the time and realized it was only 9:30 p.m. She couldn't get "PAN" out of her head. Feeling a surge of energy, Naomi got out of bed and walked over to her book bag near her desk. She pulled out a pen and paper and started writing potential meanings for the acronym PAN.

She then pulled up the emails from PAN and wrote more potential acronym meanings. After creating and trying about twenty different options, Naomi groaned in frustration and rubbed her hands over her face. She gazed around her room, and her eyes focused on her diploma.

"You've gotta be kidding me." Naomi shook her head. "It can't be my name...could it?"

Naomi typed in "Porter Alexandria Naomi," which took her to a prompt that said, "Good Job! You passed your first task. We will contact you tomorrow with your next objective."

Naomi let out the breath she didn't realize she was holding. On the one hand, she felt good about finishing the first task. However, Naomi was in a state of befuddlement and hurt because someone used her initials to terrorize her. She wanted to talk to someone who would understand, so she contacted Reed.

Naomi: *Hey, are you up? I have a huge update on the case.*

Naomi waited a few moments before getting up and using the bathroom. When she came back, she noticed she had a message notification. It was from Reed.

Reed: *Hey, I am. I'm hanging out at a bar not too far from your house. Wanna come down?*

Well, it wasn't like she was doing anything and she couldn't sleep so she thought, why not?

Naomi: *Sure. Send me the address, and I'll try to be there in 25 minutes.*

Thankful that she showered before bed, she went back into the bathroom, brushed her teeth, and took her scarf off her head. Luckily, it took no time for her to fluff up her curls, put some mascara, cover-up, and a little lipstick on before she headed into her room to figure out what to wear. She checked her phone and saw that Reed had sent her the bar location. She checked the weather and grabbed a pair of jeans and a fitted sweater. Naomi then called a car to pick her up and take her to the bar. While she waited, she walked into the living room and saw that Diane must have gone to bed. Naomi sent Diane a message letting her know she was going to meet up with Reed and the location of the bar before heading toward the front door. She grabbed her coat and put on her knee-high boots. She checked herself in the front hall mirror before leaving to meet the car out front.

Fifteen minutes later, she was getting out of the car in front of a bar named the Hen House. She opened the front door and was shocked to find what looked to be a dive bar. Naomi placed her phone onto the scanner at the front door. The front door opened once it confirmed that Naomi was over the age of eighteen. The bar lit up with neon lights; human bartenders were behind the bar, but the option to order a drink off of the computerized menu was there too. Naomi liked the atmosphere of the bar. She spotted Reed in a corner booth near the back of the bar with his eyes transfixed on the TV screen in his booth.

"Baseball fan?" Naomi asked after she strolled up to him. Reed looked up and smiled at her. He stood, grabbed her coat, and hung it on a coat hanger near their booth. "Nice spot. I'm feelin' the atmosphere."

"Thanks, and yes. I'm a big Nats fan," Reed said before he glanced at the TV screen.

"I can tell...especially the way you're having a hard time not looking at the screen," Naomi said teasingly.

"Yeah. I'm just happy the bar is replaying the game 'cause I missed it earlier. Anyway, what update did you have about the case?" Reed asked as he took his eyes off the screen.

"I figured out what PAN meant. It's an acronym for my name backward."

Reed thought about it for a second before asking, "What's your middle name?"

"Alexandria."

"Like the city?"

"Like the city," Naomi confirmed.

Naomi and Reed stared at each other for a few seconds before Reed replied, "That's interesting. So, this person or these people are targeting you specifically. And us finding out why might help get Paige back."

"Yeah, I wasn't sure what to think, which is why I texted you." Naomi's and Reed's eyes briefly drifted back to the TV screen as the batter for the Nats swung and earned a third strike.

"Shit," Reed mumbled. He took a sip of his beer before he

turned to Naomi. "Please excuse my crappy manners. Do you want something to drink?"

"Can I taste what you're drinking?" Naomi asked, and Reed handed his beer to her. She took a sip before saying, "I'll have that. It tastes good."

Reed got up and walked over to the bar to order the beer for Naomi. Naomi examined his profile as he turned to look at a television that was closer to the bar. Reed raked a hand through his hair as he watched the next batter come up to bat. He lightly bounced on his feet as he got excited since this was one of the stars of the team. The bartender placed the beer in front of Reed, and he took it back to their booth.

Naomi took a sip of her beer before asking, "Do you like any other sports besides baseball?"

Reed nodded his head and took another sip of his beer. "I also watch the Skins and the Steelers when I get a chance. Don't have strong feelings toward either team, but I guess based on me being from Pitt, I should probably be a part of Steelers Nation."

"True," Naomi said as she glanced at the game again before looking back at Reed. "So, what do you think our next move should be? I don't want to just wait around for 'PAN' to send me another email."

"I agree. I think we need to figure out the kidnappers' connection to you and why they've made this personal. We were so focused on trying to figure out what PAN stood for, and this being a political attack that we never thought Paige could be a way to get to you. Now maybe Paige's cybersecurity work is still at the center of this kidnapping, but these people want you to know this is personal."

Naomi didn't reply as she was taking what Reed said to

heart. She couldn't think of anyone off of the top of her head who would have anything against her. "I'm stumped. I try to mind my business, so I don't understand how this would be related to me."

Reed finished his beer and placed the glass back on the table. "Yeah, I agree. But there has to be some connection."

Naomi lowered her voice. "Could it be related to my work at Edmon? My team is small, so it wouldn't be hard for someone to have picked me. But I'm also so low on the totem pole that going through all this trouble to get my attention is pointless."

Reed stared at Naomi for a moment before replying, "It could be. What do you do for Edmon?"

Naomi was curious about the confused look he gave her briefly but put it temporarily to the side as she tried to focus on getting Paige back. "I do mostly database work, which involves uploading data into the cloud. A lot of the data I see is confidential because it contains personal information from various companies, but like I said, I'm low-hanging fruit. Why me, of all people?"

Reed knew this was a rhetorical question. Naomi fluffed her curls briefly before saying, "I feel like I'm missing something that would connect everything." She took a long gulp of her beer.

"That's usually how these things go. Once we find the missing piece, everything usually falls into place." Reed refused to look at Naomi while he shifted in his seat. "Can I get you another beer? I was going to get one for myself," Reed said as he stepped out of the booth.

"Sure," Naomi said, and she polished off her beer. Reed grabbed their glasses and walked back to the bar. Naomi pulled out her phone and searched for her name to see if there were any hits while she waited for Reed to return.

"What are you looking up?"

Naomi jumped and said, "Make a little more noise, please. Whew." She placed her phone down on the table and took a sip of her beer. "Thank you."

"Don't mention it."

"Anyway, I was doing some research on my name, seeing if it might say something concerning PAN. But I couldn't find a thing."

Reed started to say something but stopped. Then he said, "So we're still at a dead end."

Naomi raised an eyebrow and asked, "What were you going to say?"

Reed shook his head. "It was nothing, don't worry about it."

"Okay. Well, did you talk to your contacts in the police department about the woman that was following us this afternoon?"

"I did." Reed took a sip from his beer. "We have little to go on as we didn't get a good look at her or the driver's face. I mentioned to them the fact that the car could have potentially been flying, but we were one, too far away to tell, and two, if it was, it was only flying slightly. The police mentioned that if the car was flying, then it is not like any other car on the market. They are keeping an eye out, but I'm not holding my breath."

Reed and Naomi continued to chat quietly in the bar until the baseball game ended. As they were getting ready to leave, Reed helped Naomi put her coat on and went to the bar to pay the tab. The two walked outside and stood in front of the bar.

"Beautiful night, isn't it?"

Naomi focused on ordering a car to take her back to her apartment, was startled when Reed spoke. She put her phone away and admired the night sky. Although the chilliness and the city lights were taking a little away from the beauty, it still stunned Naomi. She looked back at Reed and saw that he was looking at her with a small, soft smile. Naomi realized that the more time she spent with him, the more she liked him.

Reed's eyes dropped to her lips for a second before they moved back up to her eyes. He leaned forward until their noses touched. He gently rubbed his nose up against hers before going in. The kiss started soft and sweet before it turned into hunger, almost needy. Reed's hands slid to her lower back as he softly pulled her closer to him. Naomi didn't know how long they stood outside the bar kissing, but the sound of a car horn made them jump apart.

"Well, that was amazing," Reed said, rubbing the back of his neck with his hand.

"Yeah, it was. I'd love to stand here and talk about it more, but my ride is here. I'll see you later?"

"Yes, definitely. Let me know when you get home, okay?" Reed asked quietly.

His concern was comforting to Naomi. "Uh, yeah. Sure. I can do that. Good night." She walked to the car, opened the door, and got inside. She put her seat belt on and turned her head as the driver pulled off. She saw that Reed stood there to see her car off before he turned around and walked off into the night.

CHAPTER 10

The next morning, Naomi awakened with a start. She could feel her heart racing and a thin layer of sweat on her palms as she looked out her window and saw that it was still dark outside. Naomi woke up thinking since she needed to complete whatever the kidnappers wanted her to do; she would have to get a better handle on her anxiety again. She had to get in contact with Dr. Evans as soon as possible.

She got up and grabbed her phone from her desk. She quickly checked her email and noticed that she still hadn't received another message from Paige's captors. She exited her inbox and logged on to her health portal. In this portal, she could see all of her stats, medications, and health history, including the dates and times she met with Dr. Evans. She messaged Dr. Evans through the portal and made a mental note to call if she hadn't heard from her in a couple of hours.

To calm herself down, she decided to take a shower. Washing her hair could be a long process, so she knew that she would kill some time while she waited to hear from Dr. Evans.

"Simon, play soft music on my phone." The music started, and she sat on her bed and leaned against her headboard. She rested there for thirty minutes before she stood up and walked into the bathroom. Naomi hopped in the shower and washed her hair.

She finished up and exited the shower. She then moisturized, put her robe on, and placed her hair into medium-sized braids before she sat in her desk chair and turned on her computer.

She skimmed her work emails and read up on the latest news. Her phone pinged just as she was finishing up researching Senator Butler's cybersecurity legislation. She flipped through her apps until she reached her messages and saw that she got something from Reed.

It was a picture of the sunrise. Naomi smiled to herself but didn't reply right away because she was speechless by the thoughtful gesture. While she thought of a response, she went back to her health portal to see if Dr. Evans had responded to her request to meet. To Naomi's relief, there was a calendar request sitting in her inbox, asking if Naomi was free to meet this afternoon. She quickly confirmed their appointment.

Naomi flicked back over to her messages and pulled up the photo that Reed sent.

Naomi: *Thinking of me?*

She turned the phone over, so it was facing down on her desk and facepalmed. Why had she said that? She felt a sense of nervousness and butterflies in her stomach. Naomi shook her head and muttered to herself as she waited for Reed to respond.

Seconds turned into minutes, and Naomi all but gave up on getting a response. Just as Naomi was about to turn off her computer, she heard her phone's ping. She briefly froze before reaching to pick up the device. Gathering up the nerve to check the message, Naomi swiped the screen to open her messages and saw Reed's response.

Reed: *Always. Did you get another message?*

Naomi was happy with his response and relieved that he changed the subject.

Naomi: *Nothing. I'm worried that I haven't heard anything yet, but maybe it's too early.*

Reed: *I ran the email through my channels. It was untraceable outside of the IP address scrambling you found, which was great work, by the way. It took my contacts way longer to find what you found in minutes.*

Naomi: *Thanks. Who else did you call? Did you find out any more information?*

Instead of hearing a ping notifying Naomi that she had an incoming message, her phone rang. Naomi picked it up.

"Hey."

"Hi, I figured it would be easier to call versus explain all of this through messages. I called a good friend of mine who is the chief of police for the Metropolitan Police Department of Washington, DC. Explained the whole situation about the video sent to Detective Thompson. We talked about how I thought the tape was not a good indicator that Paige left on her own. And he told me he had good news and bad news."

"And what did he say?" Naomi asked and thought about what Reed said. "Wait, you told the police about the video? The kidnapper said we were not to tell them!"

"The kidnapper said not to tell MPD about the email,

which I haven't. He didn't say that I couldn't use the MPD as a resource. Plus, I had to go since I believe a snitch is working for the MPD. So, I talked to Chief Hughes about it. He thought my assumptions were plausible and said he would conduct his own investigation to determine how this happened, which is great news. The bad news is that they cannot open the investigation into Paige's disappearance again until this is taken care of as not to arouse suspicion and because the video is official proof that she is safe. He doesn't know how deep this goes, but he will find out."

"So essentially, we're still going at this alone."

"Yep."

Naomi sighed. "Okay. Random question that you probably already thought of, but I figured I'd ask anyway. Is there any way we might figure out her location based on the glitch in the background?"

"That was another phone call I made last night. I have a friend who works in digital forensics. He has a lot of experience with spotting video manipulation, which we suspect might have happened in Paige's case. I'll be heading over to his place in about an hour if you want to join."

Naomi glanced at her phone and saw that she still had plenty of time before her session with Dr. Evans.

"Yeah, that sounds like a great idea. Please send me your friend's address, and I'll meet you there."

* * *

INSTEAD OF TAKING the metro to Chinatown, Naomi walked. She figured in case anything happened; it was better to be out in the open. Naomi wished Diane had come with her to have some company, but she understood that Diane needed to stay back and continue trying to field calls from her contacts about who might have kidnapped Paige. She could only imagine how frustrated she must feel that not only was her daughter missing, but the people that she had reached out to help had led to nothing but dead ends.

Feeling the cool, brisk air on her face and hair, she was thrilled that she took out her braids and let her curls run free. Thankful that she put on black tights under her black skirt, she tightened the belt on her deep green pea coat as a gust of wind picked up. Being outside helped Naomi relieve some tension she had been feeling over the last few days. As she was walking across the National Mall, she stopped to stare at the Capitol.

"Where are you, Paige? And what am I missing?" Naomi whispered to herself. Although people were walking down around the Mall, she had never felt more alone.

Naomi pulled out her phone and realized she spent more time than she thought looking at the Capitol Building. She turned around and looked at the Washington Monument briefly before continuing on her way to Chinatown.

About fifteen minutes later, she ended up in front of a building that had no signs. Naomi took out her phone to double-check the address. Just as she was about to put her phone back in her pocket, Reed opened the door and smiled at Naomi. She was distracted by how good he looked in the black suit and white button-down. He dressed down the look by not including a tie and leaving the first two buttons of his shirt unbuttoned.

"Glad you could make it. Let's go to Levi's office." As she stepped across the threshold, Reed placed his hand on the small of her back as they walked to a door down a long hall-way. The feel of Reed's hand on her lower back was a subtle touch that made Naomi feel warm and secure.

After Reed opened the door to Levi's workspace, Naomi was surprised. The space was stunning. It was designed beautifully with bright pops of color that lit up the hallway. As they entered the space, Levi greeted them in the seating area.

"You must be Naomi! It's super nice to meet you. Reed has told me so much about you. I'm Levi Cannon." Levi gave a warm smile to Naomi, which made her feel even more at ease. He was a couple of inches shorter than Reed and slim. He dressed in a stylish red blazer, white button-down, blue jeans, and brown dress shoes.

"Naomi Porter. It's nice to meet you. I'm sorry, but Reed hasn't mentioned as much about you besides your work in digital forensics. Nice digs you have here. Reminds me of a bar I was at recently." Naomi's eyes slid over to Reed briefly, and when their eyes met, Reed gave her a smirk. There was that spark again that ran straight through her.

She and Levi shook hands, and she thanked him when he offered to take her coat. She sent Reed a knowing look before they followed Levi to a waiting room.

"Thank you, but I can't take all the credit for it. I had interior design help 'cause there is no way I would have been able to come up with it myself. What Reed told you was correct. I have worked as a digital image analyst for over ten years. I am finishing cleaning up the background. If you don't mind, please follow me. It will only take a few minutes for me to have this background cleared in a jiffy!" Levi adjusted his glasses and turned on his heel and hurried to another door, which she assumed led to his office.

Naomi looked at Reed and raised her eyebrows before she laughed, amused at Levi's enthusiasm and infectious personality. Reed smiled back and gently squeezed her hand. She expected him to let her hand go, but he didn't. Levi worked while Reed rubbed small circles on the back of her hand with his index finger. The wheels in Naomi's mind were spinning at a hundred miles an hour.

"Is everything okay?" Naomi asked while glimpsing at their hands and then back up at Reed.

"Peachy." Reed placed a little more pressure on the area he was rubbing. Was he trying to tell her something?

"What can you tell me about Levi?" Naomi whispered as the duo followed Levi to his office. "Just a quick summary while we wait for him to complete his analysis."

"Levi and I met in college, sophomore year, and have been best friends ever since - we joined the same fraternity, became roommates when we lived in the same frat house, and we moved to DC and began our careers down here after graduation, and the rest is history. He also sometimes works as a consultant for the MPD. I gave him an overview of this case."

As they entered the office, Naomi's jaw dropped. It was stunning. It had all the latest technology that one would need, including a big-screen TV that she could see doubled as one of his three computer monitors. The TV had to be at least sixty inches. The room was decorated similarly to the sitting area that they had just left. Levi pulled up the video of Paige onto the television.

"Before we get started, do you guys want anything to drink? I could have Simon whip up something for ya." Naomi and Reed shook their heads.

"I have a Simon too. It was one of the best inventions."

"Yep. Simon is super helpful. I've been trying to get this dude to get one for his condo, but he refuses." Levi gestured to Reed.

"But back on topic, so here is the original image," Levi said as he rotated his office chair. Reed dropped her hand when they walked closer to the TV screen. On the TV was a screenshot of Paige sitting on a chair in front of a black background. "And here is the image with that fake background removed. Simon, please pull up the next image. "The image switched. Paige was now seated in front of a hologram green screen.

"Is there any way we can get rid of that green screen?" Reed asked.

"I'm offended that you asked. Simon, next image." The green screen was no longer there.

Paige was now sitting in a room that looked…cold. It had what looked to be concrete floors and walls. It was bare from what they could see, besides a small fridge in the far corner of the room, but that was it.

Reed spoke again. "That looks like she's in a basement or cellar of some sort." Levi nodded his head in agreement.

Naomi's stomach turned as she thought about the circumstances Paige could face before she reeled herself back into reality. "I can't even guess where she is. It could literally be anywhere. She might be in another state, for goodness' sake." She threw her hands up in the air and walked away from the computer. She paced as her thoughts spiraled out of control. Reed looked on with concern while Levi didn't know how to react. Levi spun around and went back to analyzing the screenshot.

Naomi stopped pacing and said, "No. I think whoever did this wouldn't have kidnapped her and taken her out of state. I think she's still in DC right under our noses, especially since we know that at least one email came from that internet cafe. We have a hint about where she might be, but I guess we need to wait a little longer to be able to connect the dots."

"Well, maybe I can help. There are a couple of more things I wanted to show you guys." Levi typed a few things on his computer, and the picture zoomed in on the small fridge. On the door were a few magnets. "Do you see what I see?"

Reed's mouth dropped open slightly. "If you are talking about those magnets on the fridge, then yes, I do. That is definitely a DC state flag. So that raises the chances of Paige still being in DC..."

"And there's also this. Simon, go to image number four." The image of Paige holding the plane ticket was on Levi's TV screen. There was a circle around the ticket. "Zoom in on the section labeled 'ticket.'" The computer enlarged the ticket displayed on the phone, Paige held up, and the group could read the sections that were visible to the camera.

"This proves the ticket isn't hers. The date on that ticket was before they kidnapped Paige. Whose plane ticket is that?" Naomi asked.

"Dunno. It looks like the only letters that we can see from the person's first name are *Y-N*, and their last name is *A-M*. It could be anyone."

"But it's a great lead. Awesome work, Levi."

Naomi checked her phone and realized that it was time for her to head out to her meeting with Dr. Evans.

"Hey, I need to go to an appointment. Please let me know if you both find anything else, and I'll be in touch if I find out something. Thanks so much for all that you have done, Levi. It was also great meeting you."

"It was nice meeting you too. I'll let Reed know if I find anything else. Hopefully, we'll see each other again soon."

"And I'll walk you to the door, Naomi," Reed said. The trio left Levi's office and walked into the sitting area where Levi grabbed Naomi's coat and handed it to her. He waved goodbye and hurried back into his office. Reed and Naomi strolled out the office door and back down the long hall in silence. When they got to the front of the building, Naomi turned to Reed.

"Levi has a lot of energy, huh?"

"Yeah, he keeps me on my toes, that's for sure. He's always on the go."

"Anyway, I'll call you when I get the email from Paige's account." Naomi tightened the belt of her coat.

"Okay. I'll probably stop by later if that's okay."

"Do you have something else related to the case that you want to talk about?"

"I wouldn't be surprised if something else comes up, but I just wanted to check on you."

Reed's concern for her well-being was touching. "Well, then, I look forward to seeing you later. Let me know when you want to come by." Naomi gave Reed a small wave as she walked away. The uneasy feeling in her stomach grew and had a feeling that it was only a matter of time before everything would explode.

CHAPTER 11

*N*aomi got back to her apartment with about thirty minutes to spare. She called Diane's name but didn't get a response. She walked toward the refrigerator to get a glass of water and found a note from Diane saying that she went for a walk to get some fresh air and that she would be back soon.

Speaking of parents, Naomi hadn't heard from her mother or Logan recently, so she sent them a message through her phone. She then walked into her room and made sure she had set her computer up to hold the therapy session.

A few minutes later, Naomi was sitting on a videoconference call with Dr. Elise Evans.

"Hi, Naomi. How is everything going? I know you wanted to speak immediately," stated Elise as she readjusted herself in her chair. She gave Naomi a soft smile as she waited for her to respond to her question.

"Things have been insane, and I need to fill you in on a lot. Someone kidnapped Paige. Well, we think she was kidnapped but don't have legitimate proof." The words flew out of her mouth before her brain could process what she was saying. She took a deep breath and continued, "I think it's my fault, and I'm putting on a brave face in public, but in private, I'm not handling this well. I've had another anxiety attack, and I know it's hard to control them, especially when you don't know the trigger. But even though I know what triggered it, I still couldn't keep it together."

"Paige is your best friend and roommate, right?"

Naomi nodded before Dr. Evans continued, "Are the police involved?"

That question led Naomi to launch into her story. She appreciated Elise sitting there and listening to her without trying to interject comments while she was trying to explain everything that had happened recently, including her anxiety attack.

"You have a ton on your plate right now. What are you doing to help manage your stress and anxiety?"

"I've been practicing my breathing exercises, and I was trying the sun setting exercise you mentioned a while ago."

"That's great. And how is that working out for you?"

"It has worked mostly. Not only has it helped with my anxiety, but it also helps me refocus my energy if that makes sense. Like I realize how grateful I should be for the things I have now."

The conversation between the two continued to be free-flowing, and when it ended, Naomi was in a better headspace.

Dr. Evans nodded before asking, "Understandably, we didn't get to talk about you going for the promotion for your job, but we can table that for another time since I'm sure that is the last thing on your mind."

Naomi nodded, having forgotten about the promotion entirely. It had been a while since they last spoke due to Naomi not scheduling the appointments. She typed a quick reminder to herself to schedule her next appointment.

"I hope Paige is located soon, and if you need me at any time, just message through the portal again. I'll have my assistant watch for a message from you and flag it immediately. Oh, and before you leave, it's okay to take the medicine that we prescribed for you to manage bad anxiety attacks. I know you've been concerned about taking them in the past, but you're under an enormous amount of stress. It's okay to get help." Naomi nodded again and said goodbye to her psychiatrist. Not knowing how to feel, she gave herself a half an hour to decompress from her session before checking her personal email. And there sat an email from Paige's personal account.

Naomi clicked the email and read what PAN wanted her to do.

Naomi,

Your next task is to create an algorithm that will be able to accept a determined amount of data sets as a parameter. This data would include personal information, and it will need to be secured. I need this algorithm to process large amounts of data quickly, and once completed, I will need to store everything in a secure database that you will create. We will be in touch with the data sets. You have three days to finish this.

PAN

Feeling more uneasy about this email, Naomi called Reed.

"Reed Wright."

"It's me. Didn't my name come up on your phone?"

Naomi heard some shuffling on the other end before

Reed responded. "Sorry, I was distracted and didn't look at the screen before picking up. What's up? Did you get an email?"

"Yep, I just got it."

"Wait. Can I talk to you about it in person? I'm in Southwest and could be at your apartment in fifteen minutes."

"Sure. See you soon."

Naomi thought it was oddly convenient that he would be near her apartment right now unless he lived nearby. Then again, getting around DC wasn't too hard since the city itself was small compared to other major cities. Fifteen minutes later, Naomi heard knocking at her door.

She checked her phone and confirmed that it was Reed. She walked over to the door to let him in.

Reed walked over to the couch and sat down, placing his book bag on the floor beside him while Naomi checked Paige's room and noticed that Diane still was not back from her walk. She sent her a quick message on her phone to make sure she was okay.

"Do you want anything to eat or drink? I can have Simon throw something together."

"A glass of water would be great."

"Simon, please pour me a glass of water." Naomi grabbed the glass and brought it back over to the couch. She handed it to Reed and sat down to tell him everything about the mysterious email.

"I don't know anything about the data, but if personal information is involved, it makes sense to have it secured. I assume they would want me to create a nonrelational database since they haven't sent the data sets." Naomi's right leg bounced up and down.

"How hard would it be for you to do? And how long will it take you to do it? A week to two?"

Wait, this is something that Reed didn't know the answer? Was he deferring to her on this? He seemed to know the answer to just about everything in the brief time that Naomi had known him. Even though this was her field of study, she was shocked she had a leg up on him in this case.

"It might have taken a week or two eighty years ago. I would need to think about it more, but I think I can complete it in a day or a day in a half. Which is great given that I don't know how much time we have to get Paige home safely. They gave me three days to complete the project, but who knows if they'll keep their word."

Reed didn't have a response to that.

"At least nothing they've asked me to do so far is illegal?" Naomi tried to lighten the mood and appear more confident than she was. She checked her phone and saw that Diane had messaged her back.

Diane: *I'm so sorry I didn't tell you where I was going, especially given what had happened to Paige. I lost track of time and ended up wandering around the Native American Museum. I'll be back at the apartment shortly. See you soon.*

"Sorry about that. I wanted to make sure that Diane was okay."

"Don't worry about it. Anyway, I don't see any other choice but for you to create this database. As you said, nothing the kidnappers asked you to do was illegal, even though I'm worried. This might lead down a rocky path where we are debating whether something is legal. This request is probably the biggest lead we have to go on right now...."

Naomi sighed. "I know." She stood up and paced. "This reaffirms the fact that this is all about me. Maybe there is still an angle about politics and cybersecurity being a hotly contested topic recently. But no. This is about me. The acronym was a hint, but this task is a blaring siren. And they kidnapped Paige to get my attention."

"What makes you think so?"

"Because this is part of what I do for Edmon. And what's even more interesting is that very few people know what I do, yet whoever this is, tailored it for me."

Naomi went back into her room to grab her laptop and started working on the project for PAN. She thought Reed would head home after their conversation, but he sat next to her on the couch, took his laptop out of his bookbag, and began working as well. While Naomi was gathering everything she needed to work on the database, Diane came back to the apartment.

"Hi Diane, is everything okay?" Naomi's eyes shifted away from her laptop to Diane.

"I'm okay. Exhausted, but okay. Was getting ready to head to bed." Reed filled Diane in on the latest news the duo had about the kidnapping.

"I'm...so grateful for all that you guys are doing." She looked at Reed and then at Naomi. Naomi could see tears forming in her eyes as she continued, "I'm heading to bed now so I can be up in case there is any new information. Have a good night." Diane headed into Paige's room to get some sleep.

* * *

AFTER WORKING on the database for a couple of hours, Naomi got up and stretched. Her eyes and head were hurting from staring at her laptop. She rubbed her temples, and Reed looked up from his laptop.

"Are you okay?"

"Yep. Just tired from looking at my computer screen for a long time." Although she knew that wasn't helping matters, she thought the stress of it all was getting to her, even after her session with Dr. Evans.

"Are you getting hungry? There's a great Chinese food restaurant in Northwest, but it might deliver out here." Reed pulled up the restaurant's contact information. At that exact moment, Naomi's stomach growled. "Guess that's a yes."

Naomi rolled her eyes at Reed. "You don't want Simon to put something together? Then again, Chinese food sounds amazing right now." With that, Naomi picked up his laptop when he pulled up the menu. After quickly picking what she wanted to eat, Naomi handed the device back to Reed.

"Where in Northwest do you live?"

"I live pretty close to Union Station."

Naomi revised her mental note. Union Station was not too far from her apartment in Southwest but was definitely in Northwest. Although Washington, DC, as a whole was expensive, however, the housing prices near Union Station were astronomical.

"Oh, wow. Are you renting an apartment, or do you own your place?"

"I own a condo." Reed didn't look up while fiddling with his phone. Naomi waited for a few beats for him to elaborate, but he didn't.

"Well…how about you tell me about your family?"

"Is this a date?" Reed looked up from his device and smirked. The intensity of his stare took Naomi aback.

"Uh….no? I was just curious about your life since I don't know much about you."

Reed stayed silent for a few moments before responding. "My parents have been married for almost forty years. They still live in Pittsburgh, along with my siblings. I have two sisters and a brother. One of my sisters has two kids, so the dinner table is full around the holidays. I miss them a lot and don't visit nearly as much as I should."

"That sounds like a lot of fun."

"Yeah. It really is." Reed gave Naomi a genuine smile. His family meant a lot to him, and that made her like him a little more.

She reached for her laptop again as Reed stood up. "Do you need anything? I'm going to get some water."

She shook her head and watched Reed leave. Her mind wandered to thoughts of what Paige might be going through. She shook the thoughts from her head before she got choked up, and it clouded her ability to work on the database. Naomi turned her attention back to her computer.

About twenty minutes later, Naomi took a small break to grab her food when Reed set their takeout delivery in front of her. She kept working for hours into the early morning. Reed would work on his laptop and his phone on and off. He would also offer to get Naomi whatever she wanted without complaint. Around 6:30 a.m., Naomi thought she had a working database that would suit the needs of PAN-based on the information provided to her.

"I'm going to run a couple of tests to see if everything works properly, but I think I have completed this 'task.' What have you been working on?" Naomi took a sip of the coffee that Reed had placed on the end table closest to her.

"I've just been following up on a couple of leads from the other cases I've been working on." Reed stretched his limbs and yawned.

"Do you have any leads on this case?"

"Yep. Right now, I am trying to secure a meeting with Senator Graham."

"How the hell did you manage to get their attention?" Naomi exclaimed as she spun to face Reed.

"Called in a favor to Chief Hughes after I potentially discovered that someone on his force might have their hands involved in something dirty. MPD is hosting an event to honor some officers, and Senator Graham will also be in attendance. We might get a meeting with her before or after the presentation. I think she holds a vital key to this case. Plus, it would be a neat event to attend."

"I agree. I just didn't think we could get a meeting with Senator Graham."

"You know the saying 'It's not what you know; it's who you know'? Well, it's part that mixed with some hard work and a bit of luck. Maybe more than luck. And I haven't finalized the meeting yet, so let's not get too excited."

Naomi nodded. "Still, it's good progress. And that makes sense, and I'm sure some people have moved up in my field via who they know, but you need at least some technical skills to go the distance."

"Hey, look outside."

Naomi looked out of the glass doors leading to her balcony and saw the sun rising. "It's a start to another beautiful day."

Reed glanced at her and smiled before turning back to his laptop.

Naomi picked up her laptop and started running the tests she needed to run to make sure the database was running properly. Getting the results she wanted, she made the database live and sent all the information back to PAN. She then closed her laptop.

"I think we should get a few hours of shut-eye and then maybe grab lunch around two? Maybe by then, we will have heard from Chief Hughes or Senator Graham's office about whether we can have a meeting with her."

"That sounds like a plan." Reed stood up and gathered his things. Just as he was about to head out the door, he swung around and told Naomi, "I changed my mind."

"Huh? About what?"

"You know how I said that getting lunch, later on, sounded like a plan?"

Naomi nodded her head.

"I meant to say it was a date." And with that, Reed strolled out of Naomi's apartment.

Naomi knew she couldn't dwell on his comment, for it would lead her down a spiral of overthinking. She gathered her things and walked to her bedroom.

She put her laptop back on her desk and placed her phone on her bedside table before getting into bed. She grabbed her phone once more. She saw that there was a message from her mother.

Mom: *Sweetie, we are still on track to be in DC by tomorrow.*

Diane told us she'd meet us at the airport and we'll head straight over to your apartment if that's all right. Talk to you soon. Love you, baby.

Naomi felt a sense of warmth come over her after reading Jada's words and knowing that she would be back in the city in a short while. With that, Naomi put her scarf over her hair and tried to go to sleep.

She ended up tossing and turning for a while before she had enough and hopped out of bed.

"I might as well do something productive if I can't fall asleep," mumbled Naomi as she opened her laptop. But what to do was the question. She checked her work email and saw nothing she could do there. She checked her personal email and saw nothing from PAN. Then she decided that if they got a meeting with Senator Graham that she should probably at least know the basics about her.

She found out that Senator Graham was the junior senator from Washington, DC, and was first elected in 2090. Her election was a nail biter, and she won her seat by a tiny margin. Naomi saw the senator also supported increasing cybersecurity legislation wholeheartedly for years, including joining some legislation that Sen. Butler sponsored. But that all changed within the last year.

"Interesting," said Naomi under her breath. What caused Senator Graham to stop supporting cybersecurity legislation? Naomi kept digging. She stumbled upon photos and videos of Senator Graham at events, and Naomi noticed something fascinating. Whenever Senator Graham and Senator Butler attended an event, they were stuck together like glue, whether it was them being seated next to each other, soft touches on the shoulder here, or a hand on the small of the back there.

"Are Senator Butler and Senator Graham dating? Or were dating?"

Naomi continued looking for definite proof that showed that they were dating, but she couldn't find anything that confirmed or denied that they were.

"I'll keep that in my back pocket," Naomi mumbled as she opened a new tab. She went to the Federal Election Commission's website and pulled all the records of who contributed to Senator Graham's campaign this election cycle. Naomi organized the data from most money donated to the campaign to the least. She figured for the senator to change her position entirely on cybersecurity, the person or people in question might have contributed a lot of money at once or over time.

Naomi reviewed the data and figured that she was looking for a needle in a haystack. She saw that Edmon's political action committee had donated a nice sum of money within the last couple of months.

"Interesting. I assume Edmon's is pro-cybersecurity because it would benefit the company." She took a screenshot of the page and made a note to look at Edmon's position on cybersecurity issues and to see if they have commented on Senator Butler's legislation.

She kept looking through the data when she came across a company named PAN, LLC. When she clicked the name, barely any information came up for it.

"Strange," Naomi mumbled to herself. She would almost bet that PAN, LLC, was related to the people who kidnapped Paige. And why would they have donated $100,000 to a junior senator from Washington, DC?

Naomi then tried to research PAN, LLC, but the company didn't have a homepage, nor was it listed on any of the review websites. Naomi felt she was at a dead-end but figured she could try one more thing. She reached the DC Business Center website and typed the company name into the search bar, but nothing came up. Naomi growled in frustration.

Frustrated and pissed off, Naomi called it a night.

CHAPTER 12

𝒩aomi awakened to her phone ringing.

"Hello?" She hoped the grogginess in her voice let the person on the other end know they had interrupted her sleep.

"Oh, I thought you would be up by now... Sorry to disturb you." Reed.

"No worries. I should have been getting up anyway to meet for lunch. What's up?"

"I wanted to ask where you wanted to meet?"

"Well, how about…. Wait, are you seriously exercising right now?" Naomi could hear that Reed was out of breath.

"Yep, I got a few hours of sleep and headed out for a jog. I'm almost back at my condo. I could be ready to head out in about thirty minutes."

Naomi pulled her phone away from her face and checked the time. It was 12:55 p.m. "Random question, but does the Hen House serve lunch? I assume it does but wasn't sure."

"Yep. You really liked that place, huh?"

Naomi smiled to herself. "Yeah, I did. How about we meet there at 2:30?"

"That's perfect. See you then."

Naomi raced to her bathroom and was ready to leave her apartment by 1:50. She quickly checked herself in her mirror to make sure she looked okay. Her curls flowed down her shoulders, her dark purple dress fit almost perfectly, and her black tights and black boots almost completed the outfit. She grabbed her gold earrings and a black belt and finished the look.

"Hopefully, this isn't too dressy." With one last look, she left her room. When she walked into the hallway, she saw Diane in her kitchen, wiping down the countertops.

"Hi Diane, I'm about to head out to meet Reed. Did you want to come with me? If not, is there anything you need?"

Diane looked up and smiled, but Naomi could see that her eyes were bloodshot. "No, I'll stay behind. I have a few calls to make related to getting the word out about Paige's disappearance. I don't need anything, but thanks for asking."

Naomi thought for a second before saying, "Please wait until I get back or at least until my parents get into town. We don't want to do anything to anger her captors, even though I'm wondering if doing this will kick things into gear."

Diane slowly nodded her head and said, "That makes sense. I'll wait for Jada and Logan to get back into town. Have a good time!"

Naomi left her apartment. She couldn't shake the eerie feeling she had about the whole interaction. Before heading to the car that she called before she left her apartment, Naomi quickly checked her email to see if she had anything from PAN. Seeing nothing, she went on her way.

Naomi got to the Hen House about ten minutes early, and Reed was already there.

"And here I thought I would be waiting for you," Naomi said as she walked up to the table where Reed was sitting. She noticed that he was wearing a suit and tie.

Reed smiled, walked over to Naomi, and helped her remove her coat. He then pulled out Naomi's chair and then sat back down.

Naomi scanned the menu and picked what she wanted. Their server came by, and the duo ordered both their drinks and meals.

"How's it going? Did you hear any more from Senator Graham's office? And why are you in a suit?" Naomi let loose a ton of questions just before she drank from a cup of water. She hadn't underdressed.

"We have a meeting scheduled with her today."

Naomi did everything in her power not to choke. She coughed before clearing her throat. She placed her cup down and looked at Reed. He looked concerned.

"Are you okay?"

Naomi nodded before clearing her throat again. "Really? That's amazing. Will any of her staff be joining?"

"I don't think so. We will meet Senator Graham at an official police department event with Chief Hughes. Not sure how much time we will have to chat with her, so we need to make it count."

The thought of talking to the senator one-on-one or, in this case, two-on-one was perfect. Naomi thought back to the research she had done on the senator, and she thought of a list of questions she wanted to ask. There was one question in particular that put butterflies in her stomach. Naomi was dying to tell Reed about what she suspected about the relationship between the two senators, and just as she was about to, Reed excused himself to take a call. When he returned, the thought flew out of her mind.

"Fantastic. Do we play good cop, bad cop, or something? I think that might be a bad pun…" Naomi took a bite of her meal.

Reed shook his head and smiled at her. "Yes, that was a horrible pun."

The two finished their meals and declined dessert. To burn some time before they had to be at Senator Graham's event, they chose to walk there from the restaurant.

Naomi checked her email and saw that there was still nothing from PAN. Fighting the urge to worry, she tried to put her focus on what she wanted to learn from the senator.

"So, do you think Senator Graham is involved in Paige's disappearance?" Naomi glanced at Reed as they strolled down the street.

"I'm not sure. I think Senator Graham has some information we need for the case. Do I think she kidnapped Paige? No, even though stranger things have happened. I'm curious to see if we can find out why she has done an about-face on cybersecurity issues."

"To add to the potential questions we have for the senator, I think she may be or might have been dating Senator Butler."

Reed stopped for a second and then began walking again. "Really? What made you think that?" Naomi recounted the research she found that morning. Reed nodded along as she talked.

"That's very fascinating, and I didn't pick up on it. Even if it isn't true, it could still be a good question that will take the senator off guard. I like it. Excellent job."

Naomi beamed. Although she would not admit it out loud, she was happy to provide information on something that Reed hadn't picked up on.

"Changing the subject a bit, I'm concerned that I haven't heard from PAN yet. Maybe what I sent them wasn't what they were looking for, and I did more harm than good." Naomi sighed and brushed a hand over her curls.

Reed stopped walking again and grabbed Naomi's hand. "Don't say that. You pulled together what they wanted in half of the time that it should have taken. Don't diminish what you did or your accomplishments. You kicked ass."

"You're right. I did what the kidnappers asked of me, and I shouldn't question it. My insecurities and worry for Paige are messing with my confidence. Ah, I shouldn't be talking about this with you." Naomi pulled back her hand.

"Why shouldn't you? I enjoy hearing things about you. I enjoy knowing what you're thinking."

"Because I don't like to burden other people with my problems." The silence that her statement caused was prevalent. Happy that this part of the conversation had ended, Naomi checked her phone to see if she had any messages and emails. Seeing none, she placed the device back in her pocket and motioned with her head that they should continue on their way.

Reed grabbed Naomi's hand once again to stop her from moving. "I want you to feel like you can tell me anything. Don't feel ashamed." He then squeezed her hand and continued walking with Naomi following suit.

The two moved along for a few moments before Reed said,

"After we get Paige back, I would like to ask you out on a proper date. I planned to contact you after we met at happy hour, but our paths crossed more quickly than I had expected."

Naomi gave a slight smile. "I think I'd like that too." Although they spent a significant amount of time together over the last few days, and she was happy he wanted to see her outside of all of this, she still felt a bit of weariness about the situation. On the one hand, she trusted him and wanted to go out on a date with him. She couldn't get rid of this nagging feeling that he wasn't completely truthful with her. Her gut said he wasn't forthcoming with information about himself, and she didn't understand why. She wanted to attribute it to them both, mostly being focused on Paige, but she had an inkling she was missing something important.

"So. tell me something that few people know about you."

"I'm ambidextrous. Not sure if there is another word for that."

"Wow. I never noticed it."

"Yep, certain things I can do better with my left hand than my right. For example, I can dribble a ball well in my left hand, but if I am writing with a pen, I'm right-handed."

"That's pretty freaking cool."

"You?"

"I...I don't know. I kind of feel you know a lot about me already." She chastised herself in her mind because of how insecure she thought she sounded.

Reed paused for a moment. "There is no way I could know everything about you. Only just some things I've picked up here and there. There has to be something."

Naomi thought for a second and then said, "I loved

learning so much that I would read my SAT book for fun when I was in the seventh grade."

Reed didn't respond right away. He said, "Who does that?"

"Me apparently," Naomi laughed, the first genuine laugh she had let out in a long while.

Reed and Naomi arrived at the Violet Hill Hotel just before 5:15 p.m. They surveyed their surroundings before grabbing a drink and moving to stand in a corner of the room.

"I guess we wait." Naomi took a sip of her drink. Reed nodded as he took a pair of glasses out of his suit pocket and put them on.

"I didn't know you wore glasses."

"I do, but these aren't them. These are very similar to our phone devices in that they have many functions, including being able to record. Figured it might be handy to have just in case."

Naomi was impressed once again. "That makes sense." Before Naomi could say anything else, Reed interrupted her.

"The senator just arrived, and the police chief is with her." Senator Graham, Chief Mark Hughes, and what looked to be a staffer for each walked around the room chatting with the guests. Just before the group reached Naomi and Reed, Chief Hughes looked at Reed and gave him a slight head nod.

The duo waited for the senator and the police chief to finish their conversation with the other guests. Chief Hughes walked toward Naomi and Reed first. He introduced himself to Naomi and then shook both of their hands. Although there was an air of authority that surrounded him — it would normally make Naomi feel intimidated — his brown eyes showed kindness.

He smoothed a dark brown hand down his tie and said, "Please call me, Mark." He smiled at Naomi before turning to Reed. "It has been a while since we've seen each other in person."

"Yes, it has. We should get drinks sometime soon."

Naomi looked between the two as she tried to figure out their connection. Mark smiled.

"Reed's father and I grew up together in Pennsylvania. I helped mentor Reed when he was on the police force. He still helps with cases every so often."

Naomi hoped her shock wasn't apparent on her face. Was Reed a former cop? She made a note to ask him more about it later. "Ah, okay. That's great."

Mark nodded, and Senator Graham walked up to the group.

"Hello, I am Evelyn Graham. And you are?" Senator Graham shook their hands. The senator's navy suit looked to be tailored to fit her and she had twisted her dirty blonde into a fancy updo. The bracelet on her arm was Angie & Pam; Naomi thought it must have cost a small fortune. Naomi and Reed introduced themselves and waited for the senator to continue.

"Thank you for coming. Mark mentioned that you wanted to chat with me, so let's go over here where it's more secluded," said Senator Graham as she started walking toward a door on the left side of the room. Reed and Naomi waved goodbye to the chief and followed the senator.

"So, how can I help you? I only have a few minutes before the presentation starts."

"Senator, we will only take a few minutes of your time. We were hoping to talk to you more about your stance on cybersecurity. You seemed to be a vigorous supporter a few months ago, and now you aren't."

Senator Graham's eyes shifted again. "Our beliefs and stances change and evolve as we come across additional evidence. The cybersecurity bills brought up in the Senate aren't as good as they have been in years past. The devil is always in the details."

Reed responded, "I don't doubt that. Are you against cybersecurity all together, or is it only in certain cases?"

Senator Graham thought for a moment. "I think we need cybersecurity. But the things I want haven't been addressed."

Naomi felt her patience wearing thin, and although she tried to control her emotions, she knew this might not end well. This conversation seemed to be going in circles, and Senator Graham was just a politician speaking like a politician. She had had enough.

"Did your sudden distaste for cybersecurity bills have anything to do with the fact that Senator Butler is the sponsor of a lot of them?" Naomi's question interrupted the flow of the conversation.

Senator Graham just stared at Naomi. And then she started stuttering as she tried to figure out a way to respond. "Senator Butler has nothing to do with this."

"Well then, why did you have a meltdown when you and he met a few days ago about the cybersecurity bill?"

Senator Graham looked at Naomi wide-eyed. Then she looked down at her shoes and then back up at Naomi before answering. "I'm not sure I know what you are talking about."

"I think you do." Naomi glanced at Reed, and his face was unreadable. Naomi turned back to Senator Graham.

"Does your sudden change in position have anything to do with your dating Senator Butler?"

Senator Graham shook her head, but her eyes told another story. There was a moment of silence before she sighed. "Who told you?"

"No one. It was apparent just by watching how you acted around each other. I wasn't sure but figured I would drop the question and see what happened." Naomi looked at Reed again, and his face was still unreadable. She worried she had done something wrong. She shook it off for the time being and asked another question. "Did your outburst have anything to do with Paige Harris, one of Senator Butler's staffers?"

"A little. I was jealous because Paige had been spending a ton of time with him recently, even though I didn't suspect that anything was going on between them. I think the outburst was related to the desire to spend more time with him and being stressed by everything going on the Hill right now. The reason I've changed my stance on cybersecurity is more complicated."

Naomi waited for her to elaborate.

Senator Graham pulled out her phone, and after fiddling with it for a few seconds, she turned it around and showed Naomi and Reed her screen.

"I try to represent my constituents' interests across the board. A few of the ways we do that is by reading constituent letters and emails, listening to their phone calls, what they mention when we have meetings, and when we host events. Over the last several months, here is how the priorities of my constituents have shifted."

Naomi and Reed looked at the graph and noticed that

cybersecurity went from being one of the most important issues to residents of Virginia to be in the lower middle tier.

"During this shift, we also started receiving calls from constituents stating the internet is already very secure, and we didn't need to spend more money on this, and money should be going elsewhere."

Reed asked, "Do you know what caused this shift? Did something happen that suddenly became more important?"

"We have been trying to investigate what happened, but as of now, it came out of nowhere. Usually, we have been able to detect a trend, but there isn't one here, well, at least not that we could find yet."

While Senator Graham continued talking about how the concern for cybersecurity fell in a downward spiral, Naomi debated telling her about Paige's disappearance. She decided that since Senator Graham had been forthcoming with information that could be helpful, she might as well tell her.

"When did you last see Paige Harris?"

"During a meeting with George, Teresa, and her. Why?"

"Well, Paige is missing."

"She's gone? What? I need to call George. We haven't really spoken since I lost my cool at that meeting. Now I feel even more terrible."

Naomi asked the senator not to mention the disappearance to anyone else, as they were trying to keep things quiet for now. Both Reed and Naomi then thanked the senator for her time, and Senator Graham gave both Reed and Naomi her personal phone number to call her if there was anything she could do to help find Paige. She walked back into the event, leaving Naomi and Reed alone.

Reed turned to Naomi and said, "Could you warn me

before you go off the handle like that? That could have gone way worse than it did."

Naomi took a step back as if someone had slapped her. She couldn't believe he said that. "What did I do wrong?"

"You became very emotional and snapped at a US senator!"

"Well, this an emotional situation, and she wasn't directly answering our questions. It all worked out."

"Thankfully."

Reed walked out of the room first, and Naomi followed slowly behind him. They joined the event again and stood off to the side, watching people in silence. After a few minutes, Naomi felt like someone was watching her. She surveyed the room and turned to a tall man with amber skin staring at her from the other end of the room. His brown eyes made her pause, and Naomi narrowed her eyes in return. Something about them was familiar, but she couldn't place it. Naomi gently nudged Reed. Reed turned to her, and when she gestured toward the man across the room, he looked in that direction. The guy turned and walked away quickly.

"Who was that?" Reed asked, their previous conversation forgotten.

"I have no idea, but he seemed to know me. I hope you caught his face on those glasses of yours."

CHAPTER 13

*R*eed invited Naomi back to his condo to look at the footage that he collected with his glasses. It was not too far from Capitol Hill, so they got there in record time. Reed opened his door, and Naomi immediately started looking around, trying to learn more about the man. The decor of the living room was simple but homey. The room featured different tones of gray with a big-screen TV on the wall.

"Nice place," Naomi said, turning around slowly. She walked past his kitchen toward the dining room, which was in the back of his home. The doors to his balcony were right off the dining room. "Your view is better than mine. I'm resisting the urge to go outside even though it's cold out."

"Your view is nothing to sneeze at either," said Reed as he moved behind Naomi to stand on her right. The sun had almost set, and there was a low glow in the sky.

Naomi stepped back and headed over to Reed's couch and sat down. Reed walked down a hallway and entered a room. A few seconds later, he came back with a laptop and took his phone out of his pocket. He turned on the laptop and opened up an application.

"My glasses automatically send footage to my laptop and the cloud within two seconds," he explained as he pulled up the video of their interview with Senator Graham. Before he started, he looked at Naomi and said, "I'm sorry for snapping at you earlier about throwing down the gauntlet with that question to Senator Graham."

"No, you were right. I lost my cool. So, I apologize too."

Reed nodded and then smirked. "So, was this our first fight?"

Naomi playfully side-eyed Reed and said, "I wouldn't call this a fight, but why are you counting our fights?"

Before Reed could answer, their meeting with Senator Graham started playing on the screen. After the interview ended, their disagreement appeared on the screen, and Reed cringed and mouthed to Naomi that he was sorry again. Naomi waved him off. The two focused on the end of their video until the mysterious man appeared. He was only on there for a second, and the image that Reed captured was blurry.

"I'll send this to Levi right now to see if he can fix the blurriness. Would you like anything to drink?" Reed stood up and walked into his kitchen.

"Red wine would be great if you have it." Reed held up a bottle of red wine and poured some for Naomi. He grabbed a beer out of his fridge and brought both drinks back to the living room and placed them on the coffee table.

Reed looked at his phone and saw a message from Levi. "Levi's cleaning the image up now. Said he could get it back to me in fifteen minutes. How about I give you a tour of the rest of the place?"

"Sure," said Naomi as she got up and followed Reed.

"I think you saw the kitchen when you walked in, but here it is again." Reed gestured to the kitchen. She looked around and noticed the darker appliances immediately. They were relatively new, which led to Naomi's question.

"Do you cook a lot?"

"As often as I can."

"That's great. I love your kitchen. It's almost perfect."

"What would make it perfect?" Reed stood in front of Naomi with his arms at his sides.

"If you had a wine fridge." Naomi winked at Reed and strutted out into the living room while she waited for Reed to show her the rest of the house. Reed chuckled as he continued the tour. He then showed her where the bathrooms and his guestroom were before showing off his office.

"Here is my office. As you can see, Levi and I share similar tastes in terms of high-powered computers, but I didn't want a huge TV monitor in this room. But I have an evidence board and everything else you'd probably find in an office." Naomi strolled over to Reed's evidence board and saw that the documents were related to Paige's disappearance.

Before she could get a good look at the board, Reed put his hand on the small of her back and said, "I have a couple more things to show you. Let's go." Reed led Naomi to the last room that she hadn't seen yet: his bedroom.

There wasn't much clutter besides a few things on his nightstands, including lamps. The room also had a dresser and a TV. There were some black-and-white photographs on the walls that went with the darker tones of the furniture.

"Wow, these photographs are amazing," Naomi said, examining one photo.

"Thanks. I took them myself."

"Oh, really? You are very talented." Naomi admired another photo.

"I took up photography after I started working as a PI. I took photos for some of my cases and then started taking photos on the side. It just kind of fell into place." Naomi glanced back at Reed and noticed he was by his bedroom door.

"My closet is behind that door, and the bathroom is behind that door." Reed pointed at each door, respectively. "Come on. Let's see if Levi got back to me yet."

"Did you decorate your home yourself?" Naomi took another sip of the wine and followed Reed out of his bedroom.

"Nope. My sister did, actually. She's an interior decorator. I told her what I envisioned, and she sent me samples, and I okayed the things I wanted. It worked out great. She also designed Levi's office space. She caught the designing bug that runs in my family."

"That's awesome. I would love to do something similar in our place, but I feel weird decorating a place we don't own. If Paige is fine with it, shit," Naomi mumbled, shook her head, and closed her eyes.

"I'll give you my sister's contact information when we find Paige and the assholes who kidnapped her," said Reed.

Naomi nodded, and the two walked back into Reed's living room. Reed checked his phone but did not see a message from Levi.

"Did you get an email from PAN?" asked Reed.

"I haven't checked in a while because I was obsessing over it. Let me check now." Naomi pulled out her phone. She scrolled through her messages and saw that there was nothing but spam.

A few seconds later, Reed's phone rang. "This is probably Levi. But why would he be calling instead of just sending me an email...?" Reed trailed off as he answered his phone and put the person on video.

"Hey, man. I have you on speaker. Naomi is here."

"Hey, Naomi. I figured it would be easier to call you versus explaining it via email. I sent you the cleaned-up photo. Let's get started. I'm going to share my screen."

Levi's face disappeared off the screen, and the original photo that Reed screen grabbed from the footage his glasses captured appeared on the screen.

"Here is the before. And here is the after!" Levi exclaimed.

The transformation stunned Reed and Naomi. The screenshot went from a blurry, contorted mess to something that looked like Reed took it at a magazine photoshoot. The features of the mysterious man were clear.

Reed remained silent for a bit before asking, "Do you know who this guy is?"

Naomi shook her head. "There is something very familiar about his eyes," Naomi whispered. She couldn't take her eyes off the photo. The tall, tan man with the dark eyes had a sinister look about him that made Naomi feel uneasy. But there was also a bit of vulnerability there too.

"Is there anything else you wanted to show us?" Reed turned his attention back to Levi and the photo.

"Actually, yes. This guy was wearing a nametag."

Naomi's heart dropped into her stomach. Would this be their big break?

"So, I couldn't pull his name off of the nametag unless it was PAN, LLC." Levi clicked through the slideshow again, and another photo popped up. It was a photo of a sticker on the mystery man's suit jacket that said PAN, LLC.

"You've got to be kidding me. He was right there?" Naomi yelled. She stood up so fast that she made Reed flinch. She paced because it helped her to think and would hopefully help her with her anger.

"Good job, Levi," Naomi mumbled while pacing. "So this is the guy who has been stalking me. I knew someone was following me, and it was not just paranoia." Her anger dissipated.

"I'm going to send this to Chief Hughes to run through their database to see if anything pops. Hopefully, I'll have something to share soon."

"And you promise that he won't make a big fuss about this? The kidnappers—well, potentially that guy—told us not to say a word to the police."

"I'm one hundred percent confident that this won't leak."

Naomi doubted that he could have that level of confidence in anything right now but said nothing. "Thanks for doing all of this work last minute, Levi."

"Not a problem. Let me know if I can help with anything else." Levi disconnected the video.

"Okay, I'll head home because my parents should be there by now. Would you like to come with me? Diane was talking about putting together some plan on her end, but I asked her to wait until I got back, and my parents got into town before she did anything." Naomi gathered her coat and phone.

"I'm meeting the parents already?" Although he didn't say it, Naomi could tell that Reed was pleased that she offered for him to meet Logan.

Naomi shook her head with a smile. "Sure, but you've already met my mom. Do you want to come back with me or not?"

Reed nodded and grabbed his laptop and other essentials. He packed the items in his bookbag, and the two hopped on the metro to head back to Naomi's place.

* * *

When Naomi opened her apartment door, she was greeted by the smell of something good. She looked around and spotted Diane, Logan, and Jada in the kitchen.

"Hey, Mom!" Naomi yelled as she quickly walked toward the kitchen. Jada turned around with a big smile and hugged her only child. Naomi also hugged Logan and Diane before turning around to introduce Reed.

"Mom, I know you know Reed, and of course, Diane does, but I'm not sure if you've met him, Logan."

Logan smiled at Reed and said, "I haven't. Logan Porter," as he held his hand out for a handshake.

"Reed Wright. Nice to meet you."

"Oh, you made brownies. Fantastic! Thanks so much." Naomi grabbed a brownie and walked into the living room.

"Any news on Paige? Diane was just filling us in on everything she knew." Jada took the plate of brownies, and the rest of the group followed Naomi into the living room.

"We have some facts and speculations, but things are up in

the air at the moment." Reed filled the rest of the group in on what they had encountered that day.

While Reed answered questions, Naomi walked into the kitchen and checked her phone.

She saw an email from Paige's personal account. Dread immediately flowed through her veins. Her heart sank when she clicked on it. She scanned the email and saw that PAN thanked her for her work. He told her it was perfect. She felt a small sense of pride for being complimented but was also disgusted, and she kept reading.

"I can't do this," Naomi mumbled while she reread the email.

"Can't do what?" Naomi didn't hear Reed walk over to her. He gently placed a hand on her shoulder.

"I just got another email from PAN. I can't do this next task." Naomi stood up and began running her hands over her face and hair.

"Wait. Why not? What does the email say?"

"No. It's just the fact that I could go to jail if I create what the kidnappers want."

"Can I see the email?"

Naomi handed over her phone, and Reed read the email. He, too, ran his hands through his hair as he placed the phone down on the table.

Naomi,

Good job with the last task, your next project is to get the data sets that are located in Edmon's Cyber Edge file and insert them into the database. Once you have done this, we will think about letting Paige go. You have two days.

PAN

"Cyber Edge?"

Naomi looked up at Reed before looking back at her phone. "I've only ever heard of it in passing, but apparently, the file contains some data on some important people. I would essentially be stealing this information."

Reed gripped the table.

"Are you okay?" Naomi noticed that Reed had tensed up.

"No. I'm pissed. I don't want to be stuck between you potentially going to jail and something happening to Paige." Naomi could see that Reed was doing everything in his power not to lose control.

"I'm upset too, but we need to think about this with clear heads. Also, I wonder how smart these people are."

Reed looked over at Naomi. "Why would you say that?"

"Based on this email, the guy who was at Senator Graham's event doesn't know that we know he's involved. Now he knows I saw him, but our encounter happened so quickly that he might not have gotten suspicious. I only say that because there wasn't anything in the email that alluded to the encounter."

Reed calmed down as he was comprehending what Naomi was saying. He turned and gave her his full attention. "That's a good point. You sure that you weren't a detective in a past life?"

"Maybe, but I think this is mostly instinct and gut more than anything."

"Those are both very important characteristics that you should have while investigating. I don't think it's a coincidence that this guy showed up today. I also noticed that PAN didn't mention us telling MPD anything, which was a big relief."

"That's true. And we need to keep it that way. Did you hear

anything from Chief Hughes? Did he say anything else about the person or people who approved that video of Paige?"

Reed checked his email before putting his phone down. "Nope. Haven't heard anything from Police Chief Hughes yet."

"Okay, I'll grab my laptop and try to think of a way around this project." Naomi left the kitchen and headed to her bedroom. When she entered her room, she noticed something was amiss. The picture frame of her and her parents was turned over.

"Hey, guys? Can you come here but stay in the doorway?" Everyone in the living room came running into Naomi's room but did as she asked. She turned around and looked at the group.

"I think someone has been in the apartment."

CHAPTER 14

"Diane, when did you leave the apartment?" Naomi tried to piece together when someone could have accessed her home.

"Late afternoon? It had to be around three because I remember checking my phone when I left to double-check that I wouldn't be late in meeting Jada and Logan. I needed to get out and think, so I walked around, and then I met Jada and Logan at the airport and brought them back to the apartment." Diane looked somewhat weary. She needed a break.

"So, this person had maybe an hour and a half to do whatever he or she did. I'll check with the front desk to see if they saw anything."

"I'm going in to look around, but I won't touch anything." Reed slowly wandered into the room. He analyzed the room, much like he had done when he saw it for the first time.

"Someone was definitely in here and that someone couldn't stand having this photo of you all looking back at him or her. That sounds personal. But the question was, what were they looking for and why?"

Reed continued looking around the room before spotting something sticking out from Naomi's laptop.

"Did you find anything?" Naomi noticed that Reed was studying her laptop.

"If I had to guess, I would say that is the reason the person came to your room." Reed gestured to a small device that was attached to Naomi's laptop. "I think that's a tracker." Naomi didn't move at first but followed Reed's gaze with her own.

"I don't want to grab the tracker because of fingerprints and disturbing evidence. But based on what I see, this is an old school homemade tracker. I don't believe there's anything like this on the market today."

Naomi looked at the tracker from other angles, all the while trying not to touch it. "Yeah, definitely not." She didn't mention this out loud, but she knew about some trackers that Edmon was testing lately, and this looked nothing like them. Although she didn't directly work with trackers, she still made it her mission to find out the latest and greatest things that Edmon was testing. "Someone must have bypassed Simon to place that on my computer. Which furthers my thoughts about them having some kind of background in the tech field."

"I'll call Chief Hughes, but we should all leave Naomi's room alone." Reed walked back into the living room and grabbed his phone. He called the chief and told him what he suspected had occurred at the apartment. Her eyes were trained on him as she watched him walk back and forth. Naomi could only hear Reed's side of the conversation, and she was eagerly waiting for him to get off the phone. When he finally hung up and put his phone down, it took everything in Naomi to not pounce on him.

"So, what did he say?"

"Nothing. Absolutely nothing."

Naomi didn't realize how much she depended on his answer until she got one that she wasn't expecting. The stress and pressure from the last few days caused her stomach to churn. "I—I need to go outside for some fresh air." Not waiting for a response, Naomi dashed to her balcony doors and stepped outside before closing the door. Once she reached the balcony railing, she closed her eyes and took a deep breath as she tried to tame the anxiousness roaming through her veins. Attempting to ground herself, and her feelings were the first steps she wanted to take to stop another anxiety attack.

"Are you okay?" Naomi hadn't heard Reed follow her outside, and although she would usually be annoyed that someone was interrupting her, she was relieved to see him. She still felt tiny pangs in her stomach, but she was happy that the pain in her stomach was beginning to ease.

Naomi nodded but said nothing.

"Is there anything you want to talk about?"

She shook her head before replying, "No. I felt myself getting anxious, but it settled down once I was outside, breathing in the fresh air. Your arrival helped too." Naomi gave a small smile over her right shoulder before turning attention back to DC's landscape in front of her. Reed walked over to her right side and joined her. She didn't know how long they stayed there, but a stiff breeze blew one of her curls over her shoulder and into her face. Naomi laughed, and before she could do anything, Reed reached over and softly pushed the curl back over her shoulder.

She turned her head to gaze into his eyes. Naomi didn't

realize that she had stopped breathing under his intense stare until she took a breath several seconds later.

"Can I kiss you?" He whispered so low that she almost didn't hear him. Naomi was speechless but could nod just as Reed cupped her cheek. When their lips met, everything briefly disappeared, Paige's kidnapping, the bull's-eye on Naomi's back, everything. She could feel Reed relax under their kiss and knew that frustration was leaving his body as they broke apart.

"Well, that was...something else" whispered Naomi.

"You felt that, too, huh? I've been wanting to do that again since we stopped kissing at the Hen House. Hell, that was a lot better than our kiss outside of the Hen House, and I couldn't imagine anything would top that." Reed gave Naomi a small smile as he brushed one of her curls back behind her ear. He leaned forward and bent down as if he would kiss her again, but whispered in her ear, "I'll do a sweep of the apartment manually and transfer the results directly to Chief Hughes myself. I have everything I need to do that in my bookbag. We'll be as discreet as possible to make sure we don't tip off whoever broke into your apartment. I suggest you and your parents, and Diane get rooms at a hotel, and I'll meet you there when I finish. Okay?" Reed leaned back to look into her eyes.

Naomi nodded again and stood on her tiptoes to whisper in his ear, "How about I help you briefly? I'll send Diane and my parents to the hotel to get situated and book my room, and I'll run checks on my laptop to see if they did anything else to it. I highly doubt they could break into my laptop, given Edmon's security features, but you never know. If I run the scanner now, I can take my laptop with me worry-free. If you can scan for fingerprints on my laptop, desk, computer chair, and anything else in that general area first, that would be great. While the scanner is doing its thing, I'll talk to the front desk and see if they have any information."

"Sounds like a plan, and you sound even more like a detective," said Reed as he quickly placed a quick peck on her lips.

"Damn right, I do," said Naomi. She smiled, and the two walked back into the apartment. Naomi escorted Diane and her parents outside and told them their part of the plan since Naomi wasn't sure if someone had bugged other areas in the apartment. She also told them she would join them later, and Jada offered to book her hotel room for her. After saying a quick goodbye, Naomi joined Reed, and they got to work.

Reed scanned her office area to check for any fingerprints and bugs in that section of the room. After that was complete, Naomi got to work on making sure her laptop was still secure. After she finished setting up the scan, she went to the lobby to check who was sitting at the front desk. She breathed a sigh of relief when she saw that Ann was back on her usual shift.

"Ann! How are you doing?" Naomi said as she walked up to the desk.

"Good, can't complain about anything. How about you? Any word about Paige?"

"You know life can be crazy. I'm glad things are quiet for you. We heard some things here and there about Paige, but she hasn't come home yet." Naomi tried to keep the amount of information that she gave Ann to a minimum. "I had a few questions, though. I know I saw you when I came in, but when did your shift start?"

"My shift started around two. And yes, I saw you with

mister tall and handsome." Ann winked at Naomi. Naomi felt her cheeks grow a little warm, but she kept her cool.

"Oh, so you were on duty. Did you notice anyone out of the ordinary between 3:00 and 4:00 p.m.?"

"I vaguely remember seeing someone, but he came in and left so quickly. I reported it to my superiors so that it might make it up the chain of command there. I see so many people daily. We have cameras set up, though, and they work. Let me see if I can find that timestamp and scan it."

While Ann made quick work of scanning the video footage from this afternoon, Naomi sat down in a chair checked her work email on her phone. She tried to reply to a few emails, but she found herself unable to concentrate. Naomi checked her personal email instead and reread the email from PAN. She was trying to think of potential solutions to the request when Ann called her over.

"So, this was the guy I was talking about." Ann showed Naomi the video. Naomi held her breath since she was expecting that she would see the tall, tan complexioned man from Senator Graham's event. In the video, a man dressed in a dark baseball cap and dark clothes appeared on the screen, scanning the room. He looked up at the camera briefly, and Naomi could see his face. He was an older black man with a salt-and-pepper beard and piercing dark-colored eyes. He seemed to be of average height and slightly overweight.

"I swear I've seen this man before, but I can't place him. Is there any way I can get this shot printed?"

"I'm sorry, but I can't do that because there hasn't been a warrant presented. I could even get in trouble just showing you this video."

With that, Naomi took a step back from the front desk and

said, "I definitely don't want that to happen. You've been a great help, Ann. Thank you so much!" Naomi waved goodbye and headed back up to her apartment. Even though she did not have a physical photo of the guy, she knew that she wouldn't be able to forget his face.

CHAPTER 15

*N*aomi walked off the elevator and opened the door to her apartment. "Reed?" She replayed the interaction with Ann over in her head.

"In your room," said Reed. Naomi entered her room and saw Reed on his hands and knees, looking under her bed with a scanner.

"I hope I don't have anything embarrassing underneath there," Naomi said. "Did you finish scanning this area of the room?" Naomi pointed at her desk.

Reed nodded and said, "I'm just wrapping up your room so we can talk freely as long as we speak low. What did you find out?"

Naomi relayed her conversation with Ann to Reed. Reed nodded here and there but mostly stayed silent until the end. "You're confident you would be able to ID him if it came down to that or if this guy pops up elsewhere?"

"Without a doubt. There was something eerily familiar about him. I'll never forget those piercing eyes." Naomi sat at her desk and checked her computer. It had run the scanner to check for any viruses, virtual tracers, and a host of other items that could hack into the computer. It found that someone had attempted to turn on her laptop, but Edmon's technology had blocked the attempt.

"Good job, Edmon," Naomi murmured as she finished some manual checks. She concluded that her laptop was more than likely fine and could go with her to the hotel.

"Naomi, I found this." Reed handed Naomi an envelope with her name on it. "I already inspected it. There were no fingerprints." Naomi opened the envelope and read the letter inside.

> *Naomi,*
>
> *I know more about you than you could ever dream. And you can see how easy it was to enter your personal space, your sanctuary. Don't doubt what I am capable of doing. If you want to see Paige alive again, you must connect the database you created to Edmon's cybersecurity clientele database in the cloud. You must then extract the data to the database you made. Email Paige once you have completed this objective. We'll be in touch.*
>
> *PAN*

"Is this enough to get the police on the case?" Naomi said sarcastically. She rolled her eyes and sat down at her desk. It took everything in her to not pace, and she was thankful that the stomach pains she had grown to suspect weren't there.

Reed didn't have an answer she wanted to hear. She knew there was nothing he could say that would make her feel better. She knew she couldn't dwell on the current state of affairs and had to keep putting one foot in front of the other.

"So, I'll pack and head to the hotel in a bit," Naomi said while she threw things into an overnight bag. Reed nodded his head as he started moving his equipment into Paige's room.

Naomi went to her dresser and noticed the photo of her and her parents was sitting upright again. She appreciated Reed taking the time to do that, even though it was minor. She then walked over to her window and observed how quiet Washington, DC, was on this cool, crystal clear night.

"I wonder if whoever entered my apartment was the same person with the red laser who was spying on me," she said out loud. The thought of it caused her heart to thump harder.

When Naomi finished packing, she grabbed her laptop bag and her overnight bag and called out to Reed to tell him she was leaving.

"Did you call a car to come to pick you up?" he asked. He left Paige's room and walked over to her.

"Yes, but it won't be here for ten minutes," replied Naomi as Reed took the bags from her hand. He leaned over and kissed her. He then headed out the door with Naomi staring behind. Naomi quickly snapped out of it and followed him to the elevator. She gently grabbed his hand when he attempted to press the button to summon the elevator.

"What if the person who broke into my apartment is the same person who shined that red laser at my windowsill a few days ago? Maybe the red laser wasn't just being used to scare me. Maybe it was to measure the distance between the two buildings."

"That's not a bad assumption. Let me do a little investigating after I wrap up all the scans here, okay? You go to the hotel and relax as much as you can." Reed pressed the elevator button, and this time Naomi didn't stop him. When the elevator opened its doors, he loaded her bags and then held the door open for her to enter.

"I would take your bags all the way downstairs, but I don't want to leave your apartment unattended. I'll lock up when I leave, and I'll shoot you a message when I get to the hotel so you can tell me what room you're in."

"Okay. I'll see you soon." Naomi initiated the goodbye kiss between her and Reed before stepping onto the elevator and watching the doors close. They needed to talk about what was happening between them.

Naomi arrived at the hotel within fifteen minutes and checked in with ease. She unpacked a few things that she'd need for the night and then took out her phone to message her mom about meeting everyone for a late dinner. Jada responded that Logan got pulled into a call for work, and Diane was resting for a bit, but she could meet Naomi downstairs at the hotel bar for a drink or two in thirty minutes.

Naomi thought this was a great idea and decided to put some makeup on. As she pulled a tube of lip gloss from her bag, her phone rang.

She picked it up and saw that the number on the screen was not a number she recognized. Usually, she'd let it go to voice mail, but just in case it was related to Paige, she answered the device.

"Hello, this is Naomi."

"Hi, Naomi. My name is Jenna Cross, owner of Jewelry by Jenna. I am returning your call."

Naomi's stomach almost touched her feet. She quickly recovered and said, "Hi Jenna. Thank you for calling me back. I called about the kidnapping of my friend. I believe it occurred near your business. My friend was taking a yoga class at the studio next door, and she never made it home. The studio's camera only had visuals on their front door. Based on what we could see, everything was fine when she walked out of the view of that camera, but all we know is that she walked toward your jewelry store. Would it be possible to view your video feed from that time? It would have been between 7:30 and 7:45 or so on Monday morning."

"I am so sorry to hear that your friend disappeared. I'll get right to it and send you the video from that time. What is your phone code? I should have it to you within the next ten minutes. Please let me know if I can help with anything else."

Naomi read off her code, and profusely thanked Jenna for her time. She knew the ten-minute wait would be excruciating, and she paced to burn off the nervous energy. Almost eight minutes after the call, Naomi received a notification saying that Jewelry by Jenna wanted to send her a file. She quickly accepted it, downloaded the file, and pressed the play button.

The first few minutes were nothing special, but by the six-minute mark of the video, Paige appeared on the screen. She was walking with her head down and suddenly looked up. A man in a dark coat, pants, and a hat approached her, but Naomi couldn't see his face. Paige's face went from surprised, to confused, to smiling while talking to the man, and the two walked off together off-screen.

Naomi played the video several times but noticed nothing different. Naomi's attention diverted when Jada said that she would have to cancel drinks and dinner with the group tonight because she, Logan, and Diane were trying to work on putting together a tip line. Naomi shrugged her shoulders and went back to looking at the video. She'd order from the room service menu in a little while.

"It looks like she recognized the man," Naomi mumbled as she watched the video once more. When she was about to play the video again, Naomi's phone pinged. She picked up the device and found a message from Reed.

Reed: *Would you be able to come over to my condo instead? I got caught up in something that I should have wrapped up by the time you get here. I hate to ask you to travel this late at night, but it seems to be unavoidable.*

Naomi: *Sure. That shouldn't be a problem. I also have some new information for you.*

Reed: *Great. I'll also order dinner if you haven't eaten so tell me what you want. See you soon.*

Naomi packed up her laptop and other things she thought she might need to take over to Reed's. She grabbed her phone again and noticed that Reed had sent her his address. She quickly sent him her dinner request, sent a message to her mother about her whereabouts, and caught a taxi to his condo.

CHAPTER 16

*N*aomi arrived at Reed's condo twenty minutes later and was let into the building once Reed verified her identity. When she knocked on the door, Reed opened it almost immediately with a smile on his face. But that smile quickly turned to a look of concern once their eyes met. Naomi's eyes welled up with tears as she fought the urge to cry.

"What's wrong?" Reed asked as he stepped aside to let Naomi into his condo. He grabbed her bag and coat. He quickly placed them in the closet as he grabbed some tissues from the kitchen before he guided Naomi to sit on the couch in his living room.

"I think everything that has been happening over the last few days has gotten to me. I was able to calm down my anxiety earlier, but I'm having a hard time doing it now." Naomi paused as she wiped tears from her eyes. "I'm sorry I came here this upset."

"Why are you sorry? I want to be there to help you when

you're upset and be with you when you're happy. You are under a tremendous amount of stress, and no one's perfect. I'm glad you came over."

"I just don't understand. There has to be something I'm missing. What am I doing wrong?" Naomi pleaded with Reed, but they both knew he couldn't answer the question. But he could hug her, so that was what he did.

Naomi didn't know how long they hugged, but when they broke apart, she felt better. "Thanks for that," she whispered.

Reed smiled at her. "Can I get you anything? If talking about the case is too stressful, we can find something else to do."

"Could you grab me a glass of wine if you don't mind? Hey, that almost rhymed." Naomi inspected Reed for the first time since she had arrived. She noticed that he had changed into a white T-shirt, dark wash jeans, and was barefoot. He looked peaceful and understandably comfortable in his house.

Reed chuckled as he grabbed his phone. "I'll grab you that glass of wine."

A couple of minutes later, he returned with a glass of wine for Naomi and a glass of water for himself. "Do you want to talk about the latest information you found?"

"Sure. I want to sort this out." She filled Reed in on what she heard from Jenna and showed him the video of Paige walking past Jewelry by Jenna.

After the video ended, Reed was silent for a few seconds before responding, "I agree she knew the guy. I know the angle isn't the best, but are you sure you don't recognize him?"

She shook her head. They were thinking for several moments in silence before Reed talked again.

"Quick question. I remember back when we first met—well, met again—right after Paige disappeared. You told me she was supposed to be going on a coffee date with someone. Did she tell you what he looked like?"

Naomi tried to recall what Paige told her about this guy that asked her out for coffee. "Um. I think she said he was a tall guy with short, curly hair." She paused again. "Oh! She focused on his eyes. She said his eyes were dark brown and that they were intense if I remember right."

Reed was silent for a moment before he snatched his phone off of his coffee table. He fiddled around with it before showing her the screen.

"I know it's a broad description, but couldn't that describe him?"

Naomi studied the photo again before she closed her eyes. "I'm such an idiot."

"No, you aren't."

Naomi brushed his comment off and continued. "I just remembered that Paige told me he had a small scar near his left eye." She pointed to the picture. "And there it is. A scar near the left eye." Naomi took a big gulp of her wine, polishing it off.

"We have two faces, but not a name. Let me send these to the chief to see if there's a hit."

"How are you sending these things to him?"

"Top secret and secure line. I think Edmon was a part of the production team for it, but it is not released yet. I'll be right back."

Nor had the news of that been released to its employees, Naomi thought as she watched Reed leave the room. She got up and headed into the kitchen, taking her wineglass with her.

Naomi wiped her face, then poured herself a glass of water. She closed her eyes once more as she tried to shut down all the drama from the case and move it to the back of her mind temporarily. When she did that, she finally realized what she wanted: him.

Reed interrupted Naomi by clearing his throat to get her attention. She smiled at him before brushing one of her curls behind her ear.

"Did you hear anything back from the sweep yet?" She walked back to the living room and folded her feet up underneath her.

"Nope. I'll probably hear something tomorrow, so it would probably be wise for you all to stay at the hotel one more night if possible."

Naomi nodded and pulled her phone out to adjust her stay. She soon realized that when her mom booked the hotel reservation, she set it for two nights anyway. Naomi breathed a sigh of relief and placed her phone and the glass of water on the coffee table. When she sat back, she noticed Reed was staring at her lips before he looked into her eyes.

"You know, Paige was always trying to push me to step outside of my comfort zone. She said we only have one life to live, and we should live it up to the fullest." Naomi turned her body toward Reed. "Maybe it's finally time I took a deep dive into that philosophy." She leaned forward and gently kissed his lips.

"Naomi, what are you doing? I mean, I know what you are doing. And I'm not complaining…" Reed said as he broke the kiss; this was the first time she had seen him flustered.

"I'm doing this," she said as she kissed him again. This

time, Reed had no problem keeping up. The kiss went from soft and gentle to hard and intense. Their hands were all over, and their limbs were tangled. Reed stopped again.

"Are you sure about this? I thought we agreed to explore 'this' once Paige was back home?" Reed asked as he gestured to himself and her.

"I need something to take my mind off of this. I'm tired of being worried. I'm tired of being sad. I'm tired of being angry. I'm tired of feeling like this is all my fault. I want you and a small escape for just a little while. Can you do that for me?" Reed saw the pain in Naomi's eyes and knew he wanted to do whatever he could do to help take the pain away, even if it was temporary. But he still wanted to be cautious.

"I just don't want you to regret this in the morning."

Naomi caressed his biceps with her hand and said, "I promise you I won't." And with that, Reed's lips were on hers. She threw her arms around his neck while her legs ended up around his waist as he carried her into his bedroom. He gently placed her down on his bed and walked over to his nightstand.

"I've been thinking about this moment for a while." Reed found what he was looking for and tossed it on the bed. Naomi looked down and saw it was a condom.

"Well, you don't need to think about 'this' any longer," Naomi said as she repeated the same gesture that Reed made a few moments prior. Reed smirked before he bent down and slowly took off Naomi's boots and tights. He kissed up her legs and took his time making his way his way to her inner thighs.

"Ahem."

"Is everything all right up there?"

"Yes, just wishing you were up here… and moving faster."

"That could be arranged."

And with that, Reed joined Naomi on the bed. He softly caressed her cheek before his lips found hers once more. She got lost in his kiss. She felt his hands everywhere on her breasts, on her thighs, and everywhere in between. But it still didn't feel like enough. When his hands slowed down, Naomi opened her eyes, having just realized that she had closed them.

"What's wrong?" Naomi could see that Reed was frustrated.

"How the hell do you take off this dress?"

Naomi giggled and pointed to a zipper on the side that started a few inches below her armpit. Reed rolled his eyes and unzipped the zipper slowly. The lower the zipper went, the more butterflies flew into Naomi's stomach. She shushed her thoughts and her nerves as she concentrated on what was going on in front of her.

As soon as Reed removed her dress, his eyes drank in all of her body. His eyes swept over her purple lace bra and panties. "You are…stunning." The warmth that she felt from his words was indescribable as her cheeks warmed. His mouth laser-focused on the column of her neck before he worked his way down to her breasts. He gently massaged her breasts while her bra was still on. He pulled down one of her bra cups and took one of her nipples into his mouth. She couldn't control her body's movements, and while the sensation felt good, she wanted more. She sat up, took her bra off, and flung it behind her.

"Sorry you were taking too long." Reed gave her another

smirk before he grabbed her breasts once again, but this time teased her nipples. He put her other nipple in his mouth, and her head fell back. She leaned into the way Reed was touching her, into the way he was making her feel.

Reed kissed down her body and made his way to her stomach. The next thing Naomi felt was her panties slipping slowly down her legs, while Reed continued to kiss all over her stomach. She briefly looked down at him and noticed that he still had all of his clothes on.

"You are way too overdressed." Naomi ran a hand through his hair just before she sat up. Reed stood up and took a small step back. He pulled off his white T-shirt, but before he could undo his jeans, her hands were working fast to unbuckle his belt. Once she undid his belt, she quickly unbuttoned and unzipped his jeans. Soon the only thing standing between them was his boxer briefs.

Naomi took her time admiring his body before her gaze met Reed's, and something happened that she couldn't explain. She could see his strength and his vulnerability in his eyes, and it made her both excited and frightened. He broke eye contact with her as he leaned back down to kiss her on the lips. This kiss was different. It was needy and completely took her breath away.

"Reed…please." Naomi didn't know how he had done it, but next thing Naomi knew, Reed had maneuvered them, and he was waiting at her entrance, condom on. She looked up into his eyes and slightly nodded.

The two stared into each other's eyes as he entered her in one slow swoop. Naomi didn't realize she was holding her breath until she let it out in a big huff.

Reed looked down and froze. "Are you okay?"

"What? I'm fine! Please keep going." She panted as she tried to catch her breath and moved her hair, so she was more comfortable. Reed started moving again. He quickly found a rhythm that made both of them happy. All they heard was their moans as his hands grabbed her waist tighter.

Her hands moved from her sides up to his shoulders as she gripped them to regain some semblance of control. But there was no control to be found as they both worked to bring themselves to euphoria.

Reed started moving even faster and gently pinched her nipple. She matched each of his movements and could feel her pleasure building. He stroked into her a few more times, leading to the release that she had been seeking. His release followed, and all he could do was lie on her with his head on her shoulder. He flipped them over, so she ended up on top of him, and she could hear nothing but his heart pounding out of control. He brought his head up and gave her forehead a quick kiss as he tried to catch his breath.

"Damn. That was something else." Reed grabbed the blanket at the foot of his bed and placed it over him and Naomi.

Naomi chuckled. "And I don't even know how to describe what that was. Wow." She could barely get the words out since she too was trying to catch her breath. Reed gently played with some of her curls mindlessly.

"Are you okay?" Reed asked after Naomi had said nothing for a while.

"Oh yeah. I'm fine. Great, even." She hadn't realized that she had been short with him until he stopped playing with her curls.

"You don't regret any of this?" He sounded unsure, and that made Naomi pause.

"Nope. I enjoyed every second of that, thank you. It was amazing, and being perfectly honest, I can't wait to do it again. After a little recovery time," she said with a laugh. She traced imaginary circles on Reed's chest. Naomi thought about how nice it felt to be in his arms and how she might want to feel this regularly.

She knew their relationship, whatever it was, had just dramatically changed, and she wasn't sure if it was for the better. Naomi stopped drawing circles on Reed's chest and lay with her back directly on the bed, next to him.

"We forgot about dinner."

Reed laughed. "Yeah we did. I probably have something in the k—"

"I should probably go."

Reed looked over at her. "Why? It's late now, and you would go back to a hotel room alone. You can stay here."

Naomi knew he was telling the truth, but she also didn't know how she felt staying over at his home. "True, but I don't have any clothes to change into nor any of the things that I usually use for my nightly routine."

Reed rolled over to his side and wrapped his arm around her waist. "Can you miss your routine for one night? I really was hoping you would stay."

Naomi thought about it for a few more moments before typing out a quick message to her mother to let her know where she was. "Okay, I'll stay as long as you promise to have an Americano served to me in bed in the morning."

Reed looked over at her and stated, "That can be arranged," as he leaned down and kissed her again.

* * *

Naomi woke up again with a start. Her heart was slamming into her chest, and she was sure she was sweating. Naomi tried to figure out where she was since she could tell she was not in her bed. Her brain connected the dots as she felt a heavy arm around her waist. Naomi felt around the bed, and her hands landed on a hard chest.

"Reed?" Naomi asked, but she didn't get an answer. All she heard was heavy breathing coming from the man behind her. After Naomi realized she was in Reed's bed, she relaxed as her breathing turned back to normal. Reed had not woken up during her episode, and for that, she was grateful. She tried to go back to sleep, but after a few minutes, she gave up.

Naomi slowly moved Reed's arm and rose from the bed. She felt around for something to throw on her naked body, and she found the shirt that Reed had on yesterday. With that, she walked into the kitchen to see if she could find something to eat.

Making herself at home, Naomi found a mug and Reed's coffee machine and made herself a cup of coffee. It had not been served to her in bed, but this would do. She checked the time on his microwave and saw that it was 7:00 a.m. She walked through his home toward his balcony and watched as the sun rose over the Capitol. She then strolled back to his couch, set her mug down on the coffee table, and grabbed her bag. She took out her laptop and checked her email accounts but saw nothing pressing. She then thought about Paige's disappearance.

"There has to be something I'm missing," she mumbled while she looked at the last email PAN sent her. Nothing new stood out to her, so she placed her laptop down as she tried to go over all the evidence they had collected in her head. A few moments later, she sat up swiftly.

"How the hell did I miss this?" she questioned herself as she ran toward Reed's bedroom to wake him up.

CHAPTER 17

*N*aomi jogged into Reed's bedroom and had to do everything in her power to stop herself from jumping on the bed. She slowly crawled up the bed and was thankful that he had readjusted himself so that he was lying flat on his back. She smiled as she lay down beside him and gave him a quick kiss on the cheek. He didn't stir. Naomi tried again, and he still didn't move.

"Reed?" She tapped him on the shoulder. Reed swung his hand around and tapped his lips. Naomi gave him a sweet kiss on his lips, and as she leaned back, Reed opened his eyes and gave her a huge smile.

"Are you ready for round four?" Reed's smirk and words made her chuckle and quiver.

"No, I need you to wake up so we can go look at a couple of things concerning Paige."

Reed stretched his limbs and leaned over to his nightstand to grab something. When he placed a pair of glasses on his face, she grinned at him.

"I like these. When did you take your contacts out last night?"

"Sometime in between our second and third sessions. You had fallen asleep, so I figured it was all right to turn into a pumpkin."

Naomi gently punched him in the shoulder and said coyly, "I think you should wear them more often." She got up out of bed and gestured toward the doorway. "I want to talk to you about something." Reed followed her into his office.

"Can you pull up that screenshot that shows the plane ticket that Paige showed the camera?"

Reed nodded as he tried to find the screenshot she wanted. As she waited, she wandered over to his evidence board and looked at it more closely.

"What are you looking at?"

"Nothing, it's just weird looking at the evidence laid out like this." She quickly spun around and ended up knocking a couple of papers off of Reed's desk. She bent down to pick them up, and the paper on top was the guy who walked into the lobby of her apartment a couple of days ago.

"How did you get this photo? Why didn't you tell me?"

Reed glanced at the photo she was holding before looking back at his computer.

"The security company at your apartment provided the information directly to Chief Hughes, who then gave it to me. Between me trying to make sure I did the sweep of your apartment by the book and submitting it quickly, it must have slipped my mind. I apologize. Here is the screenshot."

Naomi nodded as she placed the papers back on his desk. She quickly analyzed the image before saying, "We need to talk to Senator Graham again."

"Why is that?"

"I'm pretty sure that ticket stub is hers."

Naomi pulled up the senator's official social media accounts and showed them to Reed. Low and behold, on October 17, she created posts that alluded to her being in NYC, and then on October 19, her posts showed she was back in DC.

The senator offered to talk to them that afternoon, and while they waited, Naomi caught up with Jada, who rescheduled dinner with that group for tonight. She mentioned that she wanted to get drinks with Naomi before dinner, for which she was grateful. She hadn't had an opportunity to catch up with her mother one-on-one yet, and she knew it would help her immensely.

Naomi and Reed called the senator that afternoon and cut to the chase. Naomi thought that she would have been nervous about talking to the senator after their last encounter, but she wasn't.

Naomi placed a hand on Reed's before saying, "Senator Graham, it's great talking to you again. We don't want to keep you as we know you are very busy, but we just had a couple of questions for you."

"Fire away. As I said before, I want to help in any way I can."

"Thanks. Were you in New York City in mid-October?"

"Let me check quickly." Senator Graham was silent for a few moments. Naomi's heart was in her throat as she waited for the senator to respond. "Yes, I was in New York for a fundraiser and came back on October 18. Why?"

Naomi squeezed Reed's hand before responding, "I think your ticket stub was used in a video involved in Paige's disappearance. We could only make out the last few letters of the first and last name. The first name ends with a *Y-N*, and the last name ends with *A-M*."

The senator gasped. "What? I shouldn't have had a ticket stub at all. I use my phone as my ticket when I travel. I'll need to check with my staff, and I'll get back to you. Did you have any other questions for me?"

"At the event, we met you at a few days ago, who was the person that was there representing PAN, LLC?"

"PAN, LLC? Ah, I believe his name is Jett, but I'm blanking on his last name. The company is apparently a secret investor in the technology and cybersecurity industries."

Reed shook his head quickly as if he snapped out of a trance. He shared a look with Naomi before speaking up. "Senator, if you don't mind, would you be able to send us any information you have on them?"

There was a brief pause before Senator Graham responded. "I can send you as much public information as I can, but anything more than that I can't."

"That's fine. Thank you for your help."

"Goodbye."

"Well, now we have the name of a potential suspect, which is more than what we had about twenty minutes ago. I need to head back to my hotel room and throw on some new clothes to meet with my mom." Naomi had already showered with Reed and put on the clothes she had on the previous day. She packed all of her things up in record time, and Reed walked her to the door.

"I'm going to work on a few things back here, but I'm hopeful that I'll get some information about the sweep and a few other things today. I'll stop by the hotel this evening, okay?"

She nodded and stood on her toes to kiss him.

"I'll see you later."

And with that, Naomi headed back to the hotel.

* * *

After a fresh change of clothes, Naomi arrived at the hotel bar, which she noticed was relatively empty. She chose a seat at the bar, and the bartender gave her a computerized menu. Naomi ordered a glass of soda and pulled out her phone. Her soda appeared immediately, and she sipped on it as she browsed the web, waiting for her mother to come downstairs.

"HEY, SWEETHEART," said Jada as she sat down next to her daughter at the bar. Naomi leaned over to hug her mom, and Jada settled in her seat. Naomi handed her mother the computerized menu, and she ordered a glass of wine.

"Hi, Mom. What's going on?"

Jada took a sip of her wine and dabbed her mouth with a napkin before replying. "So, you know that Reed has a pretty good relationship with the MPD? He and Diane talked and decided that it would be a good idea to start a tip line. There would be a reward for information on Paige's kidnapping. That way, we are getting Paige's name and picture out there yet aren't directly working with the police. It also might force Senator Butler's team to respond to Paige's disappearance publicly, therefore shining even more light on it."

"This is a great idea. I wonder if it will also help push the police to act. Did you contact Senator Butler's office?"

"Yes, actually. Diane called them yesterday before we officially launched this endeavor because we didn't want to catch them off guard. They are planning on releasing a statement about Paige's disappearance at any minute now."

Naomi cleared her throat. "That sounds perfect. Thank you."

"How are you doing?"

"What do you mean, how am I doing?"

"In terms of your anxiety. I know your anxiousness was rising due to your job and trying to get that promotion, but I can only imagine how it is right now with all of this going on."

"I'm doing pretty well right now but had a pretty bad anxiety attack a few days ago. I talked to Dr. Evans, and that helped quite a bit. And finding out new information that might assist Paige has also been helping." Naomi filled in her mother on the latest news she found out about Paige's disappearance.

"Did you hear anything else from Reed about the sweep of your apartment? Aren't you happy I called him?"

"Nope, nothing yet. He's hoping to hear something today." Naomi paused before she responded, "Yes, he's been super helpful throughout this whole ordeal."

Jada nodded and took another sip of her wine. "So, is there anything going on between you two?"

Naomi choked on her soda. She recovered without spitting any of her drink out. Thankfully.

"To be honest, I'm not sure. We haven't put a label on it like said we are dating or anything, but I do think Reed likes me. I'm not trying to think about it much. Mostly due to Paige's disappearance."

Jada nodded but stayed silent.

"It's also feeding into my anxiety," said Naomi. She paused again before continuing her train of thought. "Would I love to date someone like him? Yes, well, based on what I know about him, I would definitely consider a second date. But there is also a lot I don't know about him, but I am very intrigued if that makes sense."

"It does. And I think Reed likes you too."

"Yes, he has mentioned wanting to date after we get Paige back, and she gets settled again."

Jada smiled and continued sipping her wine. She checked her phone and a frown appeared on her face.

"Sweetie, Logan just sent me a message and I need to head up to my room briefly before dinner. I'll be back down in a minute, okay?"

Naomi nodded and said goodbye to her mom.

She pulled out her phone again and checked her messages. Seeing nothing from Reed or anyone else, she decided to check her personal and work emails. She felt someone approach her from her left but didn't look up from her phone. She heard the person who was seated next to her clear their throat but didn't pay it much mind. The person cleared their throat again, and she looked up. The man sitting next to her was the same man from Senator Graham's party.

"Excuse me? Who are you?" Naomi whispered, trying not to cause too big of a scene.

"I'm just a man who would like to buy you a drink." He turned toward the bartender and said, "She'd like another of whatever she is having." She tried to keep her breathing leveled, although she felt her heart racing.

The mysterious man smiled briefly at Naomi, making her feel uncomfortable. Since she already had her phone out and a message to Reed up, she was able to turn on the record function so that she'd hopefully be able to capture the interaction. She was also thankful that he had not realized that she was drinking a nonalcoholic beverage.

"So, then you wouldn't mind if I asked you a few questions?"

"Be my guest. Whether or not I answer the questions is up for debate, Naomi."

"Is your name Jett?"

"Yes. Didn't Senator Evelyn Graham already confirm that for you?"

"Wait. First, I catch you staring at me at an event, then you approach me in a bar, and now you know my name. Are you intentionally trying to be a creep? And where's Paige?"

"You find it creepy, but all I am trying to show you is that I find you particularly interesting," Jett said coyly. "Who is Paige?"

Naomi grew even more wary of Jett. She knew that he knew more than he was letting on about Paige. She tried to catch the attention of the bartender with her eyes. Naomi finally was able to make eye contact with her, and just as the bartender was walking over, Jett stood up from his barstool and handed Naomi a large tan-colored envelope.

"It was great to meet you in person, Naomi, finally. I'm sure we'll be seeing each other again really soon." The bartender was almost in front of Naomi before Jett got up and walked away.

"Sir, you didn't sign your electronic receipt!" the bartender exclaimed as she put the device down on the bar.

"Oh, he had to leave quickly and asked me to sign the check for him." The bartender handed the receipt over and walked away to continue tending to other customers. Naomi opened the receipt and saw that the name under the line for the signature was J. Was.

Naomi closed the receipt without signing it. She walked into the lobby to wait for her parents and Diane and decided to call Reed while she waited. She first sent the audio from the encounter with Jett and then waited a few seconds before dialing Reed on her phone.

"Hello," answered Reed.

"Hi." Naomi's heart rate slowed down at the sound of his voice.

"Are you okay?"

"Sort of, can you listen to the audio I just sent you and then call me back?"

"Sure," said Reed, "I'll do it right now, and I'll call you back."

"Thanks," said Naomi as she hung up. She paced a couple of times around the lobby and then sat down in one of the chairs across from the front desk. While she was getting comfortable in her seat, Reed called her back.

"You have got to be kidding me, he found you? How? We took special precautions when selecting this hotel, and he just waltzed past security. I need you to stay with your parents as much as possible until I get there, okay? I know you can take care of yourself, but this guy has me worried. We can chat more when I get there."

Naomi nodded, even though Reed could not see her. "Yeah, I'll stay with my parents and Diane until you get here. He also handed me an envelope. Hold on a second." Naomi opened the envelope and looked inside.

"There is a piece of paper inside of it that says, 'Open your eyes.' What the hell is that supposed to mean?"

"I don't know."

"I'll talk it over with my parents and Diane at dinner. Speaking of that, here they are now," said Naomi as Jada, Logan, and Diane exited a nearby elevator.

"Perfect, I'll see you soon."

"Great. See you soon."

Naomi walked over to her parents and painted a fake smile on her face.

"So, who's ready for dinner?"

CHAPTER 18

*D*inner was uneventful, besides discussing the envelope Naomi received, as well as relating what happened between her and Jett, and she couldn't have been more grateful for the support. Her parents and Diane were rightfully concerned, and Naomi felt safer being around other people, so she hung out with them until Reed sent her a message to let her know he was at the hotel and would be in the lobby shortly. About fifteen minutes later, Reed met Naomi in the hotel's lobby. She took him up to her room, and once the door closed, he gently grabbed her arm and turned her around. He opened his arms to hug her, and she stepped into them without a second thought. They stood like that for at least a minute, neither one of them wanting to break the connection.

"Are you okay?" Reed asked a few seconds later after he pulled back to get a better look at Naomi.

"Yes. Still a little shaken up, but I'm okay."

"You know that I'm here for you, right?" Reed slowly rubbed Naomi's arms as he tried to soothe her.

Naomi nodded and then paused before continuing. "I'm freaked out, to be honest. I'm stressed, and I'm not sure what else we should do," said Naomi as she gently pulled her arms from Reed's grip and paced. "Like I can't do that database project that they want me to do because I could end up in jail. Heck, I would probably get thrown under the jail."

Reed nodded his head as he watched Naomi pace.

"But I can't think of any other way." Naomi began another lap around the room. Again, Reed grabbed her arm gently and stopped her midstep.

"I was so worried about you after you sent me that audio from your meeting with Jett," Reed said.

"You were?" she asked as she looked Reed in the eyes.

"Very much so. I knew you were in a public place, and chances were that nothing would happen, but still, not being able to be there to at least try to help you was rough. It made me feel like things were out of my control, and it was…scary. I'm glad you're okay." Reed hugged Naomi again and whispered sweet nothings softly in her ear.

Naomi looked Reed in his eyes, and she saw the vulnerability that had been in his eyes last night. This vulnerability was one of the few times that Reed had gotten personal and let Naomi in on what he was feeling. Naomi warmed to the idea that Reed wanted to do his best to help keep her safe.

Reed gently cupped her face with both hands and leaned in for a kiss. There was nothing gentle about this kiss. Naomi's arms were around Reed's neck as she tried to get as close to him as possible. Reed's hands traveled south from her face down her neck, and before Naomi realized, they were cupping her breasts.

"If you want to stop, say it." Reed briefly broke the kiss

and before he began kissing her neck. His hands traveled down to her legs and picked her up so that her legs could wrap around his waist. He turned her around and held her up against the hotel room door.

Reed's hands gravitated to Naomi's shirt. His hands drifted underneath the hem of her shirt as he went back to kissing her lips.

"You are so damn beautiful," Reed said as his hands moved toward her breasts again. Just as he was about to raise her shirt, Naomi's phone pinged.

"Are you kidding me?" Reed gently lowered Naomi down until she could balance her weight and helped her fix her clothes. As she continued to fix her clothes and hair, Reed readjusted his shirt and pants.

"Talk about bad timing," Naomi said before she walked over to read the message on her phone.

Mom: *We received similar envelopes under the doors of our hotel rooms. We will be over soon.*

"It looks like Diane, and my mom also received large tan envelopes too. She, Logan, and Diane are headed over here in a few minutes."

"Well, while we wait for them, why don't you open the envelope that Jett gave you?"

"That's a good idea. I put it over here." She went to the dining room table and sat down. Naomi took the envelope and played with it briefly. Although she knew what was inside, it still made her nervous.

A few minutes later, Naomi heard a knock on her hotel room door. She checked herself one more time to make sure she didn't look like she'd had the hell kissed out of her before opening the door. As expected, her parents and Diane were on the other side.

"Oh great, Reed, you're already here. What did you find out?" Jada asked as she entered the hotel room.

"What do you mean, 'what did he find out?' I thought you came over here to talk about the envelopes you and Diane received? I received one too. We should probably figure out what's in these first," Naomi said as she gestured to the envelopes in Jada's and Diane's hands. Both women placed the envelopes down on the dining room table as everyone else gathered around.

Naomi watched as Diane grabbed her envelope and opened it. Inside, the group found a code and a link to a website. Naomi dashed over to her laptop and did a brief virus scan on the link and found that it belonged to a photo-sharing website and had no known viruses. She swiftly typed in the link, followed by the code. As Naomi was doing this, Reed walked over and stood behind her, looking over her shoulder. When the webpage loaded, she gasped as her blood ran cold. Inside there were photos of Paige and Naomi doing their daily/weekly routines, going for a jog, grocery shopping, to the movies, and more. Some photos featured them individually and together.

"Holy crap, whoever took these photos must have been following us for a long time. I remember when most of these pictures got taken. It definitely had to be over the last several weeks."

Reed said nothing as he analyzed the photos. Naomi wasn't sure if he had heard her. "Reed? Is everything okay? What's wrong?"

Naomi stared straight at Reed but he wouldn't meet her

eyes. A feeling of uneasiness set in her mind as she tried to shake the feeling that something was about to go wrong. Very wrong.

"So, what else did you need to tell us?" Naomi grasped her mother's hand as she prepared for the worst.

"You know how we thought Paige's disappearance was directly related to you? We assumed that it was, but there is no doubt in my mind that it is."

Naomi didn't move a muscle but knew that Reed could read her emotions in her eyes. She went from feeling uncertain to being angry, to being disappointed.

"What do you mean? I thought we thought it was a combination of my skills and her job in Congress. What's going on?"

"Do you know a Morris Washington?" Those words sucked the air out of the room.

Naomi didn't reply immediately. She took a deep breath and said. "He's my...he's my biological father. Did he kidnap Paige?"

"Well...I'm not sure. I know he was the man at your and Paige's apartment the other day."

"How do you know that?"

"I showed a photo of him to Ann at the front desk. She recognized him immediately and pulled the screenshot she had of him from the security footage. Perfect match."

Naomi couldn't think straight. The hatred she had for this man had been dormant for years but was now rising back to the surface. She had not seen her father in years. He had given up his parental rights years ago, and that was the last she thought she'd see or hear of him, even though Logan thought he might one day make an appearance.

"He also fits the very broad description that we got from Isabelle at the internet cafe."

She nodded and added, "The last time I saw him, he left and never came back. He abandoned us a long time ago, and I was hoping he'd stay gone."

Naomi stepped back from her mother before asking, "Mom when was the last time you heard from or saw Morris?"

Jada sucked in a deep breath before replying, "Sweetheart, it's been quite a while. Years." Jada wrapped her arms around herself and rubbed her hands up and down her arms for comfort. Logan looked at Jada, laid his arm on her shoulders, and brought her into his chest for a one-armed hug. "What made you think it was him?"

"Because I saw him outside of Naomi and Paige's apartment the night before Paige got kidnapped."

Jada looked at Reed in disbelief and exclaimed, "You saw him?"

Naomi did a double-take. She looked at Reed and then back at her mother and then back at Reed. "What do you mean you saw him?"

Reed didn't say a word while he rubbed his neck with his hand.

Jada's eyes widened as she pieced together what happened. "Naomi, I thought I told you in one of my messages on the ship. I hired Reed to track down your father and to watch you to keep you safe."

CHAPTER 19

*N*aomi's heart was racing at a million miles an hour. She closed her eyes and rubbed her temples. "When did you hire Reed to do all of this?" she asked. The side-eye that she sent Reed could melt ice.

"A few weeks ago. I should have told you sooner, but I knew you would freak out. And I couldn't exactly tell you why I was having someone keep tabs on you. A friend told me Morris might be looking for you. Your biological father is a very dangerous man and I was trying to keep you as removed from this as possible to protect you."

"Were you in on this?" Naomi asked. Her eyes darted over to Logan. He nodded his head.

Naomi shook her head in disgust and glared at both Jada and Reed. "What makes him so dangerous? And try not to leave out any details."

"Morris always had an interest in technology and computers. That is what he was into when we met, and everything was great. He had a lot of stress from his job because of the amount of pressure he was under while working at one of the biggest tech companies in the world. One day his boss approached him about a project that needed to happen under the table, and everything snowballed out of control from there. He turned into a different person. He would stay out to all hours of the night, and when he was home, he would talk to people all of the time but was very secretive about it. You could imagine how I felt about this behavior, especially with a toddler in the house I had to protect."

Jada shuddered because a memory resurrected itself in her mind. "He fell in with the wrong people. I was worried at first but got even more concerned when some of his late-night conversations turned into talks of cybersecurity. I could only hear bits and pieces, but it was enough for me to make plans to leave. His name popped up again recently at an event I was at, and I was concerned since you now worked for one of the biggest cybersecurity companies in the world. I asked Reed to tail you and dig up as much information as he could about Morris. Including if he could figure out where he was."

Even with Jada's explanation, Naomi could feel her anger increasing. She understood her mother's reasoning, but that didn't change the fact that she was an adult and could handle her own affairs. Reed had known that Naomi had no idea that her mother initially hired him to trail her, and he said nothing, even with how much closer they seemed to get over the last few days. She knew she should try to keep her emotions in check, but frankly, she didn't want to. All she could see was red.

"I assume the envelopes we received under our doors are a match to the envelope that was handed to you by Jett at the bar." Jada placed her envelope down on the table.

"Do you mind if I open this?" Naomi pointed toward the

envelope, and Jada nodded. Naomi ripped open the flap and pulled out the contents. They were photos that showcased how Reed had also been watching her from different locations. One photo stood out to Naomi. Naomi was at a coffee shop, having a meeting with a coworker. She could see Reed in the photo, sitting directly behind her. Although she believed her mother when she told her about hiring Reed, seeing evidence of it was jarring. She couldn't remember seeing Reed that day, but he had been there.

Naomi turned to Reed while trying to control her emotions. "Were you tailing me outside of Edmon when I went to get lunch the other day with June? I mentioned that I had a feeling someone was watching me, and you kind of waved me off."

Reed didn't hesitate when he said, "That was me."

"So, you let me believe I wasn't getting stalked when you were stalking me? And Morris was too? And was the meeting at the bar a coincidence? Or did you plan that too?"

"I planned it."

Naomi's lip trembled. She tried to do everything to stop the tears that were threatening to shed. "When we were at the bar, and I told you about how I felt like I was missing the connection. Did you know then it was my biological father?"

Reed paused for a moment and closed his eyes before replying, "I had a suspicion but wasn't one hundred percent certain."

Naomi's heart broke with every answer he gave. She clenched and unclenched her hands as she felt the tension forming in her shoulders. She hoped the stomach pains that had just started were not a sign that an anxiety attack was on the horizon. "I am such an idiot. I thought it was weird that you knew so much about me but didn't second guess it more even though I was suspicious. Such an idiot."

"I'm so sorry. If you—"

"Please. Don't. I hate to be rude, but would all of you mind leaving my room? I need some time alone."

There was complete silence as everyone moved toward the door. Reed looked like he wanted to say something more but refrained as he walked toward the threshold.

"What was the good news?"

Reed turned and said, "The sweep found a couple of things in your apartment outside of the tracker on your laptop that are still being analyzed but you can go home tomorrow." And with that, he left.

Jada was the last person out of the room, and she gave Naomi a small hug. "Please know I was only doing this to protect you. And Reed was doing what he was paid to do."

"But you should have told me so I could have tried to protect myself."

"I know, I know. But please know I was only acting out of concern for your safety and trying to do everything I could to protect you." Jada gently hugged her daughter and left the room.

Naomi paced for a while to calm down, but her anger only grew stronger. She knew now that Morris and Jett had Paige, but what was she going to do about it? A strong urge to vomit was rising in her stomach. But she couldn't let her anxiety get the best of her if she could help it. She knew she had to try something else, and after a few moments, she formed a plan.

She called room service and asked for a bottle of Malbec along with a random assortment of snacks and dessert. She turned on a TV show, but it ended up just being background noise since she was deep in her thoughts. Naomi didn't know how much time had passed, but a knock on her door pulled her out of her daydream. She answered the door and grabbed the wine, dessert, and snacks and set them on the table. Naomi then went into the bathroom and started a bath. While the tub was filling up, she grabbed a wineglass in the kitchen. She poured the red Malbec and took it and her phone with her to the bathroom. After seeing several messages from Reed that she ignored, she placed her phone facedown on the counter.

She tied her curls into a ponytail and got ready for her bath. When she first put her foot in the tub, a warm sensation rose up her leg, and she almost instantly felt relaxed. Just sitting in a tub with warm water and nothing else had a calming effect on her. She didn't keep track of how long she was in the tub, but by the time she exited, the water was cool, and her fingertips looked like prunes. She put on a robe and grabbed her glass and her phone, and left the bathroom. When she reached the kitchen, she poured a little more wine into her glass and walked over to the living room. She sat down on the couch and checked her phone and read through the messages that Reed had sent her.

Reed: *Naomi, I am so sorry. I should have told you all of this earlier.*

This thing that's going on between us has nothing to do with Paige's kidnapping.

I know you aren't speaking to me right now, but I just wanted to tell you that.

Please call me whenever you want.

Deciding not to, she set her alarm and walked over to her bed. She grabbed her bag and pulled out her moisturizer, PJs, and headscarf and put them on. She placed her phone on her bedside table and got into bed. Naomi fell asleep without incident.

* * *

AFTER NAOMI WOKE UP, she received a message from Jada asking if she could meet her at Naomi's room. Although Naomi was still hurting from the night before, she agreed and pulled herself together with several minutes to spare. She heard a knock on the hotel room door, and Jada was on the other side.

"Hi, Mom."

"Hi, sweetheart. Did you sleep well?"

Naomi shrugged her shoulders. The two sat down at the dining room table in silence as they both tried to decide what they wanted to say to each other.

"Naomi, I am so sorry about how things unfolded yesterday. You should have been brought into the loop much sooner than you were. You're a grown woman, and doing things without your consent was terrible. I apologize," Jada whispered.

"I accept your apology. I know you weren't trying to be malicious, and I trust your judgment. I deserve to know what is going on, especially when a situation will affect me," said Naomi with a firm tone.

"I agree. It was silly to try to hide it from you. Let me start by telling you everything that happened over the last few weeks." She took a deep breath. "As you know, Morris is…an interesting man. I heard through the grapevine that he was talking to people about how his daughter is one of the youngest women in her field to move quickly up the ranks of Edmon. I knew then he would probably seek you out, and I panicked. I didn't think he would try to hurt you, but I figured he'd do something. I paid Reed to track you and him. I didn't want him to tell me your every move, but I wanted him to tell me if Morris tried to initiate contact. We didn't expect Paige to get kidnapped."

Naomi nodded her head as she digested the information. "Did you tell Reed not to tell me anything related to you hiring him to track me?"

"No, in fact, I told him it might not hurt to tell you since you all were spending so much time together. I thought he might have, and that's also why I mentioned it in a message that apparently never sent."

They sat quietly for a minute before Naomi asked a question.

"I am very proud of what I have done at Edmon. But why would Morris want to contact me now, let alone go out of his way to the kidnap my best friend?"

"If I had to guess, he got caught up in something and needs your help to get out of it. Kidnapping Paige meant he had your full and undivided attention."

Naomi repeated her mother's words in her head. What she said made perfect sense, and it made her briefly shiver to the point where Jada put her hand on her daughter's knee, concern in her eyes. He had what he wanted. Her full attention.

"When was the last time you heard from him?"

"Probably right after we split. Maybe I heard from Morris a year later? But it hasn't been since Logan came into the picture."

"Can you tell me more about him? And your relationship with him? You've mentioned tidbits about him over the years, but I guess I just...stopped asking."

Jada shifted in her seat. Naomi knew that this was probably making her uncomfortable, but it's about time that this discussion happened.

"As you know, Morris and I met soon after we graduated from college. I went away for college and moved back here because I thought it might be a good place to get into the nonprofit world. He moved here following some friends that had moved here after college. We met one day at a coffee shop and hit it off immediately. There were some red flags that I wish I had paid more attention to when we were dating."

"Like what?"

"He was horrible with money. I ended up taking over budgeting when we got engaged and then married because I didn't want us to end up in a lot of debt. Or so I thought. Little did I know, he was still racking up debt behind my back, and it didn't come out until after we had you and ended up getting separated and then divorced. I wouldn't be surprised if he is currently in trouble with someone and it's about owing money. I should have told you more about this a long time ago, but you seemed so happy and hadn't brought him up in years, so I just kept putting it off or waiting for you to want to know more information."

As her mom was talking about her history with Morris, an idea popped into Naomi's head. "Do you know if he has any living relatives?"

Jada stuttered for a second. Naomi assumed the question caught her off guard. Jada took a moment to gather her thoughts before responding. "His mother used to live in the area, but I haven't seen her since right after I left him. I tried to keep in contact with her for your benefit, but she never returned my last phone call. I'm not sure if she's still alive or if she's still in the area. He didn't have any siblings. His father died several years before we met."

"So, it might be worth looking into...my grandma." Naomi had a hard time saying those words. "She might know where he's staying. What's her name?"

"Irene Washington. She used to live in DC, but as I said, I have no idea if she's still alive or not. She was always so sweet to me, and I regret how things turned out between us. I could've done more to keep the communication alive but didn't," Jada said before going silent.

"I'll let you know if I find out anything about her. Changing the subject, how did you hear that Morris might try to find me?"

"I heard about it at a fundraiser we put together a few months ago from one of my friends who works in the technology sphere and knew about my relationship with Morris because we have known each other for thirty-plus years. I put two and two together based on what she said, and I trusted her judgment. That's when I contacted Reed."

"What made you contact Reed?"

Jada paused again. "Well...Reed and I crossed paths previously."

Naomi raised an eyebrow. "What do you mean crossed paths previously? How? Where?"

"Well, Reed is a big donor to Hazel's Temple."

"By big you mean... 'big'?" Naomi chewed on her lip. "Does Reed donate regularly, or was this a one-time donation?"

Jada confirmed her thoughts. "He donates regularly."

Naomi assumed that Reed was well off given his condo location, but if he's making large donations to her mother's foundation, he must be. All she could think about was how much she didn't know about him, even though they had spent a lot of time together over the last few days.

"I will still have to work with him to find Paige. It's just a little awkward now. I need to keep in mind that the most important thing is finding Paige."

"True. And if you want to forgive Reed and try to pursue something with him afterward, that's your prerogative," said Jada.

"Who said anything about pursuing anything with Reed?"

Jada shrugged her shoulders and smiled at Naomi. "Are you forgetting that I am your mother, and how well I know you? Your eyes are giving you away."

Naomi rolled said eyes before she asked, "How's the tip line going?"

"Good. The tip line is up and running, and Diane has had interviews with reporters about it. We expect to see some tips soon, and maybe some of them will be helpful. Did I send you Senator Butler's statement? Diane's going to the press pushed them to say something to the public."

Naomi shook her head no, and Jada pulled out her phone, and after a few seconds, Naomi's phone buzzed. "I just forwarded it to you. It is good, and I think it puts more pressure on the police."

"Have they mentioned anything about trying to track Paige down?"

Jada shook her head. "Reed told me this morning that there has been more chatter about what the police can do, but they still have their hands tied because of that video of Paige that was sent directly to them." Naomi closed her eyes at the mention of Reed's name. She knew she had every right to feel hurt, but she was trying to channel those feelings to go full throttle into finding Paige. She thanked her lucky stars that her anxiety hadn't been acting too bad recently.

Jada charged the meal to her room, and as they left their table, Jada gently grabbed her daughter's hand.

"I'm sorry for not telling you about Reed."

"It's all right, Mom. I'm not fully past it, but I'll get there."

"And that's all I could ever wish to happen. Please let me know if I can do anything to help. I'll work with Diane on her interviews and coordinating with the tip line how we would get our information. We'll probably head home today. I'll ask Diane if she wants to stay with us or go back to your apartment."

Since Naomi's parents didn't live too far from her, she thought that idea made sense. She nodded and hugged her mother. "I need to pack my things up and check out. I'll talk to you later."

"Sounds good. I love you, sweetheart."

"I love you too, Mom." Naomi and Jada hugged and went their separate ways.

CHAPTER 20

*a*fter Naomi left the hotel, she waited for the car she ordered to take her back to her apartment. Once she settled inside the car, Naomi checked her phone. She let out a sigh of relief when she saw that she had no new messages. She sent a message to her mom to let her know she was on the way home and that she might go for a jog.

Naomi got back to her apartment in record time and placed her bags in her room. The apartment was eerily silent, and she could smell some cleaning solution. She was thankful that she was able to call in someone to clean their apartment on such short notice. She felt weird being there after someone had broken in. Naomi had reached out to the management of her apartment to upgrade the security features of her unit, which included an upgrade for Simon.

Just as she was about to decide what to do with herself, her phone pinged.

"I swear if this is Reed again," she mumbled. She checked the device and found a message from Doug.

"Strange. Doug usually sends messages through our work

chat versus messaging me on my personal line," she mumbled to herself while opening the message.

Doug: *Hi, Naomi. I'm sorry to bug you, but have you heard from June? She didn't come into the office today, and I haven't been able to reach her.*

Naomi reread the message several times because she couldn't believe it. Her first thought was that Morris and Jett might have taken June, but she didn't want to get too carried away with her guesses.

Naomi: *Hey, Doug. I haven't heard from June, but if I do, I'll let you know as soon as possible.*

Naomi knew she had to contact Reed, even though she didn't want to talk to him. Naomi called, and the line rang and rang before it finally went to his voice mail.

"Reed, it's Naomi. We might have an even bigger problem on our hands regarding this case. Please call or message me back as soon as you get this. Thanks."

Naomi hung up and mentally gave herself a pat on the back because of how professional she sounded. She decided that she needed to take her mind off of whatever was going on with Reed and this case. She practiced some self-care and went for a jog. Naomi went through her pre-exercise ritual and was out the door within minutes. As she walked out the front door of her building, she noticed that it was very cloudy. Shrugging it off, Naomi put her headphones in her ears and took off jogging. Instead of running around the National Mall, she changed things up a bit and ran toward the Nationals Park.

She didn't know how long she had gone before she felt the drop of rain on her hand. Mentally cursing at the turn of events, she turned around to begin the run back to her apartment. Within a few minutes, the rain grew from a drizzle to a steady rainfall. Without a second thought, Naomi darted into a coffee shop across the street to wait for the rain to let up. She ordered a cup of coffee since she was there anyway.

Naomi walked over to a table and ordered off the menu monitor. A few seconds later, an Americano popped up from a turnstile on the table. She sat there, watching the rain for a bit and sipping her coffee and enjoyed the calm and tranquility of being by herself in a quiet setting.

A piece of paper was placed in front of Naomi as she went to pull her phone out. It was a photo of her as a little girl. She looked up at the figure before her.

"What in the world? Who are you?" Naomi asked a few seconds later as she turned to look at the person who gave her the photo. The person sat across from her and removed their hood from their head. There she was, staring into eyes that were a mirror of her own.

"Morris?" Naomi asked. "How did you know where I was?" She felt the temperature in the room dropped several degrees while she studied her father.

Before he answered, Morris, took back the photo of Naomi and played with it.

"I followed you," he said nonchalantly. He stopped playing with the photo.

"Lovely. Well, I'm adding you to the list. Where is Paige?"

"You know I can't tell you that. How is our project coming along? You realize the seventy-two hours that I gave you are almost up, right?"

Naomi clasped her hands under the table to control their shaking. She didn't want Morris to notice she was anxious.

"No, I didn't realize." She thought playing dumb might

help her here. "Is there any way I could get more time?" Naomi asked as she thought quickly on her feet. Having more time would mean the group could think of a plan that didn't involve Naomi completing this task.

"You have twenty-four hours." Morris gave her a sinister smile and Naomi gulped. Hard.

"Okay." Naomi hoped her voice was steady enough not to give way that she had done nothing related to the task. "Is she okay? Why are you doing this?"

"There is a lot of money to be made in this arena. And when you have people to pay back, you have got to do what you got to do."

"Who do you have to pay back?"

"That's none of your concern."

Naomi did all she could do not to roll her eyes since she didn't want to piss Morris off.

"Okay. Then why are you here if you won't tell me where Paige is? If you won't release her?"

"I'm here with a warning. Finish the project, and everyone will be happy," Morris chided. He took a deep breath and softly said, "I also wanted to see you in person. People told me you looked like your mom. They were right."

Naomi didn't have a response for that, so she put the focus back on Paige. "How do I know if Paige is okay?"

Morris stood up from his seat and took his phone out. He clicked a couple of buttons and then slid it across the table to Naomi. On the device was a clear image of two people lying on twin air mattresses on the ground. The room was bare for the most part besides a door on the left-hand side of the room.

"Is this video? How do I know when this image was taken?

This video doesn't prove that Paige is all right. And who is that other person?" Naomi asked frantically.

Morris pressed a button on the screen and gestured for Naomi to say something.

"Paige?"

One figure moved as if they had been startled. The figures moved into a sitting position and looked around just as the other person stirred, "Hello?"

"Paige! I am so glad you're okay! I am coming to get you, okay? Just hang on," Naomi said as Morris snatched his phone back and placed it in his pocket. Before Morris could shut off the sound, Naomi heard someone say "June," and her eyes widened.

"Is everything okay over there?"

Both Naomi and Morris turned to the barista at the cash register and Morris said, "Everything is fine. My daughter here got excited over a video I was showing her." Hearing Morris refer to her as his daughter made her want to flip the table. Morris's words brought her out of her thoughts.

"Is that enough proof? Look now, I have to go since I have other business to attend to," Morris said pointedly before leaving the cafe.

It took every ounce of control Naomi had not to go after him and do something irrational that might get Paige, and now June hurt. She took off her hat and angrily adjusted her ponytail before placing the baseball cap back on her head. She took out her phone and sent a message.

Naomi: *Please meet me at my apartment as soon as you can. Super important.*

With that, Naomi put her phone back in her pocket and grabbed her Americano. She looked out the window and noticed the rain had stopped. She checked her surroundings to make sure she was not leaving anything and left the cafe.

She thought about her interaction with her biological father as she rushed back to her place. She waved to the person at the front desk but kept her pace as she walked to the elevators. She reached her front door, opened it with her phone, and stepped inside.

She slowly walked in and took a visual inventory of the apartment. The silence that enveloped the space was something that she used to cherish, but now it seemed to be the enemy. She didn't know if Diane was coming back, but she would love the company. She had never felt more alone than she did right now.

PAIGE THOUGHT the plan to have someone join her in this prison had fallen through. Morris mentioned that this guest was supposed to be coming shortly, but that was a few days ago, so she assumed no one was coming. Paige had fallen into a fitful sleep but suddenly awoke when she heard a bang and then saw a stream of light flow down the stairs. All she could see was that two people were walking down the stairs. Seconds later, light flooded the room.

It took a second for her eyes to adjust to the light before she noticed it was Morris and a young woman. She didn't recognize the woman, but in a sad, twisted way, it relieved her to have some company, although she wished it was under better circumstances.

"Paige, meet your new roommate, June. June, this is Paige," Morris said as he pushed June forward. The rips in her light blue coat and the small cut on her forehead led Paige to believe that she put up a fight. Morris helped her sit down on the floor before leaving both women to their own devices in the basement.

Paige and June sat there in silence for what Paige thought might have been an eternity. Paige broke the silence.

"So, how did you end up down here?"

June didn't answer right away. But when she did, her words took Paige's breath away.

"I'm not sure. But I got kidnapped on the way home from my job at Edmon."

"Edmon? The cybersecurity firm, Edmon?" Paige whispered. She whispered in case anyone was listening or recording their conversation.

"Yes, have you heard of it?" June asked. Paige was happy that June followed her lead and whispered her reply.

"Not only is it one of the biggest cybersecurity firms in the world, but also my work portfolio includes cybersecurity legislation. I work on the Senate side. Also, my best friend and roommate works at Edmon. Do you know Naomi Porter?"

June's eyes widened. "Yes. We are on the same team at work. I'm a project manager."

"This can't be a coincidence. Millions of people work in the cybersecurity field, and they kidnapped both of us? This situation has to be related to cybersecurity...or to Naomi. It could be both."

June wrapped her arms around her body and said, "I don't know. I haven't been at Edmon for long, so I am not sure what they would want from me anyway."

Paige didn't respond right away. She was still trying to

figure out the connection between her and June. And all signs pointed to Naomi.

* * *

REED: *I can be there soon, wrapping something up here at home.*

Naomi reread the message. He sent that message about fifteen minutes ago, so she knew that she had just enough time to talk to Dr. Evans.

"So here goes nothing," Naomi said as she sent Dr. Evans a meeting request that was thirty minutes from now. She grabbed some grapes from the fridge, poured herself a glass of water, and walked into her room. She turned on her computer to prepare for Dr. Evans.

While she waited, she checked her work and personal emails. She saw some emails from work, but there was nothing pressing. She debated telling Doug what she knew about June, but she kept it close to the chest for now. She then received a notification that Dr. Evans was available to chat in twenty minutes. Naomi had a little time to burn and decided to do more research. But this time on Reed Wright.

"Okay. I have just enough time to look Reed up, snack, have this session with Dr. Evans, and be ready for when Reed gets here," Naomi said, laying out a plan to herself.

As Naomi searched, she was both not surprised but still annoyed not to find more information on Reed. She saw that he'd been a police officer with MPD and that he had owned his condo for several years.

Realizing that she had a couple of minutes until she needed to start her session with Dr. Evans, Naomi switched tabs to her health portal and was the first to arrive at the session. Dr. Evans showed up about a minute later.

"Hi, Naomi, how are things going? Is Paige home?" Dr. Evans said. She adjusted her glasses and her computer monitor.

"Things have been...very intense," Naomi said as she launched into an explanation of everything that had occurred since their last session. Dr. Evans did her best not to disturb Naomi as she was telling her story.

"That is a lot of things going on at once. How is your anxiety doing?"

"Besides the minor anxiety attack that I had a couple of days ago, it has remained steady. I can sometimes feel my anxiety levels rising but have done a decent job of controlling it. Which a few years ago, I don't think I'd been able to do. I know that has a lot to do with seeing you."

"No. It has a lot to do with you and how you've changed. I might give you some options or tools to use, but you are the one who is continuing to use them again and again. That is an enormous factor in helping how anxious you are. You have an immense amount of pressure on you, and for you to be doing what you're doing under that pressure is incredible. Have you had to take any more of the medication?"

Naomi shook her head. "Thanks and no. I've had some moments that I could feel my anxiety rising, but I've been able to control it. There is also one other lingering issue I've been dealing with as well. I'm not sure what to do about Reed. I was angry as hell when I first found out I was being kept in the dark about this whole 'keeping tabs on me to protect me' scheme, but now I'm feeling...more hurt than anything."

"Have you told both Reed and your mom about how you

feel? You can use the 'I statements' to help explain your feelings."

"What do you mean by 'I statements'?"

"For example, if you are telling Reed how you felt, you can try telling him by saying, 'I felt betrayed that you didn't make sure I knew you were keeping track of me.' Or with your mom, you can say, 'I felt upset that you didn't come to me first before hiring a private investigator to investigate me.'"

Naomi nodded as she took a moment to digest the information. She continued to talk to Dr. Evans about other steps she could take to manage her anxiety better. They ended their session on a pleasant note hoping they would find Paige safe and sound and that they could have a follow-up session next week unless something else comes up.

She wrapped up the conversation and dashed into the shower. When she finished with her whole routine, she took deep breaths to prepare herself to talk to Reed when he arrived at her apartment mentally. She double-checked her blue jeans, a black T-shirt, gray sneakers, and a black hoodie in the mirror. Then, she tied her curls in a ponytail and figured that this was as good as it would get. Just as she checked her phone to see what time it was, there was a knock on her front door.

CHAPTER 21

𝒩aomi opened her door and saw Reed was on the other side. He dressed in a gray sweatshirt, dark blue jeans, and sneakers. Her mind raced as she took him in. She couldn't deny that he looked good, even though she was still upset at him.

"Did you just shower?" She watched as his eyes studied her.

"Yep, just got out. Had to shower after I ran," Naomi said. Reed never broke the gaze he had trained on her. She thought she noticed a sense of longing in his eyes, but she couldn't allow herself to get distracted right now. She let Reed into her apartment, and he settled in her living room.

"Did you find out anything new?"

"Yes. Happy to share, but I came over here to hear what you had to say."

"Please tell me whatever you know first."

Reed cleared his throat before beginning. "So, I heard more information from MPD about the sweep I did on your apartment. Morris Washington was definitely in your apartment, but we don't know when. Although I didn't find any fingerprints that weren't already accounted for, the sweep picked up a single hair that we connected to him. I suspect that he might have entered your apartment multiple times. There is no way he would have been able to do as thorough of a search as he did while Diane was gone, and that includes the actual breaking in and entering."

"Well, that's scary as fuck," Naomi said. "I wonder how he gained entry? I mean, Paige and I were both working long hours over the past few weeks, so it wouldn't have been hard to miss us, unfortunately. But one reason we liked this apartment outside of location and automation features was that there was always someone at the front door."

"Hmm. My thought was that Morris could have posed as someone that would make it easy to hide in plain sight."

Naomi thought for a moment before responding. "Like a delivery driver?"

Reed nodded. "At least that's what I would guess. I know a lot of companies are using drones and robots to deliver packages, but delivery drivers are still around."

"Well, now that you say that, the only two options I could think of is a delivery driver or a smart home technician, and I am leaning toward the latter. He has a background in technology so it wouldn't be that big of a jump," Naomi said.

"That makes sense. Morris wouldn't have had to act too much because he already had a background in the area and would sound like he knew what he was talking about. We don't have a warrant. I'm not sure if I can convince security to give me that footage, plus it might take a few days to review."

"We only have twenty-four hours. And that is an extension because it was due today."

"Wait. What? How?" Reed took his glass and drank some water.

"Well, today, I saw Morris for the first time in about twenty-five years."

Reed coughed to clear his throat. "Seriously? How?"

"He was following me. Apparently, it's a trend nowadays."

Reed paused for a moment while her words sunk in. "I deserved that."

"Oh, I know," Naomi mumbled. She could feel the tension increasing in her shoulders. "I'm trying to move past this whole thing, but I'm hurt." Naomi saw the road she was about to travel down and stopped herself. Instead, she said, "I understand why you did what you did, so I want to call a truce for Paige and June. I won't make any more snide comments. Let's just focus on getting Paige and June home." She held out her hand for him to shake.

"That sounds good to me," Reed said as he shook her hand. "Wait a minute. Is June missing? She's your coworker, right? You mentioned something about checking in with her about work."

Naomi nodded before telling him about her encounter with Morris earlier that day. "Doug reached out to me about it today while I was out and about. He hasn't mentioned that he thought she was kidnapped nor that she could be with Paige, but I know that's where she is. Morris didn't mention it explicitly during our meeting, so I didn't know until I saw her in the video."

Reed sighed as he ran his hand over the back of his neck. "This is insane."

Naomi agreed and said, "Yeah, I know. I think he's trying

to keep my attention and was pissed that I've been avoiding that last task like the plague. Did you have any more intel?"

"Yes. Police Chief Hughes also ran Morris Washington through MPD's databases personally. And there wasn't much on him."

"What do you mean there wasn't much on him?"

"It was almost like he is a ghost. Not so much as a parking ticket. This guy keeps a low profile. But there was a lot of debt that was suddenly paid off out of nowhere. According to the background check, there is no way he could pull an operation like this off on his own. I mean, it could have been something like an inheritance, but I doubt it. Now do I have evidence to prove this? No, this is just my gut speaking."

"And it hasn't led us wrong yet." Naomi gave Reed a small smile. "We also still have little information on Jett."

"True. I mean, Jett could have just been the messenger? Maybe he was supposed to just hand you the photos and spy on you at the event. Maybe he just found you attractive, but I don't believe that." Reed realized what he just said and turned red. "I meant I don't believe in coincidences. Not that you aren't attractive. You are beautiful. Stunning. I'll shut up now." He shook his head.

Naomi belly laughed. It had been the first time she had genuinely laughed in a while. This situation was maybe the second time that she saw him sweating bullets. And she loved it.

"So, what you are saying is that you find me attractive."

"Very much so," said Reed. His eyes met Naomi's and the first thing Naomi noticed was the sincerity in them. There was something else there too, but she couldn't put her finger on it. "And I also know that I need to clear the air regarding our situation."

Naomi nodded and waited for Reed to continue.

"I didn't want to hurt you, but I see how my actions led to it. I should have immediately told you I was tracking you when I showed up at your door. Jada hired me because she was concerned about your wellbeing after she heard Morris was sniffing around. I also shouldn't have been secretive about hiding major details related to myself, especially after I told you I wanted to get to know you better and possibly date you if you wanted. I promise to be more open, even though it's hard for me. I'll answer any questions you have. I'm so sorry."

Naomi nodded but still was hesitant even though she thought his apology was sincere.

"So, why is it hard for you to be more open with people?"

"Well, I spent a lot of time undercover while working with MPD, so I'm used to playing a role and concealing my identity. I do the same thing when I'm working a case now. My go-to reaction is to protect details about myself. And I know that is something I need to work on."

"My mom mentioned that you're a major donor to Hazel's Temple. Why?"

"Cervical cancer has affected my life, personally. My siblings and I used to spend weeks during the summer with my grandma and my great-aunt. We had a blast and learned so much." Reed smiled at the memory. And just as quickly as the smile appeared, it went away as he continued. "My great-aunt died a few years ago from cervical cancer. My siblings and I received a huge inheritance, among other things. So, I searched long and hard to find a charity that appealed to me related to cervical cancer, and I found out about Hazel's Temple from a coworker on the force. And I've been contributing to Hazel's Temple ever since. And that is also how I met your mom."

"That's amazing. I'm surprised we hadn't run into each other sooner. Is your grandmother still alive?"

"Yep. Alive and kicking. I go to see my grandmother every couple of weeks or so."

"That's so sweet. Is she in the area?"

"Yep. She lives in Northern Virginia now. I love visiting her, and it's helpful that I don't live too far. My parents and siblings try to make it out as often as they can, but they're farther away."

"That makes sense. But it's definitely admirable since many people don't visit elderly family members that often."

"I promised my great-aunt Pam that I would make sure Nana was okay. I mean, she has her own life and friends that keep her busy, but she makes time for me when I come to visit."

"So, she is super social." Naomi took the straw out of her glass before gulping down the rest of her water.

"Her social life is probably that of someone in their early twenties. She goes to bingo nights, does Zumba classes, and she still works part-time. She said she needed to keep busy or else she might drop dead from boredom, so she just keeps going. She can definitely run laps around me and looks fabulous while doing it. She's always gifting me new items of clothing and accessories for Christmas, even though I tell her I don't really need anything. She gave me this watch for my birthday this year." Reed showed her his watch.

"Was that a pun? She sounds like a hoot."

"She is. I think you'd like her."

"I bet I would too."

Naomi grabbed her glass of water and walked to the kitchen to place it in the sink. "I noticed your watch when we first met. She has incredible taste. I know it was an Angie & Pam piece but hadn't seen it before. Then again, I guess I pay little attention to men's fashion anyway."

Reed didn't respond, so Naomi turned around to look at him. He was staring back at her. She smiled at him and asked, "What?"

"My Nana is Angie Watts, and my great aunt's name was Pam Watts. They were the co-owners of Angie & Pam. So, I guess technically she gave me her product," Reed chuckled.

"Excuse me?" Naomi exclaimed. She almost dropped the glass she was holding on the ground. "You're kidding me. Paige is a huge fan. She would...love to know this." Naomi strolled back over to the couch. She stared at her glass for a few moments before looking at Reed and wiping a stray tear from her cheek. "What do we do next?"

"I think we need to kick the hornet's nest, as they used to say. We need to force the captors out of hiding."

"What are we going to do to bring them out of hiding? I don't want to do anything that might lead to pissing them off, and they end up hurting Paige and June. And we only have twenty-four hours to do it in."

"So, this is risky. I'm hoping that doing this with what your parents and Diane are doing might lead to a breakthrough. In fact, why don't you call them and find out what progress they've made on the tip line front?"

Naomi agreed and then grabbed her phone to call Jada. Her call went straight to voice mail, so she sent her a quick message instead. Naomi asked her to call or send her a message back as soon as possible.

Naomi went to her room to check on her computer. She noticed that she had more emails from work, including an email from Doug. Naomi gave Doug a summary of how she was doing and responded to several other emails that were currently sitting in her inbox just as her phone pinged.

Mom: *Hi, sweetheart, Logan, Diane, and I are wrapping up a conversation with the company that has organized the tip line. I will call you back shortly.*

She walked back out into the living room to see what Reed was doing. He was just ending a call before he placed his phone down on the table.

"Did you ever hear anything back from Senator Graham regarding the questions about PAN, LLC?"

Reed shook his head. "I also didn't find much information about PAN, LLC, when I looked, only that it was formed a couple of years ago. I've ordered more information on it, but it will take over twenty-four hours for me to get it. I have an idea, though, that might work with the tip line."

"Well, that won't help us." Naomi stood up and began pacing.

"Is pacing a coping mechanism for you?" Reed asked as he changed the subject. His question didn't stop her.

"I guess. I think better when I pace," said Naomi. "What idea did you have that could work with the tip line?"

"I think we need to do a deep dive into Morris. Based on what your mom said, you don't know much about him from when he abandoned you 'til now. So, I think the key is finding out what he's been doing over the years. My preliminary search didn't turn up much, but maybe someone called into the tip line and provided some helpful information. I'm just hoping it's not a wild goose chase."

Naomi noticed that Reed seemed unsure about this plan, and to her, it was another side of him she was getting to know. In the short time that she knew him, he had always been this confident person who was sure of the moves he should make, and now he wasn't. It made him more human, not that she didn't think he was human before. He put on his best face when they were together, and seeing a little dent in the mask he presented to everyone else made her feel a bit closer to him. He was being vulnerable and was open to sharing it with her.

Naomi felt her anxiousness rising again. She knew how much was riding on this, so she tried to use some of the things that Dr. Evans told her about just a couple of hours before to help, but she knew she was not in the proper mental space to do them effectively. She knew that she had to push her anxiousness aside as much as she could and keep going. Paige and June depended on her, and Naomi knew they were getting close. She could feel it.

"Your plan is risky because who knows what we might find. But it is a risk that we must take to find Paige and June. Let me call my mom again. We really need to find out what tips people called in because time is a-wastin'.'"

Reed nodded.

"Let's do this."

CHAPTER 22

*N*aomi stepped into her room to call her mother in private. Jada's phone went to voice mail again, so Naomi sent another message.

Naomi: *Mom, please, please message or call me back as soon as possible.*

She put her phone down, and it immediately pinged. She picked it back up.

Mom: *Sorry, sweetie. We are working through the tips now.*

Naomi: *We really need to find out what information people called into the tip line. ASAP*

There was a pause long enough that Naomi was not sure if her mother would respond, but another ping answered that question.

Mom: *We've received so many tips and are finishing up working through them now. Hopefully, at least one is helpful.*

Naomi: *Okay. Please let me know when you have an update. I also wanted to let you know that Morris approached me today.*

Jada didn't respond. A few moments later, Naomi felt her

phone buzzing and picked it up. Jada's face appeared on the screen.

"Hey, Mom," Naomi said after she answered the call.

"Hi, honey, I asked Diane to join me while Logan continues talking to the people who helped set up the tip line. You said you saw Morris?"

Naomi took a deep breath before replying. "Yes. Morris is apparently or was watching me too. Anyway, we talked briefly, and he ended up showing me a live video feed of Paige. It turns out that he also kidnapped my coworker June. It appeared they are keeping them in a room with nothing in it, but they both looked fine psychically, at least from what I could see from the five seconds of video feed."

Naomi heard someone on the other end let out a loud gasp, and she assumed it was Diane.

"Naomi, you've got to be kidding me. Now he's involved in the kidnapping of two women? Sorry, continue with your story," Jada said.

"He pushed me to continue with this illegal project they want me to do because apparently, he owes someone or multiple people a lot of money. This information confirms some information that Reed found while researching. Morris had quite a bit of debt that was suddenly paid off out of nowhere and all at once. And Reed doesn't think he did it on his own, and he wasn't sure who paid it off."

Jada spoke once again, "None of the money issues are surprising. I mentioned he started having them before we separated, and that was one reason why he ended up giving up his parental rights. He didn't want me coming after him for child support."

Naomi found that tidbit interesting and told Jada, "When

he approached me in the cafe, he greeted me by showing me a photo of me when I was a little girl. We're also pretty sure he is the one that broke into my apartment."

Jada was silent, so Naomi continued, "There is another issue at hand. I also talked to the jeweler whose business was right next to Paige's yoga studio. While the yoga studio caught Paige leaving the front door and nothing else, the video feed from the jewelry store shows that a man wearing dark-colored clothes approached Paige. They seemed to at least be friendly with one another because she did not freak out at the sight of him. I couldn't get a good look at his face, but part of me wants to know if he was Jett, the guy that came up to me at the bar with the photos yesterday. I'm also wondering if he was also the same guy who asked her out for coffee at her job a few days ago. Which might have been why Paige recognized him."

Naomi took a deep breath before continuing, "I'm not sure who in their group kidnapped June. And who knows who the woman was that was following Reed and me when we were exercising."

"You think this mysterious guy might be involved?" Jada asked.

"Yes. I can't shake that feeling that he is. I find it very peculiar that he popped up seemingly out of nowhere. I also hadn't gotten an opportunity to look into when and where they kidnapped June. I hope to do that once I get off the phone with you. I hope it could lead to some answers regarding both of their disappearances."

"That sounds like a good plan. Let me know what you find out, and we will touch base a little later. But before you go, let me give you an update on the private tip line request. As I mentioned before, we're finally getting to the end of all the responses. At least one person was near Paige's yoga studio and saw her or at least a woman that matched her physical description get into a car with a man, but based on the angle and where they were standing, they could not tell if she got into the car willingly or not. The person said that the car took off in a direction that would have led them to believe that they were headed farther into DC versus headed out to Virginia."

"That is helpful. Too bad this wasn't a joint effort to find out if anyone saw June get kidnapped. I'll check in with Doug to see if he has heard anything before potentially going to June's apartment."

"That sounds like a solid plan. And Naomi?"

"Yes, Mom?"

"I love you."

Naomi gave Jada a soft smile and replied, "I love you too. I'll talk to you soon."

Before leaving her room to talk to Reed, Naomi grabbed her phone and messaged Doug.

Naomi: *Have you heard anything from June?*

She then opened up her laptop and found the Edmon Staff Directory. Since June was on the same team as Naomi, it would not be completely out of the ordinary to look up June's address. Naomi found the address and realized it was a five-minute walk from the Edmon offices.

"That's helpful," she mumbled as she sent the information to her phone then shut down her laptop. She grabbed her phone to see she had a message.

Doug: *Nothing. I'm wondering if I should call the police? I have also left a message on her parents' voice mail but have heard nothing back from them yet.*

Naomi sighed. Not only did this case need to be wrapped up quickly to get Paige and June home, but now it needed to be wrapped up to prevent the police from becoming involved, which could upset Morris, Jett, and whoever else was working with them. But she knew how much of a big deal it was that someone else around Naomi was missing, and that might push the police to act.

"Eh, I'll deal with the cop aspect later. After all, I'm not doing anything illegal. At least not right now," Naomi mumbled to herself.

Naomi: *Okay. I'll let you know if I hear anything.*

Doug: *Thank you.*

Naomi left her room and found Reed writing in his notebook at Naomi's kitchen counter.

"Is everything all right?" Naomi approached Reed at the countertop and placed a hand on his shoulder.

Reed nodded. "Reviewing some notes and writing things down. How did everything go with Jada?"

"It went well. They are finishing reviewing the tips they received, and one person said they saw a woman who fit Paige's description, hopping into a car with what looked to be a guy. The person couldn't tell whether she was forced or went into the car willingly. The same person said they saw the car driving in the direction that would lead them farther into DC versus going in the opposite direction that would lead them to VA."

"So, chances are Paige, and now June are being held somewhere in DC."

"Exactly."

"So, the next thing we should probably do is find out

where June was last and find out her address and where it is in r—"

"I'm already a step ahead of you. I have June's address and where it is in terms of the Edmon offices, and they're both near Metro Center. In fact, she's only a fifteen-minute walk from our office. I say we head over there now and see if we can dig up any more information." Reed and Naomi packed up their things, including Naomi's work computer, and headed to Metro Center.

Naomi and Reed arrived at the Edmon offices in record time. "Do you think it would be helpful to check around June's desk before we do anything else?" Naomi asked as they stood outside the front doors of Edmon.

"That's a good idea, but is it okay for you to go up there even though you technically aren't working?" Reed asked.

"Why not? But in reality, there's only one way to find out. C'mon." Naomi walked through the front doors of Edmon and used her phone to enter the building. Since Reed was not an Edmon employee, he had to go through security checks before being allowed upstairs. And even though he had some access, he could not go into all the rooms on that floor.

As Naomi and Reed got on the elevator and rode up to Naomi's floor, Naomi messaged Doug and told him she was stopping by for a bit. When Naomi arrived in the front, Doug greeted her with a sad smile before walking up to her. She could tell he was concerned.

"Naomi, good to see you," Doug shifted his weight from one foot to the other.

"Likewise. Doug, this is my friend Reed. Reed, this is my boss, Doug." She introduced the men, and they shook hands. "Were you able to get in touch with June's family?"

"Yes, her family should be in town shortly. I'm assuming they have called the police to report her missing, but I'm not sure where things stand there."

Naomi and Reed shared a look but remained silent. "Okay. Well, I need to grab something from my desk before heading out. Let me know if I can help with anything."

Doug gave Naomi a small nod and a smile and walked away. Naomi walked over to her cubicle, attached her computer to the docking station, and turned it on.

"I can access more files from here than I can at home. I can also get to files more easily. I'm hoping there is somewhere on our server that we might keep security footage, and it would be awesome if we could watch it before the police are officially involved." Naomi explained as she started typing away. Reed gave her a little privacy and looked around her cubicle. It was neatly organized, much like her room with a few personal items on her desk, including a few photos.

"You like photos, huh?" Reed asked after a long period of silence.

Naomi glanced at him and said, "Yeah, I guess I do. Especially ones that bring back wonderful memories. Didn't realize it until you pointed it out."

Reed didn't respond, so Naomi continued. "So, I have a random question. Why June?"

"Why kidnap June, you mean?" Reed asked. He leaned on her desk and crossed his feet.

"Yes. June's my coworker, and we have a friendly relationship, but we aren't close friends. So why June? I know it seems like I'm the connection, but you would think there are closer people to me to kidnap than my coworker if you needed to kidnap someone else. I think I'm missing a connection that's probably staring me dead in the face." Naomi took her hands off the keyboard and stretched her limbs. Reed moved behind her and started massaging her neck and shoulders.

"Let me know if you want me to stop," he said and applied more pressure on her shoulders.

"That feels amazing." Naomi let him carry on for a couple of minutes before she patted him on the hand to tell him that was enough. She continued working, and while she did that, Reed sat in an extra chair in the corner of her cubicle and browsed items on his phone.

"There it is!" Naomi whispered before she leaned back in her chair. Reed looked up from his phone and peered over her shoulder.

"I know we were still moving toward storing things in the cloud but was not sure if surveillance video fell under that. And it looks like it did. Let me cue up the video around the time June usually leaves work and let it load. While we wait on that, I'll check June's schedule to see what her day looked like when she disappeared," Naomi said as she opened up her applications to find her group's calendar. Reed went back to looking at his phone.

"Would you look at that." Naomi stared at the calendars on her screen. She turned to Reed and said, "You need to see this." Reed looked up again at the monitor.

"This event on June's calendar states she was supposed to have coffee with someone at 4:00 p.m. yesterday. Around that time was the last anyone had heard from her. Paige also was setting up a coffee date when she disappeared. I know many people drink coffee all over the world and but I think this isn't a coincidence."

Naomi clicked back to the video that would hopefully

show June leaving work. She searched through the stills of the video until she spotted June's blue coat on the video feed. Naomi rewound it one more time to catch the exact moment that June left the building. The video showed June leaving, and just as she was about to be out of the line of sight of the camera, she stopped and looked like she was talking to someone. She smiled at the man as if she recognized him, and he briefly stepped into the frame for Naomi and Reed to examine him.

"I think that's the same guy that approached Paige at her yoga studio. I'm 85 percent sure. Same coat and hat and he appears to be about the same height as the other guy too."

"And his MO is the same both times. I think we've figured out Jett's role in this operation."

"Yeah. Let's head out. One thing is for sure: we don't have to head to June's apartment anymore because she never made it home."

CHAPTER 23

"I want to cook for you sometime if you don't mind."

"I would like that, but I still haven't gotten over the whole you're tracking me thing, you know? And we need to focus on finding Paige and June."

Reed nodded and replied, "No pressure at all. Just stating what I thought. Of course this is after everything is settled and Paige and June are home." Reed paused briefly. She could feel the awkwardness of his statement clouding the room. "I'm fucking this up. On that note, let's find out what the police didn't tell us about Morris Washington."

Naomi chuckled and said a silent thank-you he changed the subject, and she got ready to work. They spent thirty minutes researching everything they could find on Morris. They used the information that Reed found as a starting-off point.

"Naomi, you won't believe this."

Naomi turned to look at Reed, who was staring at something on his computer. She stood up from her makeshift work area and looked over his shoulder.

"I found your grandmother."

Irene Washington, Morris's mother, and Naomi's grandmother lived in Northern Virginia. She was retired but worked part-time at a gym near her home.

"Reed, you mentioned your grandma lives in Northern Virginia. How far away does your nana live from my grandmother?" Saying the last part of the sentence felt strange on her tongue.

Reed looked at the two addresses and said, "I recognize the street name but am not sure exactly where it is. Let me look it up." Reed looked up from his computer after about a minute and said, "They are a ten-minute walk from one another."

"Do you know which gym your grandmother attends? What are the chances that your nana attends the same gym that my grandmother works?"

"Nope, but I would assume that it isn't too far from her house. The chances of that are very high."

"It isn't out of the realm of possibility that our grandmothers know each other," said Naomi, and Reed nodded in agreement.

Naomi grabbed her phone and said, "So it sounds like we need to take a trip to Virginia."

"How are we getting to your nana's house?"

"By car. My car is downstairs in the underground parking garage."

"Oh, I didn't know you owned a car. I just assumed that you took the metro to visit your nana."

"Don't assume," Reed said with a wink. He brought her to the elevator and tapped the button labeled *B*. "I also end up driving to Pittsburgh when I want to visit the rest of my immediate family."

"Do they ever come out to visit you?"

Reed nodded and said, "Not as much as I would like, but I also understand that it is easier for me to get to them than for them to get to me. They visit sometimes, and I try to make it worth their while by taking them to the museums, the monuments, and such. Especially for my nieces and nephew."

Naomi was gathering her things and walking to the front door when Reed stopped her. "Do you mind doing something for me? Could you take a photo with me?"

Naomi raised an eyebrow but didn't say anything, so Reed held her hand and walked her over to his couch, where the two got comfortable for the photo. Reed placed his arm over her shoulders and snapped the selfie with his phone.

They looked down at the photo, and Naomi whispered, "It's perfect."

Reed smiled warmly at her and walked with her to his front door.

The two left the condo and took the elevator down to the garage. When the elevator doors opened, they walked up to a gorgeous black sedan and Reed placed his finger on the passenger-side door. The car door unlocked, and Reed opened the door for Naomi.

"Talk about fancy," mumbled Naomi as she watched the car door close by itself. Reed had already walked over to the driver's side and pressed his finger to the door. All the car doors opened, and the car turned on. The navigation system greeted Reed as soon as they sat down on the comfortable leather seats. The car immediately started blowing warm air inside, much to Naomi's delight.

"The car's temperature depends on your temperature. It can take your body temperature when you sit down. If your temperature is higher than mine, your side of the ventilation system will blow cooler air. Oh, and if you want a massage, just click those buttons over there. The seat will start giving you a massage similar to the shiatsu technique."

"Oh, now you are just showing off."

"This is definitely my pride and joy at the moment, and it gets me from point A to B easily. Would you like a bottle of water? There are some in the little fridge in the back." They both buckled their seat belts.

Naomi turned in her seat and spotted the small fridge. "I'd love to have one. Would you like one too?" Reed nodded as he backed out of his parking space. Naomi grabbed two bottles and put them in the cup holders in the front seat.

Reed and Naomi rode in silence for a bit until they hit I-395. It was bumper to bumper traffic as it was now rush hour. Naomi thought this would be the perfect time for them to chat.

"So why didn't you tell me that my mother hired you to watch me?"

"Wow, coming out with the hard-hitting questions right out of the gate," Reed joked as he glanced at Naomi. "I mentioned earlier I didn't want to hurt you. I also didn't feel like it was my place to tell you. I thought it would be better coming from your mother since when I met you, I was just doing a job versus your mother, who was trying to do every-thing in her power to protect you."

"I understand that, but at any point did you want to tell me and just didn't?"

"I wanted to tell you when I appeared at your doorstep the day Paige disappeared. But I guess I thought if Jada wanted you to know, she would have told you. There was a lot of miscommunication."

Naomi nodded. "So, were you tracking me when we met at the V?"

"Yes, but I approached you because I wanted to. I'd been tracking you for a few weeks and reporting to Jada. Morris hadn't acted, so we thought that maybe he wouldn't, and my trailing you was winding down. I wanted to talk to you, so I thought that might be the perfect time to introduce myself in a public setting and not freak you out. I was conflicted about whether to tell you, and I thought Jada would. I didn't realize right away that you hadn't received the message."

"That makes sense. I don't blame you for just doing your job."

Reed was silent and turned his full attention to driving. After a few moments of silence, she spoke again. "Maybe we could try dating, though. Once all of this is over."

Reed smiled so wide that it transformed his entire face. He readjusted his hands on the steering wheel and said, "I'll take that answer."

"Getting back to Paige's and June's disappearances, is there anything I should know about your nana?"

"Nope. Here is one thing: I have only brought one other woman to meet her, and the only reason that happened is because she had an emergency in the house she wanted me to look at while I was out on a date."

"How did that go?"

"Neither one was impressed. Nana didn't care for her after chatting with her, and the woman I was out with wasn't thrilled that I had to cut our date short at a fancy restaurant to help my nana out."

Naomi whipped her head so fast that she thought it might fall off her neck. "You mean to tell me that this woman had an issue with you helping your grandmother?"

Reed nodded. "And that was our last date."

"That's not shocking at all…" Naomi mumbled as she shook her head in disbelief.

The trip would normally take thirty-five to forty minutes but ended up taking fifty to fifty-five minutes, but the duo survived the trip in one piece. Reed and Naomi exited his car and walked up to a nicely manicured front yard, up the stone stairs, and onto a front porch consisting of a few rocking chairs and a swing. Reed grabbed his keys and opened the front door.

"Hey, Nana. I'm here!" Reed exclaimed while he and Naomi walked through the front door. She noticed a bunch of photos hanging on the walls as they walked into the living room.

A small, older woman peeped her head out from behind a wall and smiled.

"Reed! You didn't tell me you were coming today. I'd have prepared something for you to eat."

"Now, Nana, you already prepare enough food for an army when it's just you here."

"I know, but I like to have meals that I can eat throughout the week." Angie Watts wiped her hands on a kitchen towel as she walked toward Reed. She placed the kitchen towel over a shoulder and gave Reed a big hug. "And may I ask who this is?"

"Nana, this is Naomi. I met her on a case I'm working on."

"It's nice to meet you." Naomi stuck out her hand to shake Angie's.

"Oh, sweetie, everyone gets a hug in this house," said Angie as she opened her arms to hug Naomi. Angie and her home surprised her. She expected a fashion designer to be flashier and have extravagant art on the walls of their home. Although Naomi knew Angie's home must be worth a lot of money given the location and the size, the decor was modest, as were her clothes for the day. She wore a nice white blouse, a pair of navy slacks, blue flats, and a yellow cardigan with her hair put up in a perfect bun.

After they took a step back, Angie looked at Reed and asked, "Is everything all right?"

"Well, no. Naomi's best friend and her coworker are missing, and we are trying to find them. Do you know someone named Irene Washington?" Reed was getting right to the chase.

"Irene? Of course! She works at the gym, where I am a member. I see her all the time at some events I attend there. She's so sweet. Did something happen?"

For a moment, Naomi and Reed said nothing. Naomi took a deep breath before chiming in. "She's my biological father's mother. My father is more than likely involved in this case," Naomi stated matter-of-factly, with little emotion. Reed reached over and rubbed a hand up and down her back.

"Irene mentioned having a grandchild, but I thought she said, grandson. She mentioned that she hadn't seen him in a very long time."

Naomi and Reed glanced at each other before looking back at Angie. "Do you have any way to contact her?" Reed asked.

"I do, but I can do you one better. Chances are Irene is working her regular shift at the gym right now. I usually have a swimming lesson right now and see Irene during her shift at this time every week. We have a week break before classes start up again. I could take you down there right now.

"Oh, we don't want to ruin your dinner," Naomi said.

"Nonsense. I already ate. I was just preparing meals for the week. Let me just put this food into some containers and stick them in the fridge, and we can be on our way. It's probably quicker to walk due to rush hour traffic, so let's do that."

A few minutes later, the trio walked out of the house, heading to the gym. Angie and Reed began the walk by making small talk and catching up with one another's lives while Naomi stayed silent.

"So, Naomi, how did you and Reed meet?"

"Um, we met at a bar actually," Naomi recalled. Technically she was right; the first time they met was at a bar even though he had been following her for weeks by that point.

"And what is it that you do?"

"I'm a developer for Edmon,"

"Oh, wow. Edmon is a huge company. I don't know too much about technology besides the basics, but I know they are very well known in this area."

Naomi nodded and appreciated her attempts to make small talk. "Yeah, they are. It's been fun and challenging, and I basically couldn't ask for much more."

"That's great, honey. So, Reed, have you taken this sweet girl out on a date?"

"Nana," Reed cautioned as he rolled his eyes. Naomi smirked and looked over at Reed.

"What? I figured I could ask. And if I asked in front of Naomi, you couldn't try to weasel your way out of it."

Naomi let out a snort that led to rolls of laughter. She loved seeing someone pull Reed's chain.

"If you must know, we were waiting until after the case was over. We are trying to put all of our energy into this case."

"That makes sense. But also don't forget to do what makes you happy. This case is very important, but I also want you both to take care of yourselves."

Reed smiled at his grandmother while Naomi nodded. They chatted more, and before they knew it, they had arrived at the gym. Naomi took a deep breath as Reed held open the door for both Angie and Naomi to walk through.

A petite African American woman was sitting at the front desk and stood up to greet the group.

"Hi! How's everything going?"

"Great, Irene! I wanted you to meet my grandson, Reed, and his friend Naomi."

Irene smiled at Angie and then at Reed. But when she looked at Naomi, her mouth dropped, and her face froze.

"N-N-Naomi? Naomi Washington? Oh my God, I thought you were dead," Irene said, clearly shocked. Her skin started going pale and she looked like she had seen a ghost. Naomi was worried she might have a heart attack.

Irene quickly walked around the front desk, and by the time she stood in front of Naomi, she had tears in her eyes.

"My name is Naomi Porter now. My stepfather adopted me years ago."

"It's really you. You look just like your mother. But your eyes…those are Washington eyes. Oh, my God. Can I hug you?"

Naomi was overwhelmed but nodded. Irene hugged her.

"I can't believe this. I haven't seen you since you were a

little girl. I…just can't believe this!" Irene exclaimed as she hugged Naomi again.

"Why did you think Naomi was dead?" Reed piped up. Naomi thanked him silently as this reunion was overwhelming.

"Morris told me so. He even had a mini memorial for you and Jada years ago."

Naomi did a double-take. "What? My mom told me he abandoned us."

"Now Morris has a history of lying. But it's usually small lies here and there. I believed him when he told me you both had passed away in a car accident. He even had urns made. He was so…upset, and I took it to mean that he was mourning your death." Irene shook her head as she wept. She took a deep breath before continuing, "I can't believe I missed out on so much of your life…over a big lie!" Irene angrily wiped away her tears. If someone had asked Naomi how she thought she would feel during this moment, she probably would have told them angry and upset. In reality, Naomi felt numb. It was another layer of the rhetorical onion peeling away and who knew how many more layers they had to go or if they would ever reach the core. She walked back to the front desk and found a box of tissues.

"When is the last time you saw Morris?" Reed took charge of the situation because Naomi looked out of it.

"Oh, it's been years since I've seen him. We had a falling out a long time ago, and I only hear from him when he wants a little bit of money. I rarely give him any, but sometimes I end up sending a little. I think the last time he contacted me was a year or two ago." Irene paused before she said, "What type of trouble is he in now?"

"Morris more than likely helped kidnap two people. We don't have evidence that proves it without question, so we don't want to jump the gun, so to speak, but we are sure he did. Does he have an apartment or something in the area that you know of?"

"The last time I gave him money and a few other things, I sent it to an address in DC. Hold on, let me pull it up on my phone." Irene walked back over to the front desk of the gym. She searched through the device for a couple of minutes.

"Ah-ha. Here it is." Irene showed the address to Reed, who looked it up on his phone.

"It's in Northwest. In fact, it's not too far from my place. Thank you, Irene. You've been so helpful."

"I'm glad to help. I hate to say this about my own flesh and blood, but whatever Morris has coming for him, it would probably be what he deserved. And I believe he has dragged Jett down this horrible path with him."

"Wait a minute." Naomi's eyes widened as she took a small step back. The shock was apparent all over her face. "Who is Jett?"

"Jett is Morris's son. My grandson. Your half-brother. I would assume Jada doesn't know he exists."

Naomi was stunned into silence. "Half-brother? How old is he?" Her stomach rolled. Not only had she gained a grandparent, but she had gained a sibling. Who is involved in the kidnapping of her best friend.

"He should be about twenty-four or twenty-five right now."

Naomi did the math, and it looked like Jett was conceived about a year after Morris abandoned them.

Reed followed up with another question. "When is the last time you saw Jett?"

"Um…a couple of years ago, I think. More recent than I saw Morris."

"Could you describe what he looks like or at least what he looked like when you last saw him?"

"Curly hair, tall, skinny guy. Tan complexion with dark brown eyes."

"Can you give me a second?" Reed was swiping through his phone.

Irene turned to Naomi and gently held her arms. "You're such a beautiful young woman. I thought I would never see you as an adult. Yet here you are," said Irene with a sniffle.

Naomi smiled for the first time since she got to the gym. "Thank you," she said as she handed Irene another tissue.

"Here it is." Reed showed Irene his phone. "Is this Jett?"

Irene took the device and stared at it for a second.

"Yes. That's Jett. He has a different haircut and now a small cut near his left eye."

"We need to leave, Irene, but it was lovely meeting you. You were such a big help." Reed shook her hand, and he headed toward the door.

"Do you want me to stay with you or walk you home if you need to leave?" Angie placed a hand on Irene's shoulder.

"I'll be okay, but I'll call you when I get home."

Angie gave Irene a small hug and walked over to join her grandson. The two walked outside to give Naomi and Irene a little privacy.

"I'd like to get lunch with you sometime. Can I get your number to connect with you soon?" Naomi pulled out her phone.

"I'd like that a lot," said Irene as they exchanged contact information. Irene and Naomi briefly hugged before Naomi joined Reed and Angie outside.

"Well, that was eventful. And very helpful. I'm a little concerned that Irene might warn Morris that we're onto him." Reed tried to pick up the pace back to Angie's home.

"I don't think she will. I believe that she hasn't been in contact with Morris for years," said Angie as she effortlessly kept up with her grandson.

"I hope so. I also need to talk to my mom. I have even more questions that I need answers to because I am still so confused." Reed reached for Naomi's hand and rubbed his thumb across her knuckles. She smiled at him as they traveled back to Angie's house.

The three made it back to Angie's house in no time flat and walked Angie up to her front door.

"I hope you both have a good night, and I'm so glad I could help with the case." Angie hugged Reed before turning to Naomi. Angie hugged her and whispered, "I hope to see more of you soon." Angie broke the hug with a smile, and Naomi felt her cheeks warm up. She smiled back at Angie. "Now, I want you both to be careful and stay safe, okay?"

Reed nodded his head and said, "Yes, ma'am." All three of them waved goodbye, and Reed and Naomi got into Reed's car.

Reed fiddled with his phone and asked, "Are you okay?"

"I think so, but I also think I am running on adrenaline." Naomi buckled her seat belt.

Reed set his phone into its holder, and the navigation system once again welcomed Reed into the car. Naomi noticed he set the navigation for the address that Irene told them.

"So, this might be it, huh?"

"Hopefully," Reed said, also buckling his seat belt. "Are you ready?"

Naomi took a deep breath before saying, "As ready as I'll ever be."

CHAPTER 24

$\mathcal{N}$aomi was quiet as Reed drove through the streets of Washington, DC.

"Penny for your thoughts?"

Naomi smiled at Reed briefly before looking back out the window. "You know we haven't used pennies in about fifty years, right?"

"Yes, and that's beside the point. How are you feeling?"

Naomi sighed. "I'm still trying to process that I have a living grandmother. Plus, a brother that is involved with helping my father, and possibly others, kidnap my best friend." She rubbed her eyes before continuing. "I wish I could talk to Dr. Evans right now."

"That's understandable. It's going to take time to process all of this."

Naomi and Reed rode in silence until they arrived in Northwest Washington, DC, about thirty minutes later. Reed drove by the address that Irene had given them and found a parking spot a block away. The building was a corner townhouse on what seemed to be a quiet street.

"So, what's the plan?" Naomi unbuckled her seat belt and turned to look at Reed.

"Are you nervous?" She was a little annoyed that he answered her question with a question.

"What would make you think that?" Naomi asked defensively.

"Anyone would be nervous. There is a lot at stake if we are wrong. We don't have much time to figure out a solution if we are."

Naomi was a little freaked out about how easily Reed could read her.

"Now, I don't think we are wrong." Reed fiddled with his phone before placing it in his pocket. He then started typing something into his dashboard monitor while the other hand pulled out his "glasses" from his front pocket.

"How should we get inside?"

"I'm not sure. I know there are two entrances in the back, so that might be the best option outside of climbing into a window. You can see it here." He gestured to his dashboard. On it, Reed had pulled up an image of the house that quickly zoomed out and then back in to show the backyard. After Naomi finished, he flicked it back to the home screen.

"If we had more time to study the location, I would feel more confident, but we don't. So, I'll take a look around to see what I can find. Stay here and keep the doors locked, okay? I'll leave the car keys here with you."

"Sure, but when do you think you'll be back?"

"How about we say ten minutes? If I'm not back in twenty minutes or if you haven't heard from me, hit this button right here," Reed said as he pointed to his dashboard monitor. The monitor now showed a red button on the right-hand corner of the screen.

"Why are you taking the glasses?"

"You never know when you might need to record something. See you later."

Reed grabbed her hand, rubbed his thumb across her knuckles, and gave it a gentle squeeze. Then he took off to examine the house. Naomi locked the car doors. Seconds turned into minutes, and there was still no sign of Reed. She sent a text to her mother to let her know what they were doing and where she was. When Naomi was sure he was gone for over twenty minutes, she stalled for a couple more minutes before hitting the button on the dashboard. Seeing nothing happen, she hit it a few more times. Checking her phone, Naomi saw that her mother hadn't replied. She sent a group message to her mother, Logan, and Diane before placing her phone on her lap.

"Screw this," Naomi said a few seconds later as she opened the car doors, took the car keys and her phone, and got out of the car. She locked the doors and started walking to the townhouse.

When she got within a few houses of the townhouse in question, she noticed how eerie the block seemed. There was no one on the street, even though there were bars and restaurants a few blocks away. Naomi examined her surroundings but didn't see Reed anywhere and grew worried. She was about to check out the front of the house before she thought it might be wise to go to the back due to there potentially being cameras on the front door.

"I mean, that's what I would do if I were a bad person," Naomi mumbled as she crept around the corner.

Silence greeted Naomi at the back of the house. There was a fenced-in backyard and two doors leading into the home. One led to what she assumed was the main level of the home. The other led to what she thought was the basement.

"As much as this goes against everything I stand for, I guess I should go through the basement," Naomi whispered to herself. "Plus, the video that I saw of Paige and June looked like it might be in the basement based on the lack of windows."

Before opening the basement door, she texted 911 with the address just in case. It had now been over thirty minutes since she had heard from Reed. Although she wanted to wait for the police to get there, she knew she had to go in case someone was hurt, and time was of the essence.

"Well, here goes nothing." Naomi tried the doorknob of the basement door and it opened with little hesitation. The door opened into a room that was pitch black. "I shouldn't be doing this. This door being open is telling me I shouldn't be doing this." Naomi could feel her anxiousness rising even more. "Deep breaths, deep breaths," she whispered to herself. She took a second to collect herself before she walked through the door.

Naomi turned on her phone's flashlight on low and continued walking until she reached another door leading her farther into the basement. She saw a light shining underneath that door. She looked around the room with her flashlight quickly to see if she could find anything to use as a weapon. A few feet away, there was a metal pipe on the floor. Breathing a small sigh of relief, she grabbed the pipe and went back to the door.

Naomi took another deep breath and opened the door a

crack. And it took everything in her to contain the scream that was sitting at the tip of her tongue.

There were Reed and Paige on the floor. Paige had her hands tied and was sitting up while Reed was lying completely still on the ground. A man had his back to Naomi that looked to be holding something with both of his hands. Naomi assumed that he had a gun.

"Shit," Naomi mumbled as she quickly thought about what she had to do. Reed was hurt, but she did not know how badly. Paige looked okay physically, but who knew what she was going through mentally. And where was June?

Naomi was trying to keep her anxiety at bay. Taking another deep breath, Naomi placed her phone in her pocket and opened the door softly. She tiptoed into the room. She was a couple of feet away from the assailant when she made eye contact with Paige. Paige's eyes widened briefly, and the man standing in front of her turned around to look at Naomi.

Naomi froze. She stared back into eyes that mirrored her own. Here she was looking at her biological father as he was getting ready to point a gun at her. Thankfully, Morris wasn't expecting her either as she recognized a look of shock on his face. That gave Naomi the leverage she needed. Before he could lift what she confirmed to be a gun up toward her, Naomi took a giant step and swung the metal pipe like a baseball bat. The gun flew out of Morris's hand, and he crumbled to the ground. Naomi grabbed the gun and ran over to Paige and Reed.

"Naomi!" Paige exclaimed as Naomi dropped to her knees in front of her. Naomi noticed that Paige's hands tied together with a zip-tie, so there was no way she could free her without something to cut the zip-tie. She then turned to Reed.

"Are you okay? What happened to Reed? Where is June?"

"I'm fine. Reed, not so much. It all happened so fast. Reed came in after I screamed because I heard a loud bang upstairs. Morris snuck behind him and attacked him. They fought for a bit before Morris got the upper hand. And I have no idea where June is. Jett told Morris that 'he had to take her' and went upstairs. I don't know what happened after they left the basement. That was why I started screaming."

Naomi checked for a pulse and felt that he had a strong one. She breathed a huge sigh of relief.

"Who is 'he'? Who was Jett talking about?" Naomi asked as she tried to find something that might help Reed come to.

"I have no idea. Morris seemed to know who he was talking about, however."

"Where the hell are the cops?" Naomi mumbled as she and Paige checked Reed for injuries. His handsome face had bruising and there was some blood coming from a cut on his forehead. She gently felt his head and thankfully did not find any blood coming from anywhere else.

"How nice of you to join us, Naomi."

Naomi and Paige spun around and noticed that Morris was back up on his feet, holding another gun. Naomi mentally kicked herself for not checking his body to make sure he did not have another weapon on him.

"The pleasure is all mine," Naomi said, voice dripping with sarcasm. She aimed the gun she took from Morris at him. She knew that it was probably best not to piss off someone who was holding a gun at them, but she couldn't help herself.

"Now, Naomi, do you believe you can fire that gun properly? I'm willing to bet you've never shot a gun before."

"You know nothing about me," Naomi replied. She tried

not to shake while holding the gun.

"I know plenty. I've been keeping track of you over the years and more recently took an even bigger interest in you."

"And why was that?"

"We knew it would come in handy. You worked at one of the biggest cybersecurity companies in the nation and have been rising through the ranks. You started working on data and databases related to the cloud, and we knew we had to strike. We just didn't expect him to sniff around you when we enacted our plan." Morris pointed his gun at Reed.

"And kidnapping Paige was always a part of the plan?"

"Yes. Jett knew that she would be a big enough incentive to get you to do what we needed you to do."

"But why June? And where is she?" Naomi asked. Halfway through her sentence, she decided that she wanted to keep Morris talking to buy some time for the police to get here.

"June was taken because the boss was getting pissed that you hadn't completed the project yet. She's in good hands. Now Naomi, why don't you just put the gun down?" Morris asked as he gestured to the gun she had with his.

"No," Naomi tightened her grip.

"We wouldn't want anyone else to get hurt. Put the gun down."

"No."

"Put the gun down, or I'll shoot Paige!" Morris shouted. He aimed the gun directly at Paige. Naomi heard her take a quick breath, and she knew what she had to do.

"Okay," Naomi said as she laid the gun down on the ground.

Morris smiled. "Good. As I said, we don't want anyone else to get hurt."

"So how involved was Jett in this scheme? You never responded to that question earlier, and it's been bugging me."

"He's the one who thought of this idea," Morris said without hesitation. He checked his phone briefly. "Might have to go with Plan B…"

"What is Plan B?"

"I kill these two, and you come with me to finish the project."

"That is unnecessary. I'll come with you regardless. Just don't hurt them anymore." Naomi's voice remained steady, and she slowly rose to her feet. "We should probably get going."

"You're right. Come over here," Morris demanded. Naomi walked over to Morris, and he grabbed her arm. "You probably won't believe this, but I am proud of the woman you have become."

Naomi thought about what he said for a second before replying, "And it was no thanks to you," she said, her words leaving a trail of bitterness in their wake.

Naomi saw a mixture of emotions come over Morris's face. First was hurt, then was sadness, and the last was fury. He roughly pulled her toward the stairs. "Go up the stairs!" he yelled at her.

Naomi begrudgingly trudged up the stairs, and Morris followed behind her. Once he had closed and locked the basement door, he grabbed her arm again and took her into the kitchen.

"Don't try any funny business. There aren't any sharp utensils up here anyway." Morris snatched a backpack out from a cabinet and started tossing items into it.

Naomi remembered the emotion that he showed earlier

and wondered if she could appeal to it once again. "So, why did you leave Mom and me all those years ago?" Naomi asked in a soft whisper. Although she quietly asked her question, Morris heard her and stopped moving.

"I wasn't good enough for either of you," Morris said as he continued placing things into the book bag.

"Why do you think that?"

Morris paused again. "I didn't think. I knew I wasn't. I got caught up with some terrible people, and I left because I didn't want them to hurt you guys. I even pretended like you all had died to cover my tracks. More so, that was to stop my mother from asking questions."

"I assume you know I met her recently, right?"

"The thought popped into my head that you might eventually find her but didn't know you met her until just now."

Naomi noticed that he had stopped packing his bag. "Morris, you realize that you don't have to do this, right? Just turn yourself in."

"I'm already in too deep. This job was supposed to help me get out of this mess for good. But it required dragging you down with me. The information in that Cyber Edge file is worth a lot of money, this was supposed to be my endgame."

He glanced at Naomi before he briefly closed his eyes and sighed. "You know I meant what I said when I mentioned that you look like your mother. Except you have your grandmother's eyes," Morris whispered almost tenderly. Naomi felt a twinge of something she could not identify. After all these years, she was finally face-to-face with the man who had abandoned her mother and her years ago. And it all came down to this and all of the things he had done.

"And I guess yours too."

Everything happened in slow motion. The door that Naomi had assumed led to the backyard from the main level, burst open, and a swarm of people entered the residence.

"Police. Put your gun down," shouted one of the men. Naomi put her hands up and breathed a sigh of relief. She turned around and saw that the police had come in through the front door. Naomi turned to look at Morris and saw that he was still holding the gun.

"Sir, I said, put your gun down," the police officer repeated.

Naomi looked at her biological father and said, "Morris, it's never too late. Please drop the gun."

Morris looked at the gun and then at Naomi. He put both hands up, bent down, and placed the gun on the floor. He then stood up straight with his hands in the air.

Naomi breathed another sigh of relief. She heard a police officer report that they had apprehended the suspect. Soon after that, more police officers came into the home.

Naomi started walking toward the basement as she said to the officers, "Reed and Paige are downstairs and need help. Morris locked them in the basement, but the key should still be in the door. I know there was at least one other person named Jett involved and my coworker, June, who was also kidnapped. They both aren't here as far as I know."

An officer nodded as he unlocked the door and told Naomi to wait by the stairs. A few minutes later, Paige and a conscious Reed climbed up the stairs. Naomi immediately went to Reed and grabbed his face in her hands.

"You're okay!" Naomi exclaimed. He winced, and Naomi whispered an apology. She should have figured that he, at the very least, had a headache based on the cut on his forehead. It took everything in her to not try to hug him since she saw him holding his shoulder. Tears flowed down her cheeks as she furiously tried to wipe them away.

"You thought that would have been enough to kill me? Ha," Reed said. Naomi noted the weakness in his voice. He kept waving off the EMTs that tried to get him to lie down on a stretcher. He used his hand to wipe away a couple of her tears.

Naomi turned to Paige and saw that she was crying too. "I'm so glad you're okay." She leaned over to hug Paige.

Another police officer came from the basement and held a pair of glasses in her hand. She said, "Are these any of yours?"

"They're mine, and they flew off me when Morris attacked me from behind. Hopefully, they caught some of what happened down there." Reed leaned on Naomi for support.

"If not, there should be a camera down there. I saw a video feed that Morris had when he allowed me to say something to Paige briefly a couple of days ago. I'm not sure if it recorded audio, however," Naomi explained to the police officer.

"Excuse me, coming through," said another voice from behind the group. They turned toward the sound and saw Morris escorted out in handcuffs. As he walked past the group, he stared at Naomi with a look of sorrow in his eyes. He put his head down as the police led him out of the town-house and into a waiting patrol car.

A police officer walked over to the group and said, "Hi, my name is Sergeant Tom Cummings. We need to take you all to the hospital for an evaluation and then take your statements. We are in the process of contacting your next of kin, and they should meet you at the hospital." Reed finally allowed the EMTs to load him onto a stretcher, and both Naomi and Paige joined him in an ambulance that sped to the hospital.

CHAPTER 25

*W*hen the trio got to the hospital, Reed was rushed to the emergency room while Paige and Naomi stayed in the waiting room. Paige was checked out in the ambulance by a paramedic and got medically cleared.

Naomi turned to Paige and hugged her again. "I know I already said this, but I'm so glad you are okay."

"I am too. This is not what I meant when I said you should get out more and step out from behind the computer screen, however." Paige gently nudged Naomi.

Naomi snorted and told her, "This is not what I had in mind either."

"What I really want to say was thank you. Who knows what would have happened if you hadn't come when you did."

"It's partially my fault you got kidnapped."

"No, it isn't. Never say that, okay?"

Naomi shrugged and took her phone out of her pocket. She was about to make a call when Jada, Logan, and Diane rushed into the waiting room.

"Mom!" Paige exclaimed as she jumped up from her chair. Diane turned to her daughter and let out a wail. They both ran toward each other with tears in their eyes. Naomi stood up from her chair and jogged over to Jada and Logan as they dashed over to her.

"Honey, are you all right? We were worried sick," Jada said as she looked at and touched Naomi to see if she had any cuts or bruises. When Jada finished inspecting her, Logan stepped up and hugged Naomi again.

"We were so worried." He hugged her even tighter.

"I'm fine, thanks. I probably need a lot of therapy sessions after this, but I am okay. Or at least I will be." Naomi looked over to see Diane and Paige still hugging, and she gave them a small smile before turning back to her parents.

"Did the police take your statements yet?" Jada asked.

Naomi shook her head. Just as she was about to reply, a nurse asked for Naomi.

"I'll be right back," she said as she walked over to the nurse. The nurse's facial expression was unreadable, but Naomi knew that she must've had an update on Reed.

"Reed Wright is asking for you, so I'm here to take you back to him."

Naomi let her parents, Paige, and Diane know that she would see Reed and then followed the nurse down the long, white halls. The nurse stopped at the door on the left.

"He's in this room right here," she said as she opened the door.

Naomi walked inside and saw Reed sitting up in his bed with a bandage over his right shoulder and a small portion of his forehead. His face had bruising, but other than that, he seemed fine. He looked up and smiled at Naomi as the nurse closed the door.

"How are you feeling?" Naomi asked as she walked up to his bed.

"I've been better. The hospital is keeping me here for observation since someone knocked me out cold for a few minutes," Reed said as he held out his uninjured hand for Naomi. Naomi held his hand and rubbed her thumb along his knuckles.

"You scared me back there."

"Sorry. Things definitely got hairy. I honestly think I look worse than I feel, and my pride is hurt more than anything. But are you okay?"

"I'm fine, psychically. Emotionally and mentally? Not so much. But I'll be okay. Have you heard from Angie?"

"Yep. I messaged her and the rest of my family as soon as I got a chance. Nana is on her way down here even though I told her I was fine."

Before she could react, Reed reached up to give Naomi a one-armed hug. As she was about to pull away, he placed a kiss on her forehead.

"Geez. I shouldn't have done that. I know we hadn't established what we were after you found out I was tracking you..." Reed's sentence trailed off as Naomi laid a soft kiss on his lips. When she pulled away, she gave Reed a big smile. Before anything else was said, there was a knock on the door.

"Come in," Reed said as he adjusted the covers on the bed, and Naomi stepped back and sat down on the edge of the side of the bed.

Detective Thompson and Chief Hughes walked in a

second later and closed the door. Police Chief Hughes took off his hat as soon as he shut the door.

"I'm so glad you are both okay," Detective Thompson said as she watched their reaction to their arrival.

"Thanks," Reed said. Naomi didn't say a word.

"I just wanted to update you both on a few things and take your police statements. Figured it might be easier to do it here than hauling you both down to the station."

"That's fine," Reed said as he tried to find a more comfortable position in the hospital bed.

"We found the woman who was following you the other day. She is Officer Tiffany Geller. She created and doctored the video of Paige they sent to me. We have put her on administrative leave until the investigation is complete."

With everything happening, Naomi had forgotten about the woman following them when they were jogging around the National Mall.

"Morris Washington is being charged with kidnapping, assault, breaking and entering, and a host of other crimes. Kidnapping is a felony under DC law, but it depends on what the district attorney's office wants to do."

"That makes sense," Naomi asked.

"Plus, technically, he assisted in the kidnapping Paige and June."

"Wait. What? He didn't actually do the kidnapping?"

"Nope. Jett Washington, his son, did."

"Where is Jett now?" Reed asked as he watched Naomi try to recover from her shock.

Police Chief Hughes sighed. "We have no idea at the moment. He never came back to the townhouse. We assume that he is on the run. We are doing everything we can to track him down with no success so far."

Detective Thompson took over the conversation from the police chief and said, "Reed, although your glasses fell off your face during the scuffle between you and Morris, they kept recording. They picked up some visuals, but it recorded all of the audio. That, in addition to the video files, we grabbed from the camera set up in the room. That will help nail these men to the wall."

Naomi looked over at Reed and saw him breathe a huge sigh of relief. "That's fantastic news," Reed said.

"We should probably take your statements now," Detective Thompson said as she took out her phone. Naomi and Reed relayed their version of events separately before the group came back together in Reed's hospital room.

Just as Naomi and Detective Thompson were wrapping up Naomi's statement, Detective Thompson's phone started ringing. She held up a finger as she walked away to take the call. Naomi waited for her outside of Reed's hospital room door for about a minute before she returned.

"I should probably share this news with everyone, so let's go back into Reed's room."

Naomi and Detective Thompson entered the hospital room, interrupting the conversation that Mark and Reed were having.

"I just heard that June has been found and is safe."

Naomi breathed a sigh of relief. "Was Jett with her?"

Detective Thompson shook her head no. "No. She is at a rest stop just off of I-95 near Baltimore. She found help and called the police. They are on their way up to her now."

"That's fantastic. I guess you all will have to get going to check on June and wrap this up."

Police Chief Hughes nodded, and Detective Thompson said, "Before we leave, I want to say that I am sorry. I know that I could have done more to help you with this case."

"It's okay. You did what you had to do with the evidence you had. Everyone is okay, and at least Morris is in custody. That's what matters," Naomi said as she gently laid a hand on her arm. Detective Thompson gave Naomi a small smile.

"In that same vein, you both did an amazing job solving this case. I'm sure we'll work together again." Chief Hughes nodded at Reed. "Naomi, you might want to look into this field of work," he said with a smile as he walked toward the door.

Naomi smiled back at him and said, "Never say never." At her words, Reed looked over and smiled.

* * *

"Nana, you can stop fussing over me now," Reed said as he lay on his couch. Angie was helping Reed walk over to his couch while Naomi helped bring in some get-well gifts Reed had received. Angie had come to the condo earlier to prepare for Reed's arrival after two days in the hospital.

"I'll never stop fussing over you," Angie said. She grabbed a throw blanket that she had placed on the couch earlier and put it over him.

"I need to go back downstairs and park the car, but I'll be back in a minute." Naomi turned toward the front door.

"Be careful with my baby. The parking garage in the basement is tight," Reed said as he looked over at her. After realizing what he said, he wiggled his eyebrows at her. Naomi rolled her eyes, waved goodbye, and walked out the front door, closing it behind her.

The last couple of days had been chaotic, but she would take this time of chaos over the chaos she had experienced just one week ago. She heard her phone ping as she stepped on the elevator to go back to the first floor of Reed's condo building. She saw a message from Paige.

Paige: Did you make it back to Reed's place okay?

Naomi smiled. Seeing a message she knew was from her friend and not her kidnapper was a relief.

Naomi: Yep, made it back in one piece. He's not too thrilled about Angie fussing over him, however. But everyone is okay. How are you?

Naomi placed her phone back in her pocket as she waited for Paige to respond. She stepped out of the elevator once she reached the main level and thanked the doorman, who had kindly watched Reed's car while they brought him upstairs.

Just as she was pulling into the parking garage, her phone pinged again. Naomi pulled into Reed's assigned spot and parked the car. She then pulled out her phone and checked the message.

Paige: I'm okay as I can be, I guess. I had another nightmare last night, which led to a rough night. Glad my mom is staying here for a while, though, and to start therapy tomorrow.

Naomi sighed. Paige had nightmares every night since being rescued. She was happy Paige was taking her mental health seriously by seeking out help.

Naomi: If you need anything, let me know. I'm planning on being at Reed's for a bit, but if you need me to come home, that is fine.

As she walked back toward the elevator, her phone pinged again.

Paige: *We're fine here. We were just watching some bad television shows. Have fun with your man.*

Naomi rolled her eyes again and didn't respond. Reed and she had not even gone on a proper date nor established what they were to each other. With all the craziness going on, that was perfectly okay.

Naomi knocked on Reed's door, and Angie opened it. She surprised Naomi with a hug.

"I meant to thank you before, but with everything going on, it kept slipping my mind. Thank you for everything that you've done for everyone, but especially Reed. Who knows what would have happened if you hadn't acted when you did. So, on behalf of the Wright and Watts Family, I thank you from the bottom of my heart." Angie hugged Naomi again.

Naomi smiled through the tears that were welling up in her eyes. "It's what anyone would have done, Angie."

"You'd be surprised at the number of people who wouldn't have done a thing." Angie gently patted Naomi's back as she let her in. "And please call me, Nana." She smiled before gathering her things.

"Stew is in the refrigerator if you don't want to order takeout. If you need anything else, I'm only a phone call or a car ride away."

"I think we're okay, Nana," Reed said from his spot on his couch.

"I know, but allow me to do this, okay?" Angie asked as she walked over to where Reed was lying on the couch. She gave him a gentle hug and whispered, "Don't let her getaway, you hear?"

Or so she thought she whispered, Naomi heard her loud and clear, and she felt the butterflies in her stomach flutter. Angie then walked over to Naomi, gave her a wink and a quick hug before letting herself out of the apartment.

Naomi placed Reed's keys on the counter and hung her coat up in the closet. She took her shoes off, and as she was about to settle in one of the armchairs in the living room, Reed beckoned her over to come and sit by him. He sat up and made room for her on the couch as he placed his feet on his coffee table.

"Well, that wasn't awkward at all." Naomi fidgeted with the throw blanket that Reed had put over her.

"What wasn't awkward?" Reed asked as he turned toward Naomi.

"What Angie, I mean, Nana, said."

"I have no idea what you are talking about," Reed said with a smirk.

Naomi rolled her eyes for the third time today.

"Why don't you put your feet right here?" Reed asked and motioned to his lap. Naomi placed her feet in Reed's lap, and he gently massaged one foot.

"That feels fantastic," Naomi said as she briefly closed her eyes.

Naomi was silent for a few moments before she spoke again. "You know I'm glad the case is just about wrapped up."

"What do you mean, just about?"

"We still don't know where Jett is, nor do we know who 'he' is."

"True. I'm sure the police will have more information, especially since June might tell them more. Plus, Morris is in custody, so he might talk."

"That makes sense." Naomi paused a beat before changing the subject. "So, what about us?"

"What about us?"

Naomi glanced at Reed before turning back to the television. "We said we would think more about us potentially dating after the case was closed."

"How do you feel about giving this whole dating thing a try?"

"I'm not opposed to it," Naomi said. She couldn't stop her lips from twitching.

Reed looked over at her and playfully glared. "You're not opposed to it?"

"Well, ...yeah." She winked. "But seriously, I think we should give it a shot. We started on a good foot even with you stalking me, but I would still like to try dating."

Reed chuckled and shook his head. "I wasn't stalking you. It was a work assignment. And I want to give it a shot too. Plus, we've already been on a few dates while on the case, so I have invested some already."

Naomi gently elbowed Reed and smiled at him. "So, I guess that settles it."

"I guess it does," Reed said as he changed the position of his hands as they slowly made their way up Naomi's denim-covered leg.

"Wow, that feels great too," Naomi said as she looked at Reed through heavy-lidded eyes.

"You know what else feels great? This," Reed said as he leaned over to kiss Naomi. Naomi couldn't figure out how their kisses kept getting better. Reed also avoided putting too much pressure on his right arm.

"Yes, it does. But more of that and other things later, if

you're up to it. But first, holiday movies, even if it's still a few days before Thanksgiving," Naomi laughed.

Reed playfully rolled his eyes and smiled. Together they watched a movie on his couch, and it was the first time Naomi could relax in weeks.

EPILOGUE

A FEW WEEKS LATER

*N*aomi knocked on the front door of Reed's condo. A smiling handsome face and a kiss on the lips greeted her. Reed's injuries healed completely.

"I'm sorry, I'm late. A bug popped up with a project I was working on, and I had to fix it before I could leave," Naomi said while Reed helped her with her coat.

"It happens, and technically you're still early since you did still get off work early. Dinner is almost ready," Reed said as he hung her coat in the closet.

"It smells delicious."

"I'm just glad I finally have the opportunity to cook for you."

Even though they had been on quite a few dates over the last few weeks, Reed had yet to cook Naomi dinner at his place until tonight. Naomi walked into the kitchen and checked out the food that Reed was finishing up.

"Is that risotto?"

"Yep. I'm making lobster risotto. Our starter, though, will be a salad."

"That also sounds amazing," Naomi said. Naomi was about to walk out of the kitchen when she turned and grabbed Reed's arms excitedly. "Guess what I heard today?"

"What did you hear?"

"That I am a shoo-in for that promotion I talked to you about weeks ago." Naomi let go of Reed's arms and clapped her hands together excitedly.

"What? That's amazing! Congrats!" Reed said as he wrapped his arms around her and lifted her off the floor in a bear hug. It relieved Naomi to tell someone. Finally.

"Yes! I finally leaped and applied a couple of weeks ago, but I didn't hear back right away. They are completing paperwork right now, but it looks like everything is a go."

"I'm so proud of you," Reed said as he gently kissed her forehead.

"Thanks," Naomi said as she reached up and kissed Reed. "And June came back to work for the first time today."

"That's great. How is she doing?"

"She's doing as well as could be expected. I'm not sure if her parents are still in town helping her, but she mentioned that she was happy to be throwing herself back into the swing of things."

"I'm glad. Somewhat related, did you hear anything from Irene?"

"I did! She, Mom, and I will get lunch sometime soon. I think she's ecstatic about it."

Naomi's stomach growled, and they both laughed and broke apart. Naomi walked out of the kitchen, through the living room and to the dining room.

"I also had a session with Dr. Evans today that went really well. There are still some things that I will always work through, but it feels amazing to hear her say I was making progress," Naomi said as she continued to walk.

She saw that Reed had set up a candlelight dinner for two in his dining room, with plates and placemats perfectly arranged. He placed utensils to the left of the plates, and napkins and condiments were off to the side. As Naomi walked closer, she noticed there was a picture frame on the table. She studied it and realized it was the photo that they took on Reed's couch a few months ago. The one they had taken just before they solved the case.

"You had this printed for tonight?"

Reed walked up behind her and gently placed his hands around her waist.

"No, I had it printed for you to put on your dresser at home or on your desk at work. I have a matching photo on my desk in my office, so I'll see it every day."

"That is sweet. Thank you," Naomi said as she kissed Reed on the cheek. "Ah, and now I know why you wanted to have an early dinner. Because of the sunset."

"I knew how much it meant to you, so I thought I would try to make it happen. And now we have something more to celebrate. It's a little too cold to sit outside for an extended period, so I figured we could have a candlelight dinner inside as we watched the sun go down. Do you want any wine?" Reed asked as he held up a bottle of wine.

"Sure," Naomi said as she grabbed a wineglass off the dining room table. He poured her a glass and pulled out her seat at the dining room table. Naomi sat down, and he pushed her chair back in for her. Reed then walked over to his side, poured himself a glass of wine, and then set it back down in the middle of the table.

"I'll grab our food and be back in a second."

"I can help you," Naomi said as she rose from her chair.

"Don't worry about it. Just sit there and relax," Reed said as he headed out of the room.

"Thanks," Naomi said with a smile.

Naomi checked her phone briefly while she waited for Reed to come back into the room. She placed her phone face-down on the table when Reed appeared from the kitchen with their dinner. He set the food on the dining room table, lit the candles, and lowered the lights in the room.

"Cheers," Reed said as he raised his glass.

"To what?" Naomi asked as she followed suit.

"To us. To us being healthy, happy, and in love," Reed said as he clinked his glass against hers and then took a sip.

Naomi sat there speechless for a few seconds before taking a sip of her wine. "Is this your way of telling me you love me?" They had not said those three precious words yet, and as a result, Naomi's heart was pounding out of her chest.

Reed chuckled and looked down at his dinner before he looked Naomi in her eyes and said, "Yes. I love you."

"I love you too."

Naomi jumped out of her seat and Reed pushed his seat back to make room for in his lap. He leaned over to kiss her, both of them having forgotten about the meal they were getting ready to eat.

ABOUT THE AUTHOR

B. Ivy Woods has been writing for as long as she can remember. After getting her Bachelor of Arts in Political Science and Environmental Policy and a Master's in Energy Policy and Law and working in the environmental field for several years, she decided to become a stay-at-home mom. That is when thoughts of a writing career really took off. Although she competed in NaNoWriMo multiple times, 2019 was the first year that she won. This win inspired her to make writing a career. Her debut novel was self-published in 2020.

Although she is originally from New York City, she currently lives in the DMV (Washington, D.C., Maryland, Virginia) with her husband, daughter, dog, and cat.

www.bivywoods.com

9 781735 283616